SPEAK RWANDA

SPEAK RWANDA

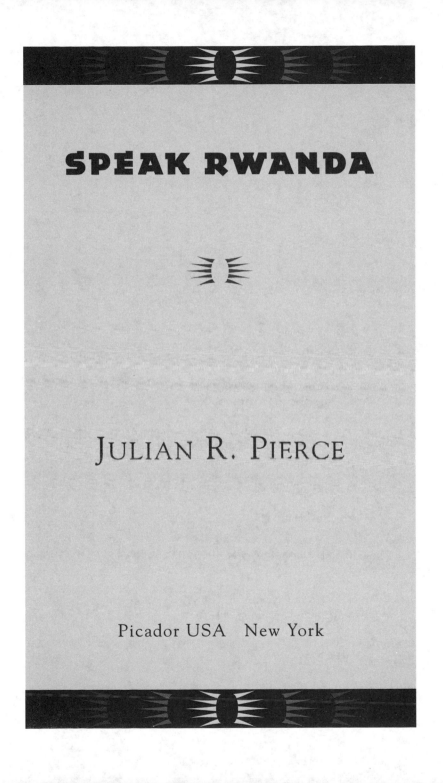

JULIAN R. PIERCE

Picador USA   New York

Picador® is a U.S. registered trademark and is used by St. Martin's Press under license from Pan Books Limited.

Library of Congress Cataloging-in-Publication Data

Pierce, Julian R.
    Speak Rwanda / Julian R. Pierce.—Picador USA 1st ed.
        p.   cm.
    ISBN 0-312-20367-5
    1. Rwanda—History—Civil War, 1990–1993 Fiction.
    2. Rwanda—History—Civil War, 1994 Fiction.   I. Title
PS3566.I3876S64   1999
813'.54—dc21   99-22079
                                                                     CIP

First Edition: August 1999

10 9 8 7 6 5 4 3 2 1

To my wife

AUTHOR'S NOTE

This novel is a work of historical fiction. Although aspects of the story were inspired by actual events, the characters, places, and incidents portrayed in the book are either the product of the author's imagination or are used fictitiously.

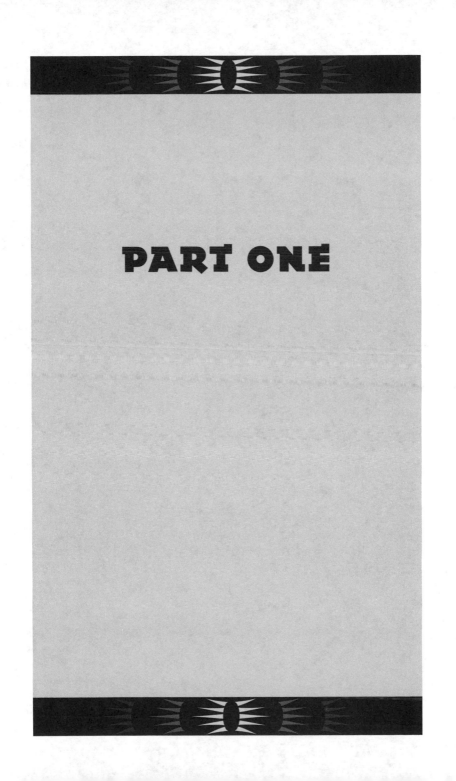

PART ONE

IMMACULÉE MAKERI

I ENVY HUTU women one thing. They can eat meat. I must admit some of us Tutsi women do too, but it isn't right and my husband, also of a good clan, would be ashamed of me if I did. Even so, now, as I knead the sorghum dough, I can smell from the opposite hill the wind-driven smoky odor of meat cooking. Tonight the Hutu women over there will sink their teeth into strong-tasting red meat, while I sit here over sorghum porridge and beans. If I told those Hutu women that I, a Tutsi of good blood, envied them anything, what would they think? That I had gone mad? What would that nice Hutu girl think, the one who once bandaged my son's cut and smiles at me each time we meet on a path? She's pretty, if short and rounded in a Hutu way. What would she think of a Tutsi woman who admitted envy of a Hutu?

But of course I would never admit such a thing. My husband is a cattle owner in Butare préfecture with standards to uphold, and I have seven children whose mother's reputation is important to them. My eldest son studies in France, the next at the national university in Butare, my girl of eighteen will marry within the year, then comes twelve-year-old Innocent, whom I nearly lost to fever in his infancy and so, secretly, is my favorite, and then the girl of seven, the boy of five. Two years ago, when

I considered myself beyond childbearing, I was blessed with a baby boy who has been baptized by our Catholic priest and awarded a legal birth certificate by the government. For such children I must look and act the part of a Tutsi mother and wife, even if circumstances have changed terribly since I was a girl.

I still love our rugo, our compound of five buildings on this most beautiful of hills overlooking the valleys of the most beautiful of lands, for everyone knows that Rwanda is God's country. It is said that if Imana walks elsewhere during the day, at night, always he returns here. But sometimes I wonder if he has forgotten the Tutsi, his chosen people, his favorite of favorites. In my grandmother's day a Tutsi woman like myself would never find anything to envy in a Hutu. The idea would not have occurred to her. She would have been too proud of her position to think of eating meat. I am ashamed of myself.

And I am sorry for my husband, who has never reconciled himself to the loss of Tutsi power. After bringing in the cattle for the day, he drinks with his friends and often stumbles home drunk. I wish he could see things for what they are. After all, Imana and Jesus have preordained everything that happens. We must do our best and accept what fate gives us. That's what I try to explain to my good husband. I tell him almost every day that he's still a patron to Hutu clients, that he rents them his cattle so they can have milk and fertilizer for their fields, that the cattle will never be theirs. My husband is aware of being less than his father, who ruled his pastureland like a king. Each month my husband's father had his clients come bow to him when they paid for the use of his cattle.

Now our former Tutsi king can't even visit his ancestral land.

They say he lives the life of an outcast, corrupted by whites in a white country, and frolics in the warm sea with naked women. Does my husband envy him? My husband used to compare my beauty to the glory of his favorite cattle, almost as if he were a court poet, an umusizi, in the service of a Tutsi king. My husband used to say his friends envied him for the way I gave him good children. And it's true, I paid back in fertility his bride-price of cattle. He'd never have to consider the old saying that the worst thing known to man is to lack children to mourn him. Imana has taken care of our family and Jesus has too with the help of the White Fathers in their mission house.

I was almost finished with the dough and getting the smell of cooked meat out of my nose when Innocent came in to ask for something. I shook my head and said nothing, because it's bad luck to speak while preparing sorghum dough. It's all right to speak while preparing maize but not sorghum dough. His eyes were bright while he panted and poked the air with his toy spear. He must have come from playing with the Hutu boy on the next hill. In the old days when we Tutsi were the warriors and they our servants, the Hutu would never touch a spear without permission. Now their children are teaching ours to be fierce. I gave Innocent a warning look that had him backing out of the house with downcast eyes. Later on, when the dough is finished, I will speak to him again about remembering the past. I don't want him to forget the splendor of our people when Imana brought them southward four hundred years ago and gave them these beautiful hills to rule as they pleased. But perhaps I'm asking too much of a twelve-year-old. Some people say the glory of our Tutsi past should be forgotten. They say it only makes things worse to remember. After all, thirty years ago many of our people left this country in fear, and for all these years the Hutu have been in charge. Or thought they were in charge. It is all so difficult to understand. When I see boys playing with toy spears and jabbing at one another with glee, I worry that someday their play will change to real violence. We have seen too much of it in our beautiful hills. A man dead by the side of the road, his throat cut with a panga as if he were a goat. Two brothers hacked down in their pastureland. Whole families murdered. A massacre of ten here, of fifty in a nearby sous-préfecture. Year after year the numbers grow. Confusion, accusations, and more hatred.

I don't understand politics, but when my husband and his friends come here to drink, I overhear them talk about such things. They discuss the civil war that has been going on for almost four years now. Tutsi refugees from Uganda crossed the border and started it all, although they haven't got very far. From what I know they stay mostly in the north and hide in the mists of gorilla forests. All they do is come out for raids that annoy the government. Even so, my husband and his friends are proud of this little war, perhaps because it gives them hope for a Tutsi victory some day. Fortunately, my two eldest boys think more of education than they do of war, and Innocent has the cleverness of someone twice his age. But what of the five-year-old? Already he begs to go with Innocent when the boys play war. And the little fellow of two? These questions make me secretly hope that the Tutsi soldiers from Uganda will go back to that place and give up causing trouble here. Our country is so beautiful. These terraced musozi are planted in good crops by Hutu farmers, and Tutsi cattlemen like my husband make daily trips into pastureland with their longhorns. We all eat well, Tutsi and Hutu, and the smoke of our cooking fires mingles in the wonderful air breathed out of the divine mouth of Imana.

But these are thoughts I keep to myself when my husband comes home. They say a hen mustn't crow when the rooster appears.

It was late when it happened and all the children had eaten and gone to sleep, but my husband still hadn't come home. He was drinking in a beer shop somewhere with his friends. So I sat under the electric lightbulb and did some sewing on a new raffia basket. I like to do close, even work. I make complicated designs with dyes just to challenge myself. No change is possible after beginning with colored designs. I'm proud of my coiled work.

There was a program of Ethiopian music on the radio that I was half listening to when a voice interrupted with an announcement. President Juvenal Habyarimana has died in a plane crash tonight under mysterious circumstances. I put down my awl. Some kind of missile had shot the plane down and all aboard were killed, including a French crew of three and the leader of Burundi.

President Habyarimana dead. Who killed him? Tutsi? Hutu? Tutsi? Perhaps we Tutsi would be blamed for the death of a Hutu president.

I looked at a Kenyan calendar pinned on the wall. Sixth of April, 1994. If this date was special in the mind of Imana, our lives would be changed by it. Six has often been a special number for me. I was married on the sixth day of the sixth month. Someone once told me that six was Imana's favorite number.

But favorite could mean important, not good. So the sixth of April could mean the day when important bad things began for us all. I wanted my husband to come home, but surely the moon was going to be much higher before he staggered back into the rugo, full of banana beer and brave talk.

SILAS BAGAMBIKI

I WAS SLEEPING with a girl in the back room of the commune's office when someone knocked on the door and called out that President Habyarimana had died in a plane crash. Getting up, I pretended in front of the girl to be surprised. In fact, I had expected for weeks that something like this would happen and should happen.

"Get out of here," I told the girl and watched her sweet ass vanish through the back door while I was getting dressed.

"We'll all have to work hard now. Not just me," I told Denis, who was waiting in the office. "So tell me about the death of our dear president."

A frightened little man, Denis explained with much stuttering what the radio had said. At 8:30 tonight a Falcon jet carrying our president and the president of Burundi and their entourages was hit by a missile and crashed near the palace.

"We must have justice," I said with a shrug. "We must have revenge."

Within minutes the office was crowded with people wanting to know from their bourgmestre the names of those who had killed our beloved president. As their representative, I told them that members of the Tutsi revolutionary party, the RPF, had planned his death and sabotaged the plane.

My people are good people, but in fact they don't understand politics. The RPF would never have killed such a weak adversary who lately had helped their cause by showing a new willingness to negotiate with them. The old fool paid with his life for failing to boycott talks that would give Tutsi politicians a new foothold in government.

My Hutu party, the Coalition pour la Défense de la République, had quite reasonably arranged for his death. Now it was time to get rid of our real enemy, the Tutsi. As I explain to my constituents day in and day out, just because I'm short and have a flat nose I'm no less a man than one of those tall, skinny, long-nosed Tutsi. If that doesn't make them think, I remind them once again that eighty-five percent of the population are Hutu. We are the majority people. In a democracy the majority rules. That's what I say.

"It's time to clear away the bush," I tell visitors with a laugh. Seeing me laugh in anticipation of doing such a thing relieves my people of fear and uncertainty. They laugh too.

I don't go home but stay for the night in the office, so I'll be up early and at work. I send Denis out to get us a pot of beer for a private little celebration, even though I still have two worries. First, our préfect in Butare is a Tutsi, I am ashamed to say— the only Tutsi with such high office in the country. Surely he won't order retaliatory action against his own kind. For us to go forward, he must be removed. Second, I wonder if everything will be accomplished by the time cassava is harvested in May and the second bean crop is planted and the maize and sorghum are harvested in June and July. A good bourgmestre wants things done in an orderly fashion, so I'm sensitive to the schedule of harvesting.

Someday I'll end my political career and let one of my friends become bourgmestre. What I'd like to do then is grow coffee again. At one time I had been a somewhat successful grower, but when world prices fell I could hardly give beans away. It's why I turned my attention to politics.

I miss the growing of coffee. I like the look of waxy green leaves a hand-length long, and the white jasminelike flowers that enjoy only a few days of beauty. In the old times I used to stand among the trees after they were topped under fifteen-feet high for the purpose of harvesting. Each day I'd watch how the clusters of green beans became golden brown and how they ripened to a bright-red color. I remember taking off the outer pulpy skin and finding beneath it the yellowish stuff around the two little beans that looked like the halves of a peanut. Like twins in the womb, though twins are a bad omen. We grow arabica around here, classed as a "mild" coffee on the world market. I'd like to have three hundred trees, twice those of the average grower, which is what I used to be. And why not three hundred? You need five pounds of coffee cherries to produce one pound of coffee beans. One tree will give you only two pounds a season, which is why I want at least three hundred, maybe four. But I don't know. If the world price fell again, I'd fail again. Tea is a possibility, although it requires much too much land. Perhaps I'd do better with bananas and beans, I don't know. But coffee is just right for this high altitude and moist soil. I'd like to study the use of new fertilizers because they say our yields here are low. I'd prune the trees correctly and spray and manure twice a year and mulch too and use Western chemicals.

When I get on this idea of a large coffee plantation, it's hard to get off it. Right now, to make extra money, I have to sell hoes and pangas—my hoes are special enough to sell for brides-wealth gifts—but I'd like to have land again. I wouldn't raise cattle, though. There's no competing with Tutsi when it comes to keeping cattle. And yet—what if there were no Tutsi? Perhaps raising cattle would be a good idea then.

This thought relaxes me so much that I put my head down on the desk and take a nap, which Denis interrupts by returning with the beer and some news. An hour after the plane crash seventeen priests and seminarians were killed in a room of the Christus Center in Kigali. No one knows who did it.

I say to Denis, "It shows our people they can't trust the Catholic Church to protect them. They need to trust *us*." But Denis points out that the Catholic Church has always supported our cause against the Tutsi.

I shrug that off. "Those priests had better support us if they want to live."

Denis grimaces at the idea of killing priests. He's such a frightened little man, but he does run errands for me and his uncle in the gendarmerie is someone I can count on.

Once a local family had complained to the gendarmerie that I had accepted a gift of cows for taking their neighbor's side in a dispute. This uncle of Denis told them, "Why shouldn't he accept a gift?" He pointed out that some judges refused to handle a case without first receiving a gift. I thought it was a reasonable defense of my position. Apparently it was, because the complaint stopped there. I like Denis and his uncle.

Even so, I don't trust Denis or anybody. So as usual I have him taste the beer before I do. My father taught me to do that. No one will ever poison Silas Bagambiki. After we drink awhile,

I feel sleepy and go to the bed in the back room, the bed still warm and moist from my body and the girl's. I let Dennis sleep on the the office floor.

Waking at dawn to the hammering of rain on the tin roof, I send Denis out for a bowl of sorghum porridge. It stops raining just before his return, so I order him to go around and help collect the civilian militia. I tell him to tell the local captain I want the Interahamwe mustered on the training field by ten o'clock.

Meanwhile, I telephone the préfect's office in Butare to see if orders will be going out today to the bourgmestres. I get connected to Butare with surprising ease. As I expect, there are no orders for action, none at all, as if nothing of importance occurred last night. I don't bother to point out that the morning radio is filled with reports of raids against the Tutsi taking place throughout the entire country. After all, I'm speaking to a clerk who tells me the Tutsi préfect and his staff are in a meeting. In a meeting!

Hanging up, I call CDR headquarters in Kigali and report that I can't hold my boys back much longer. They're thirsting for revenge, I claim, and rightly so in defense of their threatened country. It isn't right that my own préfecture still has a Tutsi cockroach in charge. He's protecting his own people by refusing to take action, I complain. An aide to the secretary-general of the CDR promises to help me. The man is respectful and a good listener, but unsure of himself. What would people in the capital do without people like me in the provinces?

Pleased by asking myself that question, I go outside and stretch in air fragrant from the recent rain and the scent of spring flowers. The terraced musozi, surrounding my cement office, glisten in their ordered greenery. What a beautiful country. I know of nearby Tutsi pastureland that would make an excellent coffee plantation. Its Tutsi owner is on file in my supply-room cabinets where I keep thousands of indexed identity cards of everyone in the commune. A photograph is attached to the name, address, occupation, and ethnic affiliation.

Today the last bit of information is vital, isn't it, I tell myself with satisfaction. In recent weeks I had Denis and two clerks update the cards in preparation for such a wished-for emergency. I pride myself on being able to locate every Tutsi and Hutu collaborator in the commune. We must not let the murderers of our country's president go unpunished.

As I walk toward the training field, people rush up to have me assure them that justice will be done, that the bush will soon be cleared away. Naturally, none of them are Tutsi, and it occurs to me, again with satisfaction, that not a single one of those tall, thin killers is on the paths today. They must be sulking in their compounds or hiding behind the broad buttocks of their cattle. I must tell people that about the buttocks of cattle. It will make them laugh.

I am absolutely confident that someday I'll become the préfect of Butare. I'll decide how many acres will be devoted to coffee and how many laborers ought to work on the roads. Each month I'll convoke the Conseil de Préfecture to tell the bourgmestres what they must do in their communes. I'll supervise debates and punish as I see fit. I'll inform the central administration of my innovative methods. I have already had limited success, of course. Even now people pay me for my signature on a document. In the last two years I have built up my constituency through tax exemptions, and I dream of the day when I can allocate lands previously held by Tutsi. Such things involve hard decisions, but being a natural-born leader I'll welcome the challenge.

Reaching the field, I watch our local Interahamwe drill. They aren't very good at it. Not like the gendarmerie, who display even more discipline than the Forces Armées Rwandaises and show respect for our people. The last time a FAR unit came through our commune, their captain raped the daughter of a good friend of mine, the drunken troops looted some compounds, and burned down a beer shop.

The militia march up and down carrying hoes because we're short of rifles in the sous-préfecture. Noticing one young fellow, I wave to him, which makes him smile proudly. Augustin is nothing much, but his sister Agnès might become my third wife—and why not. The other two are aging, dull, and devote themselves altogether to raising our nine children.

The militia captain halts his fifty men so I can address them. I tell them our destiny is at hand. Tutsi rely on clan loyalty, but we rely on local pride. We must keep the inyenzi, those greedy cockroaches, in their place. We must rise up, we majority people, in self-defense!

The militiamen are frowning. I don't think they're sure of what their reaction ought to be, so I lift my arms high in a gesture of victory. They begin shouting and waving their hoes around.

"Not only Tutsi," I tell them after reestablishing order. "Not only Tutsi, but we must root out accomplices from our own people. They deserve the same fate as the enemy. Do you understand? Do you know what I'm saying? We must pull out of our fields the most destructive of weeds. We must do it ruthlessly!"

Leaving them to their cheers, I glance back at Augustin, who is shouting lustily with the rest. Perhaps I ought to have him speak for me, but he seems so young and worthless that I wonder if Agnès might consider his support of my offer a good reason to reject it again. How could she put off my proposal of marriage? The girl has an independence and arrogance about her that I don't like. She's pretty but not *that* pretty. Perhaps she thinks of herself as important for having gone to Butare and studied to be a nurse. When I'm préfect, I'll see to it that women behave more like their grandmothers, with deference to their superiors, and a reasonably submissive acceptance of their position in life.

AGNÈS MUJAWANALIYA

HE CAME TOWARD me on the narrow path and from the way he smiled I knew the bourgmestre would not step aside and let me pass, although I was balancing a stalk of green bananas on my head. I wondered if he'd been waiting for me at this turn in the path because earlier his man Denis had passed me in a hurry. Denis must have rushed to the bourgmestre's office to tell him where I was. Now here he was, grinning as he came, with his big white teeth and goatee and shirt tight across his belly and with no one else in sight.

When I returned from nurse's training in Butare to help care for my dying father, the bourgmestre came around my first night home to ask after my father's health. Everyone smiled and of course I knew why, so later when I went out to the well, he was there in the moonlight and came up and put his hand on my arm. I could see his teeth in the milky glow when he smiled and I said outright I didn't want that and pulled my arm away. So what did he do, he proposed marriage on the spot. He kept at me, saying he wanted a nice girl who could read and write and who could understand enough to help him in his career. He bragged about his future and claimed it would lead him some day to a big government post in the capital and all the while he was reaching out to put his hand on me again and me flicking it off again.

I nearly said, "Aren't two wives enough trouble for you already?" But Silas Bagambiki is no one to insult, so I tried to calm him down. I needed to go back to Butare, I told him, and finish my nurse's training, but when I returned home maybe we could talk again about his much too generous and flattering proposal. My hope of putting this man off without trouble wasn't high, so I was surprised that he backed off and put his hands to his sides and agreed to wait.

Now I know he had another thing besides a new woman on his mind. Only a week later the plane crashed. I think he must have known something was going to happen. I heard in Butare that bourgmestres like him knew a lot about what was going on outside of their own sous-préfectures, especially if they belonged to the CDR. That's what I heard in Butare from people who often go to the capital and have knowledge of such things. They said, you watch, if Habyarimana agrees to let Tutsi back into government, we'll have plenty of trouble, and you can count on the CDR being behind it.

I didn't want the bourgmestre. He has an ugly look to his face and narrow, watchful eyes and a big stomach and looks at me as if I'm something to eat, to bite into. What bothers me most about him is his influence on my brother, who, until recently, has never much cared about anything except his friends and beer. Now he's joined the militia and his hero is a man I don't want. But you'd think my mother and three aunts are the ones who want the bourgmestre. They're always praising him to me, which only makes me more reluctant. I don't want to live with him, let alone his two wives, who treat people like dirt because of their position. So when Mother and her sisters get after me, I smile and shut my mind like a door and wait until they finish talking. Then I tell them I'll think about it.

The truth is I have enough to feel guilty about already. Father asked me on his deathbed to marry soon, as I was twenty-one and people wondered why I was living in Butare, where promiscuous girls are called *nyamuraza* and where there are three nyamuraza to every man. I promised Father I would respect his wishes. He was such a good man. Unlike a lot of fathers he didn't shout at his children and tell them what to do. I know some of his friends laughed at him for letting me go away to study in Butare. So I wanted to please him, and in fact I have been thinking of Jérome Manirakisa, who works now in Kigali as a government clerk. We have written and Jérome has offered to pay for my bus ride to Kigali for a weekend so we can get acquainted. If Jérome were to marry me, I'm sure he wouldn't ask a high bride-price because he has such a good job in the capital. I like to think he'd accept the token of a goat and laugh when we cooked it for the wedding feast. That's how I like to think of Jérome Manirakisa. I haven't been with a man in a year, so I might have accepted his offer of a weekend together, but Father's illness worsened and I had to come home.

Now Father is gone and so is President Habyarimana, who died only the day after we buried Father. There are stories coming from other parts of the country about the killing of Tutsi, but fortunately our préfecture has been spared such violence because the Tutsi préfect won't give the order against his own people. I hope he continues to refuse, though I say nothing.

Hutu on our hill are walking around hard-faced these days and silent, as if they have something important in mind, while Tutsi keep pretty much to their own kraals.

I worry about Mother. This morning she fed the chickens, fetched water, cooked porridge, weeded in the garden, went back in the house and out again to feed the chickens again, and sat on a bench in the yard and stared straight ahead for a long time. She hasn't said a word about the bourgmestre lately, as if she's forgotten him and perhaps me too. Mother and Father were close. I don't remember them talking much, but when one was in the house, I always felt the other was nearby. Each seemed to walk in the space that the other had walked in. I know Mother regrets having only two children left of the five she gave birth to. She has never forgiven God for taking away the other three before they were five years old. Now I'll be going back to Butare soon and Augustin comes home only to sleep. Mother has begged me to stay and help around the rugo, but I can't do that, I just can't. When Mother came to this hill, she brought property to her husband because, having no brothers alive, she had inherited. Now as a widow she has nothing. All the farm holdings and the compound go to my brother, who has never done a hard day's work in his life. All my mother's life she has sowed and weeded and fetched and harvested crops until the sun set. I look at her hands sometimes and see slabs of wood polished as smooth as glass from the rubbing. And for all that effort she has nothing of her own. We argue about her joining the new women's association that wants to establish credit for women and allow them more privileges as landowners. But Mother refuses even to talk to the association. She has such old-fashioned ideas. If she had it her way, we'd still be ruled by a

Tutsi king because it was less complicated. None of these political parties wrangling in the capital. Just one man telling us
what to do. That's what she says and yet look at her—she's
dependent now on my brother. I wouldn't want to be dependent
on Augustin, who was strutting today in his militia uniform. I
told him I didn't like it, but that made no difference. He's two
years younger than me, but much younger than that in his mind.
Augustin can't wait until he can go out and shoot someone.

I fear for Tutsi that I've known since childhood. I think of
Immaculée Makeri and her children. Perhaps she doesn't even
know my name, but we smile when we meet, and looking up at
her strong, calm face and long, narrow nose I ask how her boy
Innocent is. Once I bandaged a bad cut for him, and when I
see him now the two of us wave like old friends. I want nothing
to happen to Tutsi like them. When I see my brother admiring
himself, I have a cold feeling up my back. I wish Jérome would
return to the hill during these difficult times.

To feel better, I go out to the shed and with a panga cut off
a slab of goat meat left over from the funeral meal. Taking it
inside, I cook it along with some sweet potatoes. Mother loves
the smell of goat meat sizzling over the fire, so I expect it to
tempt her from the yard where she's sitting. I expect her to stick
her head through the window and sniff and give me a big smile,
but this doesn't happen, so I go to the window and look at her
sitting on the bench, staring without blinking into the glare of
midday, unaware of chickens squawking around her feet or of
flies lighting one after another on her lips and nose and eyelids.

It almost frightens me to think of marrying a man and then
losing him and having to feel the way she does now.

AUGUSTIN HAKIZIMANA

WHEN MY FRIENDS and I used to get a pot of banana wine and drink it in the shade of eucalyptus trees near that small, pretty river in the valley, we talked about having land of our own someday. But this afternoon when the four of us got our communal pot and went down there, I was given a big surprise. After we hunched around the pot and started to sip through our reed straws, my good friend Laurent Musabe gave a loud belch and said, "Look at us. We don't even have jobs unless someone wants us to pick bananas or beans. We'll never have land without taking it from those who have."

We all nodded. Then I realized the three of them were staring curiously at me. "But we won't take yours from you," Laurent said with a little smirk, "because you're a blood brother."

I asked him what he meant by not taking mine from me.

"Well, you're going to have land to take. You're not like us anymore. You're going to be a big landowner."

"Not so big," I argued, but in truth Father had left a plot for sorghum and one for beans and yet another for cassava and also a banana grove. I glanced around at each of them and said, "Anyway, I don't want to be a landowner."

They laughed, which made me furious. I got to my feet. "No

wonder the Tutsi despise us. We think of nothing but hoeing the ground."

"Isn't that your future, Augustin? Hoeing those plots up and down the hill?"

"When I get that land, I'm going to sell it and go to Kigali."

Again the disbelieving laughter. "And what will you do when you get there?" asked Laurent. Grinning, he leaned over the pot and began sucking noisily through his straw.

"I'll become a soldier."

They didn't laugh then, but made room for me when I sat down again so I could get at my straw in the pot. After drinking awhile, we were all right, yeah, with one another. I don't think they want to be farmers either, but like me they think of going to Kigali and doing something like joining something dangerous and secret like Zero Network, so that when they knock on a door and demand entry, the knees of the people inside are going to knock too. I hear the bourgmestre is a member of Zero Network, but he won't admit it to a nonmember. It's too secret. They say Zero Network is a network of Hutu death squads and when anyone gets shot by a passing car on the street, Zero Network did it. Our bourgmestre knows more secrets than anyone in our commune, perhaps in the whole préfecture. I have great respect for our bourgmestre. He has walked the halls of the presidential palace and sat around the swimming pool where beautiful women offer themselves. I believe it when he says he has lifted a glass of wine with Madame Habyarimana and her famous brothers in the garden on Masaka Hill. That's where the jet plane of her husband crashed a week ago.

The other day our bourgmestre spoke to our militia unit at

the training field and told us what to do. He said what we must do is clean up our own hills right here. And sure enough, yesterday a big man from the government flew down from Kigali by helicopter and spoke to us about our duty. We must defend our majority people from the invaders. That's what he calls the Tutsi—invaders—even though Laurent says they've lived here for hundreds of years. But if such a big man from Kigali calls them invaders, so be it. No one but the bourgmestre could have arranged for him to come down here in a helicopter and speak to us like that. He spoke so fiercely I could see the spit flying from his mouth. He promised that an order from Butare would soon let us rid our hills of cockroaches.

And this morning I heard on the radio that the Tutsi préfect had disappeared. Well, I know if they wanted to find him, they could find his body at the bottom of a lake somewhere. He can't protect his Tutsi people any longer. It's time for the Hutu people of Butare to join the rest of the country and get to work. We who belong to the Interahamwe must now be true to our name—those who work together. We must go to work, yeah, we must kill together.

We had a radio with us as usual and turned it on to hear Radio Télévision Libre des Milles Collines. It explained that the time had come to gather the harvest. We smiled at one another and turned to listen to the voice telling us what was what from minute to minute. There's no better way of learning things than through the radio. At the moment RTLMC was broadcasting death warrants for the Minister of Labor and Social Affairs and his wife and children and his mother.

Gaspard made the palm of his hand slide across his throat. "That's for them," he said.

Laurent said, "But I think they're Hutu."

"Hutu traitors," Gaspard said.

"Ibyitso," I said.

"Yes, ibyitso," said Gaspard. "Traitors deserve to die as much as Tutsi."

"Oh, well, not *that* much," I said with a big silly frown and the others laughed in agreement. I added seriously, "But here we sit doing nothing. Yeah. What are we waiting for?" I glared at each of them. "Tell me that. What are we waiting for?"

They nodded grimly, and we hunched around the pot, sipping. I let myself dream of good meals in the fine restaurants of Kigali, of fried yams sprinkled with chili powder and of matoke and beef stew and of barbecued goat meat and Primus beer, the finest in Rwanda. I'm nineteen and ready to live. Yeah, I'll sell the land once things calm down and take my money into Kigali and spend it on good food and hot women and join the Zero Network and show those Tutsi something they won't forget.

Suddenly Laurent sat back with a sigh. "You're right," he said to me. "It's better to be a soldier than a farmer."

"Sure it is. Farming is why the Tutsi despise us," I pointed out again. "They think owning cattle is the only important thing."

"And being a warrior," Laurent said.

"Yes, and being a warrior. Now we're going to show them who the real warriors are."

Just then the radio came out with a new announcement. The voice was as breathless as someone walking up our hills too fast. It said that militiamen were bringing in the harvest across the entire nation. "The baskets are only half full!" the voice told us in great excitement. "They must be filled to the brim! You must all do your job and fill them to the brim!"

"With the Tutsi préfect out of the way," I said, jumping to my feet, "we'll get the order soon from Butare. Yeah. We'll have work to do."

Even though the pot wasn't empty, we left the riverbank and trudged up the hill, each going home to try on his uniform. When I entered the rugo, I noticed Mother sitting on a bench, a bag of chicken feed next to her and both hands spread out, each on a knee. She never looked at me, but of course lately she just sits around like this and lets the rugo get dirty and the meals grow cold.

Inside the house I got my uniform on and went to the mirror in Mother's room to look at myself. And who had to come in but my studious sister, the nurse. She stood there staring at me in my uniform until I asked her what she was doing.

"I don't like you in a uniform," she said.

"Why not? Do you want me in a rebel uniform? Do you have a Tutsi lover?" I bent over to give my new boots a few swipes with a rag. "Are you and your smart friends in Butare too big for us now?"

She ignored that. "I like my brother when he's not in a uniform."

"What do you want me in, rags? Like a bean-field picker?

"You're going to be a landowner. You can dress as you please."

"Yeah? I haven't seen a franc yet." I almost told her of wanting to sell the land so I could go to Kigali, but instead I just walked out of there. She doesn't like the uniform because it reminds her of the bourgmestre who wants her. I should tell her that she might as well take him now while she can get him, because soon he'll go far in government, all the way to Kigali, and leave her and his wives behind and take up with the girls of the capital. I hear they know tricks unheard of by women in the countryside. Huh, I mean to go there too, perhaps as an officer in FAR with a driver and a car and women and a fax machine, because when we get through with our job here we're going to throw out the worthless politicians there and probably have a king of our own—not a president—but a real king, a Hutu mwami in leopard skins and crane feathers and beads and have our own sacred kalinga drum, oh yeah, oh yeah, just like the one those old Tutsi kings worshipped that was decorated with the withered balls of their fallen enemies.

Mother is sitting on the bench when I come out, but she doesn't give me a look as I hurry from the rugo into the road and head downhill for a beer shop halfway down where I know I'll find Laurent in his uniform too, and he'll be sitting there waiting, just like me, just like the others, just waiting, huh, for the word that will let us go to work and get this thing over with, and we'll have a pot together in celebration of comradeship.

IMMACULÉE

INNOCENT CAME HOME yesterday from the next hill and said that his Hutu friend's mother wouldn't let them play together and sent him home. I asked him where his spear was. It was only a toy but nicely carved along its length by his older brother, who has a gift for carving. Unable to play with the Hutu boy, Innocent had sold the spear to him for a few francs. For a moment I wondered if I should be angry that Innocent had sold what his brother had made for him, but then I found myself laughing at his way of benefiting from the situation and he laughed and fished the banknotes from his pocket and waved them at me.

But later I had to contend with my eighteen-year-old, who was crying because the young man she's to marry had suddenly left the commune. I told her to be happy that he did. Otherwise, the way things were going, the gendarmerie might arrest him. For what? she wanted to know.

I said, "For being a Tutsi."

Of course, she must have wondered about that already, but I think hearing me say it so bluntly allowed her to accept the truth of it. I assured her that she'd see him again when all of this had passed, but during the night I heard her sobbing in the next room.

I was more worried, though, about my husband, who had come home red-eyed from too much beer. He kept mumbling about the old days and bragged about the kalinga drum kept by the old Tutsi kings in honor of defeating their enemies. You would have thought he had actually seen it himself. Gleefully, he described the shriveled private parts that hung from the drum's rim.

I knew he was frightened because he would not stop talking about the old days of Tutsi glory and the power his father had once possessed in these hills. "If a Hutu client missed one payment," he said as if I'd never heard this story before, "my father would end their contract and the Hutu would have no milk to drink or fertilizer for his fields, and no other Tutsi cattleman would enter into a contract with him and his Hutu neighbors would turn away from him for fear my father would see to it their contracts ended too." Of course, I knew that his father had never ended such a contract in his life, but that didn't matter to my husband. He was pacing back and forth, fisting his hands together. "That's the way it was. That's the way it should be. These little Hutu people need a strong hand to keep them in place."

Such talk inflamed his desire as a man and he took me to bed and we were at it when the dogs started barking. Jumping up as if expecting such an interruption, he flung a sheet around his waist and went to the door. I could hear him talking to someone and when he came back, he began to dress. "It's a meeting," he said.

"At this time of night?"

"A big government man flew down from Kigali yesterday. Did I tell you? He stirred up the Hutu fools with a nasty speech and today in Butare no one can find our préfet."

"What does that mean?"

"The Hutu will put in another préfect who'll issue some kind of order."

"What kind of order?" I watched him take down from the wall a long spear that had been on hooks there ever since I came to his house. It had been his father's initiation spear. I wanted to ask what he was going to do, but I couldn't get the words out of my mouth and, anyway, I didn't want to seem frightened in front of my husband. That would be wrong. I must not shame him. And of course I knew what he meant to do. So I trailed silently behind him to the door and watched him leave the rugo with a half-dozen other men who were waiting in the moonlit yard. Four spear tips and the flat blades of three hoes appeared in a bobbing motion above their heads when they left the rugo.

Back inside, feeling a sudden chill, I lay down on the bed that still smelled of us together. The girl began sobbing again in the next room, but at least the other children were sound asleep. That was good. That was like it should be, and I thought maybe nothing more was going to happen. After all, men loved meetings and shouting at one another. They might boast awhile, and then, after a few beers, calm down and go home.

I lay there and thought of my boy safe in France. But the next oldest, who had carved the toy spear, the boy at the university in Butare, what of him? In recent years not a single Tutsi was allowed to teach there, and only a few students from our people attended. If there was violence at the university, they'd quickly single out my boy. But I believe education makes people tolerant. I believe that. University students ought to be the safest of people.

A beam of moonlight came through the small high window and lay across my hands. I have always felt that hands folded together in such light have the quiet, heavy look of death. But they were my hands and would be tomorrow. Seeing them so calm and steady made me feel better. I was glad my girl's young man got away, although he hadn't provided for her. Perhaps they really would meet again in this world or in Imana's world or in the heaven of Jesus, where the priest says we'll all meet again someday.

I can't sleep. I listen for the spaces between her sobbing until suddenly there's no sobbing but only a long space of silence. Good girl. Finally, she fell asleep. I wait for my husband to come home from his meeting; that's why I can't sleep, but he doesn't come home, he won't come home; they have gone drinking, I tell myself, until the light in the window becomes a dull blue and then a light blue like water in a shallow pond. I get up to make a morning fire. Life goes on. But what if an order does come from Butare just like the orders from other préfectures? Every day the radio tells us of our people being hunted down on roads and in their own compounds and pasturelands.

Shall I wake the children and get them out of here? Where can we go? We're known in these hills. Next to our rugo lives a Hutu family and just a few steps farther on the path, at the next bend up the hill, is a Tutsi family, then two Hutu. We all know of one another's comings and goings. But what if the big man from the capital has turned everything against us here? As the radio has been boasting of, are the Hutu going to hunt down all of our people? Where can we hide? Long ago the forests in these hills were cut for pasture and field. Instead of woods there are rows of waist-high stalks or close-cropped treeless pasture. In the valley there's a big swamp, but on the way down to it we'd have to pass rugo after rugo and the commune's headquarters and so many people coming and going on a network of paths. There's no place to hide, not one.

I'm a married Tutsi woman from a good clan, so the fear I'm feeling is shameful. I touch the amulet around my neck. It's the fang of a poisonous snake and very powerful. I stroke it three times up one side and three times down the other. Good. I'm calm now.

There's water to fetch from the well, so I get a bucket and go outside. As I leave the yard and approach the well, I see a Tutsi family coming single-file down the path beyond our compound.

Walking toward the path, I call out and ask where they're going. One man holds a bow in one hand and a clutch of arrows in the other, as if he were going hunting for antelope. The three women and a half-dozen children have baskets on their heads and extra clothing wrapped around their shoulders.

"To the church," one of the women says.

I fall into step with her as they head downhill. I know her but we're not good friends. Our clans are different. Hers is much lower than mine. Even so, at this time of trouble we look at each other with the faces of caring sisters. She tells me that the militia is assembling near the commune's headquarters and the bourgmestre is waiting for orders to go in search of lawbreakers.

"What lawbreakers?"

"Tutsi. And any Hutu who help us."

"What are the militia supposed to do?"

"Clear the bush. That's what the bourgmestre calls it."

"Do you know what 'clearing the bush' means?"

The woman shrugs instead of giving an opinion. "I hear on that hill over there"—she points at terraced musozi toward the west—"people have been killed already. A whole house was turned out and killed."

"By militia?"

"I don't think so. By some older boys with clubs and hoes. That's what we hear."

"Where are you going?"

"To the church. The bourgmestre has promised he won't let his men enter sacred ground. So the church is safe."

"Yes, that's as it should be." I thank her and return home. Roughly I wake the children and order them to get dressed. I tell the eighteen-year-old to stop sniveling and go get some jugs filled at the well. Quickly, I put on my best blue dress and white bandanna and a red sweater that was a gift from my husband twelve years ago, after the birth of Innocent. Collecting the children, the two youngest sleepily rubbing their eyes, I get us out on the path and take one last backward glance at the rugo where I have lived happily with a good man and seven children. For a moment I study the main house's thatched roof and smooth mud walls the color of straw and the dusty yard that I have swept every day for more than twenty years and the dark, cool sheds filled with rope, harnesses, bales of raffia fiber, tools. Some of our cattle are penned nearby and the rest in a kraal on the east slope of the hill. They need to be watered this morning and the cows milked. Innocent can do that, but I won't let him stay behind. Where is my husband? How can he grab an old spear and forget his livestock in such an easy way? When men carry spears, maybe they forget everything else. Maybe now it will be the Hutu who drive our cattle to pasture each day, their short bandy legs half-seen in swirls of dust raised by the herd. Maybe our forty-one beasts waiting in the nearby kraal will obey Hutu as willingly as they obey us.

But once we're out of sight of our rugo, I forget the cattle and think only of the safety of the church. It must surely be safer than a banana grove, than a cupboard or a shed. I had thought earlier of squeezing the children into cupboards, but if men came looking for us, they'd probably look first in the cupboards. I could imagine a cupboard door slowly opening and a grinning face peering in.

The church of Jesus sits on the flat top of a neighboring hill, so we must first go down, then cross a stream, and go up another path. The sun is high enough now to free itself from the hills, and I hear birds twittering on either side of the path as we cross the stream and start going up. The familiar birdcall tells me everything is going well. Birdcalls can tell you such things. Imana will provide with the help of Jesus. We must be patient because the world is still a good place to be.

I'm even more sure of it when we approach the church that the White Fathers built from red brick many years ago. It's the largest building in the whole commune, a big safe place, with a courtyard and a holy fountain of marble and a high, enclosing brick wall. At the front entrance stands a marble statue of the Holy Jesus that was shipped all the way from France. The hands of the Holy Jesus are outstretched to bring everyone in, even those who believe in nothing. As we get nearer, I see people heading for the Holy Jesus from every direction. Some families have even brought goats, which makes me wonder how long they think we'll stay inside. I imagine our cattle with udders swollen from holding so much milk. Where is my husband? It's rare that I speak sharply to him, but this time I will. He ought to be with us, and before coming along he ought to have provided for his forty-one cattle in the kraal. That's what I'll tell him when we meet. If that spear doesn't get him into such trouble that we don't meet again. That's a terrible thought. He lifted the spear as if he had stepped out of an ancient time, a Tutsi warrior going into battle to serve a great mwami. What he has really done, though, he has gone off with those hard-drinking friends of his and left our warm bed without finishing what he started.

I notice my eighteen-year-old glancing around in the hope of finding her young man in the crowd. "A strong fellow like him," I tell her, "won't be looking for a place to hide. He's gone away now so he can come back for you later."

"Do you think he'll join the rebels?"

"Maybe so. He's a brave young man." That's the Tutsi in me talking. I hope he's a true warrior, and not someone who runs off and leaves his woman behind.

Innocent, walking beside me, puts one hand against my arm. It's as gentle as the touch of a butterfly and wonderful. If I look at him, I'll have tears in my eyes, so I don't look at him. Anyway, I don't need to look, because I know his face as well as any face on earth. The high cheekbones, the slim nose, the pointed chin. He has broad shoulders, but a narrow chest and hips just like his father. His legs are not yet long-muscled like those of a male Tutsi, but his feet have already flattened out from herding cattle over so much pastureland. He doesn't yet have a pure Tutsi look, not at twelve. A couple more years will give him the necessary height. Then, of course, he'll have trouble with the Hutu, who'll be jealous of his tall good looks, but until then he's still a boy with keen watchful eyes and a clever way of getting what he wants and my favorite.

Silas

THIS IS THE way I see it. These bad people must be rooted out of the land like poisonous weeds from a garden, but when that happens some of the land will become empty, so it must be planted again and who can do that planting? I can. I can plant the land with people of my own choosing who I know are loyal majority people. If they help me root out the bad people, haven't they earned a reward? And what better reward than land? That's the way I see it, I tell my constituents who file into the office and wish to volunteer for the coming work. They ask what they must do and instead of answering that question I ask them if they have a panga or a hoe. That's all you need, I tell them with a smile. If you don't have a proper tool of your own, just remember that I sell both kinds. I explain that the cockroaches must be smashed right here, in our own neighborhood, as well as anywhere else where they crawl around and poison the land. Together we'll get rid of the inyenzi, I tell them, so go on home and wait for the signal, or if you need a hoe or panga—some people want a new and never-before-used one for this special occasion—go see Denis in the next room and he'll sell you what you need at a fair price. Today alone we've sold twenty-two pangas and eleven hoes.

A contingent of FAR troops has been assigned to help us out,

I've been informed by telephone, but so far none has arrived. Probably some of them are going to remain in Kigali now because the Tutsi rebels have attacked the capital in sudden force. This is, I must say, a surprise. We didn't expect the RPF to put up much of a fight. In the four years of their pitiful attempt at creating a civil war, the RPF has developed an annoying if nearly harmless plan. They hit a village and before we can retaliate, they melt away into the jungle. A joke has them living in abandoned gorilla nests.

But two days after the plane crash, those Tutsi cockroaches appeared with artillery on the heights above Kigali. Perhaps fear of annihilation has given them some unexpected courage. So let them make a little noise before we snuff them out. Let them strut on the heights like warriors of old. Our top officials have already left Kigali for Gitarama to establish a provisional government there. It's only a safety precaution. I don't think we have anything serious to worry about unless the world gets involved and the world won't get involved unless the UN does and the UN has chosen to do nothing but ask questions. I have seen those sweaty red faces and heard those whiny voices before. Arriving in their big cars and white suits, I can imagine them sipping tea and asking: Is it true that you're killing hundreds, even thousands of Tutsi? Ask questions, talk, do nothing. That, experience has taught me, is the UN way. Meanwhile, we'll do what we must and after a little protest the world will accept it, as usual.

I'm confident that here in the commune we'll distinguish ourselves. When the official flew down from the capital and talked to our militia and gendarmerie, I knew from his fiery speech that things were going to change in Butare Préfecture. Sure enough, the Tutsi préfect has appropriately disappeared and with him will surely disappear a reluctance to act in our region. I await the phone call that authorizes me to get started. In anticipation I have opened the identity-card files and distributed them to the eight militia captains, each of whom has been assigned a sector. Squads of ten men, carrying the identity information from rugo to rugo, will have no trouble locating each family of cockroaches, even if some of the volunteers and militiamen come from another neighborhood. Last night I got only two hours' sleep while organizing this method of cutting off escape. When the order comes through, people will say that Bourgmestre Silas Bagambiki was fully prepared.

I am smoking too much, lighting one cigarette with another, because the suspense is terrible. Only an hour ago I learned by telephone that all of the Tutsi students at Butare University have been rounded up and dealt with. We don't need Tutsi intellectuals telling the world what should be done in Rwanda. We need only the good men, the loyalists who represent the majority people and the tough workers in the Coalition pour la Défense de la République and the tireless leaders of the Mouvement Révolutionnaire National pour le Développement et la Démocratie. I tell people, I say that the high-sounding names of those political parties are perfectly matched by the dedication of their members. That's what I say. I say without boasting that we need men like myself who are willing to take in the harvest. That's what I told squads of militia as they lounged in a field and drank beer and awaited the order. A few have brought World War II guns from home, but the rest have only pangas and hoes and boards spiked with nails. When the FAR troops arrive, I hope they'll supply our boys with automatic rifles.

I called the girl's brother to me and gave him the honor of taking messages to adjoining hills. Augustin raced off at top speed.
Running errands is probably what he's good for. Yet when this is
over and if he's done his job, I'll let him speak to his sister on my
behalf. Then if the brother gets nowhere, I'll show Agnès Mujawanaliya another way for a man of my standing to deal with
youthful disrespect. Does she take me for one of these fools who
spends a lifetime lifting a hoe? None of them here yet know me.

This morning the local priest came around to the office and
insisted that his church be considered sacred ground if any violence occurs. I dealt with his insolence by pretending to take
his demand seriously. Whoever goes into your church, I assured
him, will be safe there. What do Hutu like Agnès Mujawanaliya
and Father Faustin take me for? Perhaps like so many majority
people they really believe we're inferior, even leaders like me.
After all, for generations our ancestors served the Tutsi. And
it's true that in the old times, when a Hutu managed to become
a patron himself, there was always a Tutsi higher up for him to
answer to. For more than thirty years, since Independence Day,
we have kept the Tutsi in lower echelons of government, yet
the memory of their power still walks today among our majority
people. But such a memory must come to an end. Why? After
we finish, there won't be a Tutsi left to remind us of that past.

"Bourgmestre!" Denis calls from the other room, where the
telephone is.

Rushing in there, I grab the phone from him.

The voice crackling over the line tells me what I need to know.
"Acting préfect of Butare here. Clear the bush, Bourgmestre!"

Hanging up and mashing out my cigarette, I turn to Denis
with a smile. "So at last we begin."

IMMACULÉE

IN THESE HILLS word travels by shouting almost as quickly as it did in the old times by war drum. There are few telephones here and they belong to officials like the bourgmestre, but people cup their hands and call across the hills from one terrace to another, from one kraal or pasture to another, across streams and through banana groves, until in a short while what one person knows the whole commune knows too. So it didn't take long for Tutsi to hear of the church becoming a sanctuary. The church holds maybe a few hundred on most Sundays, but a few thousand have come here today. The parish schoolrooms and other buildings are packed with Tutsi and those Hutu who have intermarried with us or in some other way have close ties with our people.

I have taken my family into one of the classrooms. I can read so I know what is written in chalk on the board. In French someone has scrawled *Waiting for the people who kill people.*

We sit in rows on benches in front of desks marked and grooved by many children over the years. Soon the benches are full and people sit on the desks too, then in the aisle, and finally they are propped shoulder to shoulder along the walls. There must be a hundred people or more and with only one small window for air. But we stay where we are. Most of the women move the air with raffia fans so there's a soft, whirring sound like insects on a hot afternoon. We don't talk much; we wait, and the only motion aside from the fans is from people getting up and stepping between legs and around seated bodies on the way to the latrine behind the supply shed. Most of us in here are women and children because many of the men have stayed with their herds and would rather take their chances in open pastureland. I suppose a few others have behaved like my husband and picked up an old spear. Some of the men here have pangas lying across their laps and bows slung across their shoulders. Their women are lucky to have them close by. If a family must go, let them all go together. But that's a thought I keep to myself.

Looking at my eighteen-year-old, who has finally accepted her young man's absence, I wonder if she can hold the same thought. Innocent probably does. Maybe the little girl, but not the two youngest boys, who don't yet seem fully aware of the danger. I hold the youngest against my breast, feeling his warm body get warmer in the close room.

But we won't die here, I tell myself, not in this holy place. Father Faustin has been given the bourgmestre's word for that. And there is this too. So many people gathered together must be protected somehow by being so many. So many can't be easily killed. Once the killing began and there was blood, those who did the killing would not want to kill more. Why? Because of the blood. Killing five chickens is worse than killing one because of the blood. This is a calming idea.

And yet when there's a commotion from the courtyard, I jump like everyone else. After awhile someone comes in and tells us that the militia have been out there trying to get in.

Father Faustin turned them away, even when they swore they had only come to evacuate us. Hearing this strange news, we look around at one another. Evacuate us? From here to go where? I suspect the militia are drinking. After all, most of them can't be much older than Innocent. Young and scared, they must be turning to the beer they brought along.

If they're young, they're scared, I tell myself. If they're scared, they won't be much good at killing, not after seeing the blood of the first few. And look at how many we are, even in this one room. Some of us can expect to live. I sit quietly, listening to the motion of fans. They're trying to move air but it's becoming as heavy as mud. It's getting hotter with the sun overhead now, but this is a sacred place so we must stay right where we are. We won't move until Father Faustin says so.

It's what I tell the two youngest boys, who are getting restless and want to go home. The youngest picks his nose again and again until I pull his hand away. An old man comes into the classroom looking worried and tells us there are men in different uniforms at the main gate now. The uniforms they wear aren't bits and pieces like those worn by our militia, who put on anything that looks military, like any khaki shirt and any leather boots, even if they don't match. A man calls out and says the new fellows might be soldiers of FAR and asks if they're wearing red berets. The old man nods.

Innocent wants to know what's going on. I tell him government troops have come to protect us. It's not true, of course, because all of the soldiers in FAR are Hutu. Innocent gives me a look that says he already knows that.

Suddenly there's a loud noise outside, so loud that many of us inside hunch over or fall to the floor or crawl under desks, trying to get away from what it means. I stretch my arms out and bring my children in.

Another explosion. Another.

Some people struggle to their feet and rush out of the room, but I hold on to my family and order them to stay where they are. We'll be right here until Father Faustin says to leave, I tell them. A man's face peering in from the door has a terrified look. Maybe he wants to squeeze into the packed room with us.

"They're throwing grenades over the wall!" he calls out. "They're going to try and get in!"

Now it's time to say it, so I motion my children to come as close to me as possible, and I look at each face as I speak. "Listen to me. You can die only once. Just that once. That one time."

"I don't want that once," says my five-year-old.

The slow awareness on his face breaks my heart, but I say, "You die only once, then go to Jesus and Imana."

"Don't want to go there. Want to stay here. I want to go home," he whimpers and clutches me hard.

Looking away from him to the others, I say, "Remember, if they come in with pangas and guns, just let them do it and get it over with so you can go quickly to God."

Shouting and cries and more explosions come from outside. A few men struggle through the milling crowd and go to the door to see what's happening. I'm not that curious and anyway, I won't move from this spot. We're going to wait right here until Father Faustin tells us to leave.

A man turns back to us on the benches and purses his lips as if thinking. "Now they're lobbing mortars in," he says.

I hear a *whooshing* sound and then an explosion. A man near the doorway has brought his bow and arrows. He fits an arrow to his stringed bow and at the doorway lets it go with a little cry of triumph. He must be trying to show his family how brave he is, but then he comes back in and sits down quietly.

I hear whistles blowing. What does that mean? Then I realize it's the militia blowing their whistles to get up the courage to break the front gate and come into the yard. Everyone's talking now, although no one's saying anything, because no one knows anything except for the fear they see in one another's eyes. Mine meet my eighteen-year-old's. She's absolutely calm now and gives me a little smile. Now that she knows her young man won't come for her, she's behaving like a Tutsi girl from a good clan should.

"You'll see him again!" I shout to reassure her. I must shout it to be heard over the terrible noise in the room and the noise coming from outside—more explosions and afterwards some screaming and yelling. I think somebody out there got hurt. And for the first time I hear a quick, clattering sound. It's like metal would sound if it could cough. It's a sound I've heard coming from a group of hunters. I have heard guns fired, but not automatic guns firing so quickly. Not until now.

"They got through the gate!" someone is yelling. "They're inside!"

"Stay where you are," I warn my children and hope each of them can feel something of me, my hands or arms or legs.

"Priest's dead." The words run like fire through the room.

"Priest's not dead," I say to no one and hug the boy to my breast. If Father Faustin is dead, then it's over. I have been a loyal wife, a loving mother, a good Tutsi woman, but now whatever I am, whatever we are, whatever my children are, we're going to be taken away somewhere. Maybe we're going to the bosom of Holy Jesus as Father Faustin promised, but already he lies dead. I say aloud, I think I say it aloud, that we are going up into the heaven of Holy Jesus. I am yelling to my boys and girls to keep close around me—close close close—and behind their heaving bodies I see people jittering back and forth, back and forth like excited flies, none of them going anywhere as they stumble into one another. A great wall of noise is getting closer, a huge wave of it breaking around my children as I see past their heads—buried, trembling against me—who is in the doorway.

It surprises me that I see them, that the killers have really come. I see boys I have watched grow up from babies carried in slings on their mothers' backs, I see them coming into the room red-eyed from their drinking, and I can't believe what I see but I am a true witness as their pangas and hoes lift and come down and lift and come down the way they would clear out weeds in a plot of land. Blood spurts up into their sweaty faces, as they circle the room and hit at anyone who tries to get past them. It's like going after chickens. I can't believe it. I feel the hands of my children around me, gripping the tree that gave them life, and I keep shouting, "Just once! Just let it get done!" as I see people holding up their arms to protect themselves and those arms hacked away, spurting, and I pull my children in as close as I can. People are trying to crawl under the desks or over them, screaming with their eyes shut the way infants scream when sick with fever. I see my eighteen-year-old's eyes not a few inches away from my own, hers white and round with the black cores like mirrors showing a terrible motion behind me. She leans against me but holds her face away. Her mouth opens to say something at the same time I hear her grunt from what is happening to her that I can't yet see, she goes *ugh ugh*, and the blood begins pouring down her lower lip. Her eyes get bigger as they see beyond me into something else, and then my poor, dear unmarried girl slumps away from me, down to my feet. I look up at another face coming close to mine. I know whose face it is but can't remember the name that goes with it, but its look was young once on the path, younger than the face of my own Innocent, a Hutu boy holding his mother's hand as we passed with a polite nod, and as I look at this sweaty face close to mine I feel on my neck a blow harder than I have ever imagined could be felt by anything living, and I see the flash of his panga as it comes down again and strikes my chest so hard I fall to one side, still hugging my five-year-old as he gives a little grunt too, a last breath of air let out of him, and I wonder frantically where are my two-year-old and my seven-year-old who were holding on to me just now but not now anymore not anymore although someone's arms still grip me from behind and I hear myself I think I hear myself yelling "Innocent?" into air filled with flying blood. I see a row of nails in a club coming down on the side of I see nothing of nothing of—

AUGUSTIN

WAITING WITH OTHER squads of Interahamwe for the order to come from Butare, we sit in the open field playing dice and bet with pebbles because we don't have money on us. We play with Laurent's dice, those ivory ones that he got from his brother who bought them in Nairobi while unloading coffee bags there. His brother used to tell us about Nairobi, especially about the Kikuyu whores in tight jeans and high-top sneakers who start smoking bhang when they wake up in the morning and drink Tusker White Cap beer all day long. Hearing him talk so bold that way used to make me want to go there myself and to other places also, so when I say I want to do something besides lift a hoe, I mean it, yeah. Listening to Laurent's brother tell his story was how I learned what I want from this life. Soon I'll get the money to go somewhere and I'm thinking of Nairobi or Mombasa or Dar es Salaam. I'll drink Tusker White Cap and smoke bhang and go with whores who wear high-top sneakers and carry health certificates that show they passed the AIDS test, that's what I'm going to do, I tell my friends while we roll dice and wait for the bourgmestre to give us the signal. A voice from the city of Gisenyi yells out of a half-dozen radios nearby. "Heroes! Don't relax! Find every one of those cockroaches who hide like cowards. Look carefully and finish them off, one by

one by one by one by one. Don't let them talk you out of it.
Don't let a single one of them get away!"

From where I sit I can see the commune headquarters, where
people go in and come out again after the bourgmestre has told
them what to do. Someday I'll tell them what to do from my
office in Kigali, where I'll be his helper and make more money
than I ever could on the land my father left me.

The bourgmestre comes out, trailed by little Denis, his present
helper, and a group of farmers. One of them holds an umbrella
over the bourgmestre's head to protect him from the sun. He's
got a bullhorn. At the edge of the field he calls out to us, "Patience, brothers! I have just learned by telephone that they
weeded out the big brains at Butare University. And they never
found the cowardly Tutsi préfect, who must have run away. So
the order won't be long in coming now. We just have to do
everything step-by-step, according to law. Hear me? Not long
now!"

We cheer and he goes back inside with little Denis and the
rest of them crowding in at his heels.

A big truck comes along, then another, then three more, and
from each of them jump thirty or forty men in uniforms. Gaspard
says they're FAR troops. He pretends to know about military
things. And we soon learn they really are FAR troops, who have
come to help us with our work, yeah. I stand up and watch them
get their equipment from the trucks. They wear zebra-striped
fatigues and their officers have short-brimmed bush hats with
soft crowns and floppy brims, the kind of hat that I'd like to
have, that I often think of having, while the soldiers wear red
cotton berets that are good-looking too. Their black-leather
combat boots are polished. I got my weather-beaten pair from

an old man who tramped through the Second World War in them. At least I have boots. Gaspard and Laurent wear rubber sandals cut from old tires.

The bourgmestre comes from the office and beckons to me with one crooked finger. I rush forward to hear him order me to go tell the militia captain on the north slope that the FAR have arrived.

I run as fast as I can, because with the FAR here I want to get back and be near them. I find the captain, who doesn't seem very interested in the news, then I hurry back to headquarters, getting there out of breath.

The trucks are parked in front, but the FAR troops have left.

Laurent says they're heading for the church, where their assignment is to surround it and wait. He holds up a pack of identity cards. "When the order comes, we'll go with these over there." He points to another hill.

"Where did you get the cards?" I ask.

"The captain gave them to me. I'm to hold them for our squad," Laurent explains proudly.

I try to hide my disappointment. Why didn't the bourgmestre give them to me? I'm his favorite. But Laurent is our militia captain's favorite.

I'm thinking about that when a shout comes from headquarters and the bourgmestre appears in the doorway, holding his arms high and waving his bullhorn. Everyone starts yelling because the order has finally come through, and we all rush to get our weapons.

"Follow me," Laurent tells our squad as if he's a captain.

I'm so excited I don't care who holds the identity cards. Anyway, we don't need cards to tell us where we're going. Everyone on that hill is known to us, except the babies. This is the important thing. We know where every cockroach lives.

But then Laurent holds up two of the identity cards for me to look at.

On one of them I see the name of Gaspard's uncle next to his photograph, a man with a fat face and thick eyebrows.

"Ibyitso," says Laurent.

"Are you sure?"

"The card's marked with a red dot."

"Why?"

"I think he and a Tutsi from Butare are buying a truck together. That's what I heard a few weeks ago."

Maybe Gaspard's uncle collaborates with the enemy, but he's also generous. Many times he's invited me for a beer. Even so, if we meet, I'll go after him because he's a proven ibyitso. I'll kill him. And Gaspard better kill him too even if he is an uncle.

It's getting cloudy. I hope it doesn't rain and make the paths slippery. We need to move fast. On the way to the next hill, we blow our whistles back and forth and start laughing. The captain went with another squad, so he won't know about it. We aren't supposed to blow our whistles unless surrounding a place and locating each other's whereabouts. We do it now to make Laurent understand he may hold the cards but he's no better than the rest of us. We're all in charge, so we all blow our whistles.

Coming up the hill, I see the Tutsi's empty kraal, which means he and maybe his sons must be taking the cattle to pasture. But there's smoke rising from the compound, so some of the family are home. Going about their daily business, are they. The idea of Tutsi living their normal lives is enough to make me angry. We fan out without being told and I think that we disappoint Laurent, who would like to remind us to fan out. In our ten-man squad we have one rifle, an old one, and Gaspard has made himself a spiked club with a half-dozen three-inch nails. Otherwise we carry pangas and hoes. I have a new hoe, bought from the bourgmestre's supply company for this special work. Unlatching the gate to the compound, Gaspard goes inside and waves the rest of us into the yard. A few chickens puff away at our feet. Tutsi won't eat chickens or eggs, but they make money by selling the stuff to us. I have bought eggs from the people here. Laurent starts blowing his whistle as we circle the house, and we all join in. I blow in rhythm to the breaths I take. They seem to be coming quick, in gusts. But we came up the hill fast, so I'm a little out of breath. It's not because I'm afraid.

Someone yells at the house, "Come on out, you cockroaches!" I join in. "Come on out, come on out, you cockroaches!" I blow my whistle just as a half-grown boy races from the house into the yard. I get to him first with my hoe and hit him hard enough in the spine to bring him down. But he starts to get up right away, which is surprising because I cracked him hard. So I hit him again with the sharp blade in the neck and watch the blood spurt, but to my surprise he starts groaning and getting up again. I never knew it takes so much to keep someone down who's been knocked down, and this is only a boy. I don't like it and throw the hoe away as if it's broken, while Gaspard comes up and whacks him with the spiked club. Then he lies there without moving, and when Gaspard yanks the spiked club free, the boy's head is a mangled bloody thing like an overripe melon.

Gaspard has a strange look on his face when we stare at each other, but then I blow my whistle in pulses like playing a drum and so does he and we turn back to the house in time to see a girl escaping. She's no older than six or seven and wears nothing but a waist bracelet. When she races out, Laurent tries to grab her but she breaks free, as quick as a fish. Running after the girl, I finally corner her near a storage shed. I could remember her coming along with her mother to sell eggs to my mother. She's crying so hard her eyes are closed tight, but somehow when I reach her she dodges the blow of my hoe. That makes me ashamed. I swing two, three, four times, each missing, but the fifth time, as she falls exhausted and crying to her knees, I catch her shoulder with the end of the blade and I feel the blow, yeah, shivering from her flesh and bone right down to my wrist. The girl is solid, something to hit, whereas when she came out of the house nearly naked she seemed like nothing but a slim little thing almost not worth hitting. I raise the hoe high with both hands and bring it down in a wide curve as hard as I can, as if I'm swinging at a full-grown buffalo, while she lies curled up on the ground. This blow goes deep, cuts her nearly halfway through, but even so, the girl still jerks like a fish, her mouth opening and closing as if trying to get more air. After the first few long spurts, the blood pumps less and less high and begins to run out in a steady flow. Looking at it, I can't seem to move my arms for another strike. Someone comes along and whacks her on the side of the head. I nearly thank him for finishing it, but instead I jam the whistle in my mouth and blow it loud in a *boom-boom* drumbeat way.

Gaspard and two others go inside the house and after a few

moments I hear a woman shriek a few times, then someone else is screaming and yelling in there, and after that the whole rugo becomes silent except for the squawking of chickens.

"No more cockroaches here," someone calls out and everyone blows his whistle, and we're all grinning.

So our work has begun. I only hope the others don't see how much my hands tremble. I won't even glance at their hands because I'm afraid theirs will look steady.

We go to the next rugo and the next, and by then I am swinging my hoe like a real soldier. We visit eight rugos by late afternoon. No one gets away. We're as careful as RTLMC radio tells us to be. Everything is searched, every shed and closet and banana grove. One tall strong Tutsi comes out of his house holding a spear, but our man with the rifle stops him with two bullets and somebody shoves a screwdriver deep into his ear while he's dying. I don't like doing the babies, but it has to be done, because they're also cockroaches and if we don't get rid of them now they'll infest the land. The bourgmestre says so. RTLMC says so. At least the ones that can't yet walk go quickly.

We're all sweating and everyone has streaks of blood on his shirt and pants. Then we get to the rugo belonging to Gaspard's uncle. His family comes out smiling because they're Hutu, but the smiling ends when all of us, Gaspard included, start circling around and calling them collaborators. "Ibyitso! Ibyitso!" we chant together.

The uncle comes out, holding a big pot and telling us we have it all wrong. He holds out the pot and invites us to have a drink of freshly brewed beer, but we're all blowing our whistles and advancing on the family, who stand in a row in front of the house. When one of the children breaks out in a run and goes down under a hoe, the uncle throws away the pot and rushes sobbing into the yard where three of us get right at him. He takes at least a half-dozen hits before Gaspard comes up. We stand back, allowing Gaspard to finish the job with his spiked club. After two hits with such a weapon we can no longer see his uncle's thick eyebrows at all. Blowing whistles in unison, our squad goes inside, Gaspard leading us. We search everywhere, just as we did in the Tutsi compounds, for anyone hiding in a closet or under a mattress. Then we check the latrine, because earlier today we found a Tutsi in a latrine, hiding up to his face in the shit and we shot him so we didn't have to get closer, but there's no one left anywhere in this rugo.

"Did we get the whole family?" I ask Gaspard, who tries to smile but can't seem to as he says, "All of them."

We have harvested six Hutu here, every one of them family to Gaspard. Leaving the rugo, we pat him on the back. "Good job, brother," we tell him, but it's not easy to look at his face.

Our squad has gone through the identity cards, so we're going to headquarters for more. On the way back another Interahamwe squad comes along, covered with blood like us. They're heading for the church where they say plenty of cockroaches are holed up, so we join them and cross over to another hill. I'm happy about this because if the FAR unit is there, I can see what real soldiers do.

When we get there, it's all over. Soldiers are sitting on tombs in the church cemetery and in nearby fields. They look tired and hot. I'm disappointed I didn't see them throw grenades and shoot mortars. We go inside the courtyard, which smells of smoke and blood. There are bodies lying around, but most are in the church itself, between pews, along the aisles, stacked

three or four deep in some places among the pots and pans they
brought and their suitcases and hymnals like the one my aunt
used to carry with her everywhere, even to the pigpen when she
threw swill. Some of our militia are finishing off people who still
breathe in the muddle of corpses. They hear a moan and go after
it with their pangas jabbing, like they were spearing fish in a
pond. Sometimes they have to root around in the mass of arms
and legs to find where the sound's coming from and then they
thrust into the bodies until it stops. I won't join in this work.
I'm too tired for more work, and that work seems nasty anyway,
and the stifling heat and the rotten-fruit smell of blood in the
church's rooms and the wide-open look of so many eyes and
mouths in dead faces have made me a little sick.

I don't say anything about it, though, and when I leave the
church I go sit with the FAR soldiers. Some of them have
bought pots of beer from local onlookers and are drinking. I sit
next to one of them who's wearing a neck towel. Every now and
then, he wipes his sweat with it. I study the oval canteen that
hangs on the rear of his web belt in a cradle of straps. I want a
canteen like that. "I want to be a soldier," I tell him.

"Really? Didn't you militia boys have enough fun today?" he
says with a frown and a little laugh.

"I want to wear a uniform like yours and fight."

"You can fight without wearing a uniform." He looks me over.
"You mean it?" When I nod, he points to an officer standing
over there. "Go ask him. But wait. Have you got money? You
have to buy a shirt with epaulets and boots. And out here he'll
make you pay to enlist. You'll pay for the use of a gun too. He
won't want to take you on and then have you run off with a
government-issue rifle."

"I can pay. I'll go home right now and get money."

He looks at me as if he doesn't think I understand, then he shrugs. "Make it fast. We'll leave soon."

I don't hesitate a moment, but race home. Lucky we live close to the church. There's no one in the rugo when I get there, so I rush straight into the room where Agnès keeps her things and in an old chest I rummage around because I know that's where she keeps her money brought from Butare. Finding it, yeah, I stuff all the francs into my pockets and leave the house, but not in time to miss her. She's coming into the compound with her head in her hands as if crying. I'm not going to stop to ask her what's wrong, but seeing me she reaches out and grabs my arm as I go by.

"What's happened to you?" She's looking me up and down, her teary eyes wide with a look of horror. "Do you know what your friends did to Mother? You fool, Augustin! Some of them told her to stop walking away from them and she didn't and they shot her, just now, not an hour ago, down the road. Augustin! Do you hear me? They shot your mother just down there at the bend in the road! Augustin!"

I'm hurrying away with her words at my back. One of these days I'll sell the land, maybe to the bourgmestre so he can grow coffee beans on it, and pay Agnès back what I took and give her a lot of brides wealth for her marriage when it comes. That's what I'll do. I'll be a good brother to my sister. And I'm sorry for Mother, so really sorry because she was such a good mother and took care of me, but ever since Father died she's been acting strange and won't talk sense or listen to anybody, so it's understandable if someone mistakes her for an arrogant ibyitso when they tell her to halt and she just keeps walking, just goes on her way the way she does lately. But I have money now and a uniform to buy and I've got to be on one of those FAR trucks when they drive away, I want to be a soldier even more than I want to be the bourgmestre's helper, I can do the work of a soldier because I know now I can do it, I have done it, I have behaved today like any real soldier, and I'm ready now to walk the streets of the capital in my uniform and someday go to Nairobi where the Kikuyu whores drink Tusker White Cap, so I can't stop now, my sister, I just can't, I can't stop.

AGNÈS

SHE'S OUT THERE putrefying in the shed because I can't get anyone to help dig the grave. They're too busy searching bushes and fields and ditches and sheds for the corpses of people they earlier chased down and killed. At least they realize that the rot can turn these hills into a hell of corruption and disease. I think too they want to keep the evidence of what they did secret from the world. I keep asking myself, Have I known these killers all my life? Neighbors, the fathers and brothers of old friends. I have known them all my life without knowing them. Yet until they picked up rocks and hoes I thought I knew them well.

A woman from my school days came by today in tears. Going to the church to see what happened there, she heard a child crying from the direction of a mass grave being dug beyond the cemetery. When she tried to go forward to the sound, militiamen stopped her. Then she said that the bourgmestre, who was there, gave the order to fill the grave. After a few shovelfuls the crying sound stopped. She said that the bourgmestre directed his militia from the back of a truck. He told them to finish off any of the cockroaches still breathing because the FAR troops had done a careless job of it. When militiamen brought a couple of wounded Tutsi men to the truck, he leaned over and shot them with his own pistol.

I have been crying most of the day, knowing my own brother is one of the killers. He's gone now with my money. People saw him waving gaily from a military truck. So Augustin is not here anymore. In his place someone is here that I never dreamed would set foot in this rugo.

It happened the day after one of the death squads killed my mother on the road, mistaking her for what they call a collaborator. She must not have realized those madmen were shouting at her to halt. Where was she in her mind when they shot her through the head? Maybe picking beans or boiling a piece of salt meat while Father sat in the shade, drinking fresh beer. She must have been thinking of him, perhaps feeling glad that he hadn't lived long enough to see what was happening on his own hill. Two boys from up the road helped me cart her home in a wheelbarrow and put her in the shed. I was thinking of the man on the north slope who used to come here and fix Father's bike. They were drinking friends, so maybe he'd come and help me get her into the ground. I was thinking of him toward dusk as I went to the shed for maize to cook.

The smoke of fires was blowing the smell of beefsteak across the hill. I knew what that meant, because a passerby told me today. People were feasting on the delicacies of Tutsi cattle that had been slaughtered in kraals along with their owners.

On the way to the shed I heard a breathy sound coming from behind it. That sound that a voice was making didn't frighten me, because it held too much fear in it of its own, so I called back, "Who is there? Come out!" After a few moments, from around the side of the shed, appeared an upright bloody shape that lurched forward and made a low, wailing sound.

It was, I could see in the last light of day, a boy covered in blood.

"Who are you?" I cried, but he only made the sound again while coming toward me. If that blood was his, he must be near death. He came shuffling, slipping, so I reached out to keep him from falling, and at the moment he fell into my arms, I saw that it was the Tutsi boy, Innocent.

"How bad are you hurt? Where?" I asked, but he just kept moaning. I folded him in both arms and led him into the house. Before going inside, I looked around to see if anyone was in sight. I didn't turn on the lightbulb, but lit a small oil lamp and sat him down away from the window. I started to examine him for wounds, but it was soon clear that the blood wasn't his, or at least not most of it. Getting a water bucket and some cloth, I began to clean him up. He said nothing; neither did I. He had a long gash on his right forearm, but it wasn't deep. Almost all of that blood had come from others.

Finally I asked, "Innocent, were you at the church?"

He didn't look at me but at something beyond me.

"Where's your family?"

He said nothing. His eyes didn't focus on anything near, so in his mind he must have been somewhere else. I had seen a look somewhat like it in Mother's eyes. It was the look of somewhere else. Innocent's lips twitched without stopping, and the sound that came from between them made my hair stand on end. I have never heard anything like it. I have never seen the look in anyone else's eyes that I saw in his, not even in Mother's. I have never had anyone grip my hand with such fierce need. After sitting with him a long time, I slowly took my hand away, got up, and went to the door to make sure no one was around.

Then using the little medical kit I brought home from the Butare hospital, I disinfected his wound and bandaged it while asking him questions. He answered none of them. I couldn't imagine what good luck had brought him here instead of somewhere else. If this Tutsi boy had wandered into any other compound, most likely he'd have been turned over to the militia or killed outright. I made a porridge of maize, but Innocent never lifted the bowl, although I suspected he had eaten nothing in a long time.

"You must eat," I told him, "to live."

I lifted the bowl of porridge to his lips and kept it right there, stubbornly. At last his lips parted over the rim so that when I tilted the bowl they took in food. He swallowed while looking at me with those terrible eyes.

"Good," I said and kept tilting until the bowl was empty. "Good," I said once more. Perhaps the boy wouldn't speak for a long time or maybe never again, but at least he would eat and live. What was going to happen next? I couldn't keep him in the rugo because passersby had told me that the militia was searching everywhere for cockroaches and traitors.

But I couldn't allow Innocent to leave, not until he was strong enough and sane enough. In our house, like many on the hill, a space had been left between the ceiling and the roof as a way of cooling the interior. This was the best hiding place I could think of, so I had him crawl up there.

Helping a Tutsi escape, I could no longer ask anyone into the compound to bury Mother. It was too risky. I might have done it myself, but the ground next to Father's grave was filled with heavy rocks and that's the only place she would want to be buried. I had to wait.

Two days later I am still waiting. I hand up food to Innocent and let him come down after nightfall to use the latrine, but otherwise he stays there all the time. I have cut down and sewed an old pair of Augustin's pants and a shirt for Innocent to wear. He says nothing but stares through those strange eyes that see beyond me. He must be looking into the church at the terrible things that happened there. Passersby tell me almost every Tutsi on the nearby hills has been murdered. Man, woman, child. As many as ten thousand in an area small enough for me to walk through in a morning. People come by and look over the wall into the yard. They wait until I approach so they can tell me what they know, as if describing it makes it less horrible for them. I only half listen because I'm wondering if Innocent is safe up there. Maybe one of the passersby will go to the commune headquarters and report something is suspicious about this rugo. If Innocent wasn't up there, I'd pack my suitcase and put it on my head and return to the hospital work that must be awaiting me in Butare. But if I leave, the militia will come around and sooner or later find him.

So I must wait. I watch the road from the wall when the killers go out, as they say, to harvest Tutsi. Like regular farmers they leave early in the morning and quit at sunset, singing work songs as they walk home, carrying whatever they have taken from Tutsi compounds. However bloody they are, they come along the road as contented as farmers can be after a hard day's work. I am beginning to understand. Through many generations they have learned to think of Tutsi as they think of animals. They see the gorilla, the antelope, the jackal. They are killing animals when they kill Tutsi. They believe this is true, I can see that. They are living a dream that they all share. But if they wake from it, what will they think?

Meanwhile, I wait under an acacia tree that stands at one end of the rugo. The top of it is shaped like a half-moon, and its shiny little leaves provide some shade. Long banana-shaped pods hang from it now. This is the greatest of trees, I was told as a child, because it can live in places that kill other trees. Father told me that. The acacia knows how to survive, he said. Now Father lies in rocky earth outside the compound wall while Mother stiffens and smells in a shed on the opposite side of the yard. I keep wondering if Innocent will know how to survive.

I want a good life. We all want a good life. I want Jérome Manirakisa to come through the gate and take me away to the capital, where he'll marry me without a dowry. I want to have children just like my mother did and live to see them grow up and have children of their own. I want to be a nurse who can help people live healthy lives. Sometimes I think I want too much. Right now, more than anything, I want to keep that silent boy up there from getting his throat cut until he can help himself survive.

I am sitting under the acacia tree when the front gate opens and Silas Bagambiki comes into the yard, followed by his little man Denis and a half-dozen armed militia. I stand up when they approach. The bourgmestre wears a military belt with a holstered pistol, a bush hat, and a wide grin.

"Poor girl," he says, halting just beyond the shade of the tree. "I hear your mother died. I hear some fellows took her for a Tutsi."

My short, plump mother for a Tutsi?

"You must think of it as an unfortunate mistake," the bourgmestre tells me with a little shrug. "Have you buried her next to your father? Now that was a fine man."

"I haven't buried her. It's too rocky next to him."

"Then bury her in easier ground."

I say nothing while he studies me as if I'm something he doesn't understand how to operate, like an airplane.

"Can we have water?" he says finally. "Our work is thirsty." He looks up at the cloudless sky as if such work has to do with hoeing in the fields.

I point to the well.

"Denis, take the men and drink and go to the compounds up the hill. I'll meet you there."

When I see little Denis smile, I'm afraid. When he and the other militiamen go to the well, leaving me with the bourg- mestre, I feel myself trembling.

"Do you have beer inside?" The bourgmestre is squinting at the house.

"No."

"No beer?" He laughs and shakes his finger at me. "And you call yourself a Hutu woman of a good clan?"

I say nothing.

He gives his goatee an impatient little yank. "Do you have water in the house?"

I nod.

"Water from the house is cooler than water from the well."

This is not true, but I say nothing.

Now he's frowning. "What's wrong? Won't you invite the bourgmestre of your commune into your house? Is my clan less than yours? If you weren't such a pretty girl, I'd think you have something to hide. Is anyone hiding in your house?"

"No," I say. "Come inside for some cool water."

As we walk toward the house, I notice Denis and the militiamen leaving the compound. One of them, turning at the gate, smiles back at us, which makes me weak-kneed when I go inside with Silas Bagambiki.

While I'm getting him a drink, he mentions my brother. "I'm surprised at Augustin leaving without a word. I wanted him to stay here so I could train him."

Train him? For what? I wonder. But I say nothing and hand over the cup of water, which he puts down on the table without sipping it.

"What a foolish boy, running off like that. I hope he doesn't bring shame on your family and inzu. You have a good ancestry."

"Augustin needs someone to tell him what to do."

The bourgmestre is looking at me in that way again. "That's what I've been saying. But now that he's gone, this compound and land will be yours."

"He'll be back to claim them."

Silas Bagambiki shakes his head, grinning. "I don't think that will happen. He won't be coming back."

"Why not?"

"Because in times like these a fool hasn't much of a chance."

"Yes," I say, knowing he's right.

He shows me his big white teeth in a smile. "Your skirt is a pretty color. So is your head cloth. You really must stay in these hills."

"I'm going back to Butare."

"No. You must stay where your land is."

He's thinking it will be his land if he marries me. But I dare not say it. Instead I say, "My nurse's training is in Butare."

"You must stay where you're needed."

"After what's happened, a nurse is needed everywhere."

"Tomorrow I'll bring you a large slab of the best beef." He is looking me up and down, while he rubs his belly with both hands in a soft, circling motion as if he's thinking of . . . oh, I know what he's thinking of. "You don't know me," he says in a soft voice. "On the wall in my house I have a framed blessing that came from the Pope in Rome, Italy. And I have a lamp painted with the faces of the Sacred Trinity. Some of the FAR troops were carrying off communion chalices, but I stopped that. It would be sacrilege, although I think the Lord Jesus wouldn't begrudge them a little reward for a job well done. People in your clan are religious, aren't they? Tomorrow I'll send some men to dig the grave for your mother. So tell me the truth. You're going to stay right here?"

"I'm going back to the hospital in Butare."

He thinks about what I said and the way I said it before leaning forward in anger. "You would go back there and use your skills to save Tutsi cockroaches?"

"A nurse doesn't choose patients."

"Who told you that? A Tutsi?"

"A Hutu nurse. My teacher."

"Such teachers won't be around anymore. And there won't be cockroaches to have as patients." Silas Bagambiki opens his hands out as if what he says is already true. This man doesn't care what others think of him. All that matters is getting what he wants. But he won't have me.

He has turned his attention to the house. Why? His eyes move from object to object. What's he looking for? Now he turns toward me, one finger to his lip as if in this way he can think better. "Have our men searched this rugo yet?"

"No."

He nods, closing his eyes for a moment. "They will. They're supposed to." Then his eyes open wide and he laughs. "You look scared! Stop looking that way or I'll think you do have something to hide." He points at the ceiling. "For example, up there. Is anything hidden up there?"

"No." I try to smile at the idea but can't make my mouth move in that way.

"Does my question surprise you?"

When I nod, he looks up again and puts one finger against his lower lip. "In the last few days we've found more than a dozen Tutsi hiding in crawl spaces, just like the one you have here. Cockroaches hidden by ibyitso."

"I wouldn't do that."

"But you'd take care of Tutsi in the hospital. So it's not much worse if you hide one of them. Isn't that right?" He grins at his cleverness. "Do you want me to have a look up there?"

Suddenly I know what is on his mind. It makes me stop trembling. I feel calm and steady because I know his thoughts. He's almost certain someone is up there, but that's not what interests him. He doesn't care about that, he only cares about having me. He could rape me, but as an important man he'd rather not. He wants me to give in. He wants me to want him for what he stands for in these hills.

So as bold as I've ever been in my life, I say, "Don't worry, there's nothing up there. But I don't want your men in my rugo, tearing things up."

"Yes, I understand that." His voice is soft, expectant.

"I would like your protection from them."

"Of course. I can make sure they don't even come through the gate." He's staring at me hopefully. I can see it in the set of his mouth, the hope.

"Come in the other room," I tell him.

"Is that where you sleep?"

When I nod, he nods too. "Good," he says. "Everything is fine now."

I try to smile but can't. Even so, my fingers move to my blouse and undo the buttons. I'm going to have sex with this terrible man. I'm not a virgin. I have slept with four men in my life so far, but the thought of him terrifies and disgusts me. Even so, I'm going to do it, because I won't give him that boy up there. So very quickly I do what is necessary. I can hardly get free of my skirt before spreading my legs and flopping down. I turn my head away and wait for his heavy body to fall upon mine, and so it does. I hold on and hold on. Mercifully, it's over almost before it begins. Now at last I can smile. I feel my lips go up in the satisfaction of having it over with so quickly.

"That was too quick," he grumbles, falling to one side, breathing hard.

I tell him that next time it will be longer. This must be the way whores do it, I think. Rapidly I put on my skirt and blouse and stand at the window.

I refuse to watch him get dressed, but stare across the valley toward a hill where Hutu cooking fires are sending the smell of charred Tutsi beef this way.

I feel it running down my legs. He's telling me that his men will bury my mother for me.

"Thank you," I say without turning, "but she's already buried."

"But you said she wasn't."

"I forgot. She's already buried." I hear him behind me, then feel his hands. I let him rub his palms across my breasts and hold each nipple gently for a time between thumb and finger. For an instant I'm amazed that he behaves so tenderly. Just like a good man. Has he ever been a good man? I wonder.

"Good girl," he whispers against my ear. I try to smile but can't. When I see him leave, strutting across the yard, tapping his holstered pistol rhythmically, I know what's going to happen next. He'll come back for me whenever he likes. Tomorrow he'll come through the gate with the swagger of someone who already owns this rugo. In the house he'll terrify me by staring up at the crawl space, and then wait for me to invite him into my bed. This will happen until he's had enough of me. Then he'll send his militiamen to search the rugo. That's my future. And the boy will die.

After Silas Bagambiki fastens the gate behind him like a polite visitor, I wait a few moments, then call up to Innocent, who must have heard everything and maybe seen some of it.

"You must get out of here," I tell him.

Looking down from the crawl space, he nods.

That he responds at all encourages me to go farther. "You must be on the road soon after dark."

He nods again.

"Good," I say, feeling tears in my eyes. "Right now I have something to do." First I wash myself with a bucket of water from the well. Then I go to the shed and the big shovel there. Yes, I have something to do, a thing most difficult, but somehow

I must do it. Oh, I will do it. Somehow I'm going to dig the big rocks out and make a grave for Mother next to Father, tonight, soon after the Tutsi boy leaves, and by sunup I'll be on the road myself, with a suitcase balanced on my head, bound for Butare and for the people who need me.

Innocent Karangwa

I SMELLED THE blood before I felt it, the slick warmth on my skin, in my hair, against my eyes shut tight and my mouth, and while I was smelling it my ears were filled with the noise of everyone around me, my brothers and sisters and my mother, all of them screaming or crying or moaning, lying on me or against me, I don't know who was where but I smelled them and felt their warm skin jerking against mine and then what was like an ooze moving along my arms legs stomach as if I were crossing a river clogged with the thick sweet smell of ripe fruit, which didn't last long though because I was jolted by a sharp pain in my arm, so I thought it had come and I waited for Holy Jesus to take me to His bosom, just like Mother said, and it was where I wanted to be because being alive like this was worse than death, buried under the bodies of my family, so I was ready, but no one finished me, the next blow didn't come, and after awhile I opened my eyes to see flesh, it brushed against my eyelids when I opened them, but whose flesh was so close I didn't know, and not to know I shut my eyes tight again and let the smell come at me until I was sick enough in the stomach to tell myself please fall asleep or die, either way, just let go of thoughts, and I was thinking about how not to think about all of this when I knew the noise around me had stopped but another had begun like a murmur in the room, like water tumbling far off in a stream, although it didn't really seem like anything I had ever heard until I thought maybe it was the breathing of people still alive in the room, and then came another sound like the stumbling motion of someone going through dense bush and a voice that kept saying "That one" and "That one" and "That one over there," and afterwards, always, came a thudding sound that sounded a little like smashing open a melon, wet and heavy, and I thought I knew what the sounds meant going around the room like that until I was sure of it, I was certain that bodies were being turned over and arms lifted so that somebody could see where the breathing came from, and the terrible waiting for them to get it over with, each time I heard "Here, this one," and then the thudding that made me shut my eyes tighter and hold on with my teeth clenched until they ached as the sound came closer, along this row of benches, my row, and I felt something moved nearby, close but not too close, the way it is when someone steps on a jungle root that travels to where you're standing, and I knew they were sorting through the bodies of my family, turning them over and searching and soon they'd find mine and get it over with so I could go with my family, all of us together, to the bosom of Holy Jesus, and sure enough, I heard a voice say, "That one," and I felt them turning someone from my family over on top of me so that I kept my eyes shut as tight as possible, not wanting to watch them looking down at me before they brought the panga down on my face, but nothing happened, they didn't do it, not even after part of someone was lifted off my stomach for a moment, because in the next moment they let it fall back on me again, the warm flesh coming down, so that I knew they thought nothing alive was

beneath that body, which might have been that of my sister or
my mother but I thought my mother's body was nearer my face,
the warmth right in front of my eyes being her arm, and they
went on down the row of benches, leaving me alive there underneath with my eyes shut as tight as possible as I waited for
something else to happen, anything, which never did, and I
stayed that way a long long time, eyes shut tight, until finally
without thinking about it I let them open, and I saw that night
had fallen and everything was left in darkness, the black empty
space giving me such a fright that I nearly screamed, because I
feared things slithering through the black room, spirits of the
dead rising out of corpses, angered by death and ready to hurt
whatever still lived, but again nothing happened, so I held on
to myself by trying to feel where every part of me was, something
bent under, cramped, somehow tangled with parts of my family
and maybe parts of other people, arm leg hand ear, I didn't
know, but everything of mine I tried to locate in that warm wet
mass until I felt changed into something else, into a spider fixed
in the middle of a web of wet threads, hanging there silent, still,
and then somehow in the hot darkness I changed all of that
into something else but not anything alive, a stone, a rock, a
big stone, a boulder in a slow-moving stream, a rock that felt
nothing, with thick water moving across me no faster than a
snail, until it dried like mud and caked every part of me, leaving
me inside a huge mound of dried mud, alone, without sound,
until I gave a little shake like a dog waking and I knew I had
been unconscious long enough for the blood to dry on my flesh,
and in the hot room I smelled the odor of rotting fruit that was
leading me into a need to scream, so I had to move quickly, I
had to get out of there no matter what happened, a thought

that had me pushing a little against flesh that no longer seemed soft or warm and pushed again until I moved the stiffened flesh away a little and pushed much harder until pushing chest shoulder arm of someone aside I got free, I felt it happening until head and neck and shoulders, all mine, were coming out into the thick smell of the dark room, and I wondered if the dead spirits were flying over me, circling, as fierce as bees, sure that if they were just above me there I had to get out, get away from them, out out out even if killers were waiting beyond the room, so I made myself move all of the way out somehow, crawling on hands and knees through the blackness across dead bodies, the lumps of them, slipping in the warm muck until I got to the doorway clogged with them and got through there by climbing up and over them and sliding down them, and then going free into the churchyard where in the moonlight, lying on my back and breathing hard, I turned my head to see large rocks lying nearby that I knew were not rocks but bodies lying there, and suddenly I found myself sitting up and wanting to go back inside to make sure my family were all dead, but I knew they were, and I knew inside that hot crowded slippery room the spirits were slithering in and out of mounds of bodies like giant snakes, ready to coil and squeeze the life from anything live, from anyone who went in there again, and so getting to my feet I stepped forward, stepped forward again, again and again and again, until the open church gate shone under the full moon and I saw through eyes not dreaming that the lane was empty, that nothing alive was around me, although spirits must have been soaring low in search of their own dead bodies because I heard them moaning, and it was only later, how long I don't know, after going forward on my shaking legs, that I knew the moaning had really been my own, that I couldn't stop the sound from coming out of me as I kept going forward on the moonlit path until my mind was calmed by the thought that I lived because Imana had decided it, and if that were true, then I must obey him and live, and I knew then that I had to think to live and by thinking I had to go somewhere safe, and in the emptiness and silence of the road it came to me that I was thinking of what I sometimes thought of in a waking dream, of that girl who once had bandaged a cut for me, the Hutu nurse who smiled on the path when Mother and I passed, and I thought then that Imana wanted me to go to her as I had done sometimes in my waking dream, and because of this secret dream of going to her compound and seeing her there, I knew where she lived in our hills, a place not far away, close enough for my legs to take me there, and so they began to take me there, slowly, away from the road and through fields so people wouldn't see me, just as Imana told me to do, and I kept from making the sounds that came up in my throat like water rising in a flooded river while going forward one step after another after another until my legs reached the rugo for me and took me behind the shed where I waited as Imana ordered me to do so I could live as he willed me to do and after a long time, while the moon went across the sky, she came through the moonlight and I stepped round the shed into it too, then she called out, "Who are you?" But I couldn't speak.

I never spoke one word during my stay with her. Not even when the bourgmestre came to the house and took her into the room. She did it for me, I know. I could tell from her voice that she didn't want to go in there with him, and when I saw her face later, after he left, I knew it. She did it so I wouldn't be found. When I left I knew I could speak, but I didn't because if

I spoke I would have cried, and I will never cry again. In the black hole above the ceiling of her house, I had time to think and so I did. There were two ways I could think about what happened. I had lived and everyone else in the church had died, so that meant I should be ashamed. I had lived and everyone else in the church had died, so that meant I should be proud, and so I am, because Imana had chosen me from all of those people to stay alive.

I am not like others. I cannot have feelings like others because what I feel is what Imana tells me I must feel. When I wanted to throw myself into the pretty nurse's arms and thank her for saving me, I said nothing, did nothing. She was the servant of Imana brought forward to help save me. My whole life I have felt different from others who think of themselves always as living and breathing within the family and the family within the clan and the clan within the Tutsi tribe. I have always felt close to myself, however, so much so that sometimes I have felt ashamed for not living more for Mother and Father and the others. Now I know that what I felt was true. I must live for myself. This is what I think as I set out on the road for Kigali. If soldiers stop me on the way and ask me, a tall thin boy, if I am a Tutsi, I'll say to them, "Give me a gun and show me a Tutsi and let me kill him for you." If they want me to prove it, I will prove to them I'm a Hutu by killing a Tutsi, just as Imana tells me to do, because I am his chosen, a favorite of God, alive on this earth to please him.

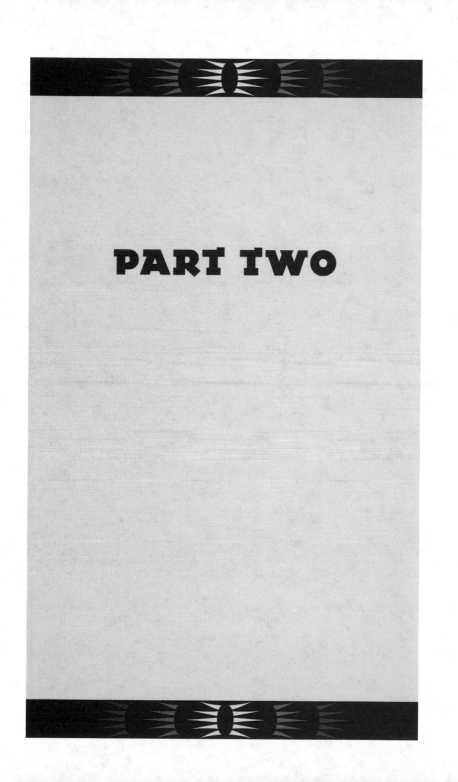

PART TWO

Captain
Stephen Mazimpaka

I never set foot in the Land of the Thousand Hills, my country Rwanda, until I helped to invade it.

Our family left for Uganda in 1962 when my mother was pregnant with me. As a boy I sat beside my father in a shed next to the kraal and listened to him describe the flight of Tutsi from Rwanda, when the Hutu came to power after centuries of Tutsi rule. He had a firm grasp of history and, unlike many of his friends, was capable of seeing events for what they were. From him I inherited a love of objectivity, even though, at times, I fail to practice it because of anger or frustration. I remember him smoking a pipe and gazing at his cattle while speaking in his calm, precise way. He explained that the German and Belgian colonials in the old days allied themselves with the Tutsi because of our success at ruling through a network of chiefs. And it is true. We did the colonials' work for them by keeping order while they grew rich.

Nevertheless, when all of Africa began to press for independence, many of the colonies feared losing more than they might gain by clinging to old alliances and patterns of power. So the Belgians shifted their allegiance to the Hutu majority, who would have the voting advantage in general elections after independence. As for the French, they took the position that the Hutu, with little political experience, would be easier to deal with than the more worldly-wise Tutsi elite. My father believed that the Roman Catholic Church supported the Hutu for the same reason.

So with independence came a profound transformation of life in Rwanda. Tutsi politicians, educators, and professionals of every sort were removed, either by legislation or force. Hutu officials could not count on generations of practice to help them make decisions. They lacked the political skill to make tactical concessions and alliances and counteralliances or to maneuver subtly in the corridors of power or to put an enemy into the position of involuntary cooperation. The Hutu ruled by a show of raw power rather than negotiation. Or so my father always maintained. This absolute change in how things were done encouraged cattle herders like him to leave the country, even when it meant abandoning most of their herds.

My father fled with twenty of three hundred cows and those he did take out of the country soon died of nagana, the sleeping sickness. "Our brains were our only wealth," he once said while describing the family's arrival in Uganda. "We weeded local gardens. That's how we kept alive, by eating weeds. Within ten years we employed many of the people whose gardens we tended." Without cattle he and others like him had to work as field hands, although by tradition they despised farming. His two brothers labored on sugar estates near Jinja as cane cutters and one died there of exhaustion. Father brought us to Oruchinga, where little by little, skimping and saving to buy cows, he stocked a small herd. To escape Idi Amin—whose hatred of refugees often led to their torture and death in what was called the State Research Bureau—my father moved his family once again. This time we entered the Kahunge settlement near Fort Portal above the great chain of western lakes, a rugged inaccessible area of little appeal to Amin's marauding but lazy troops. Again the cattle died of sleeping sickness, so when Amin was deposed by his rival Milton Obote, my father returned to Oruchinga. Once again, he worked in the fields, rebuilt the house, and started a new herd. He lived to see two sons move permanently to Europe and a daughter to the United States, another boy become an accountant in Kampala, and his youngest child, me, evolve into a revolutionary.

He was not happy about that, especially because I had made a promising start in school. He had expected me to become a professional man, perhaps a doctor or lawyer, whereas my true interest—fired by the need to recover my heritage—lay in politics. Upon entering college, I made a grandiose vow that my classmates thought was outrageous. I would never marry until my return to Rwanda, the Land of a Thousand Hills. Friends called me "the Catholic Pope" to shame me out of such folly. I was not celibate by any means, but I did remain a bachelor, which for a man over twenty among both Hutu and Tutsi clansmen of good standing was considered irresponsible.

A Rwandan exile in Uganda could enter politics only one way—through the military—and so I did. When Defense Minister Yoweri Museveni formed a rebel force to oppose Obote's corrupt administration, I joined along with other Rwandan refugees. Fortunately for us, we chose the right side in the subsequent civil war. I was a captain in the National Resistance Army when it took Kampala in early 1986.

For me and others with a Rwandan background, Museveni's

takeover of the Ugandan government was merely a step in the right direction. We had one thing in mind: return to the Land of the Thousand Hills. I had no plans to remain in this country of Uganda, where I, an officer in the Ugandan Army, could not get a passport. Anything someone of Rwandan extraction built or owned could be taken away by the simplest process of law. We worked hard to get UN scholarships and college degrees, but citizenship remained out of our grasp. As Ugandans often pointed out to us in a matter-of-fact way, "The offspring of refugees are refugees." Even though we had spent our whole lives in Uganda, we could never claim our civil rights without crossing the border into Rwanda.

With this grim reality in mind we created a political organization, the Rwandese Patriotic Front, and began to prepare for our return to the motherland. The Ugandan army, our brothers in arms during the civil war, illegally helped us collect weapons and supplies. They requisitioned far more ammo for target practice than ever before; jeeps suddenly vanished; whole truckloads of weapons never reached their destination. Commanders who knew about it looked the other way. Meanwhile, leaders in the RPF used funds solicited in Europe and America to buy rocket launchers, machine guns, and automatic rifles that we stored in sheds on tea estates near Mulindi at the border.

By 1990 we were ready to take advantage of a deteriorating situation in Rwanda. The totalitarian Habyarimana regime was in disarray and the opposition was pushing for a multiparty system that would allow for a Tutsi return to the political scene. In retrospect I know we were not as ready to return as we thought, at least not in a military way.

Even so, on a Monday afternoon in late autumn I led a small

force across the border and took the guard post at Kagitumba. Then we moved on to the resort of Gabiro and the town of Nykatare. That was the beginning. In subsequent days two thousand of us fanned out over the countryside and took what fleeing FAR troops had left behind: Panhard armored cars, Russian cannon, and even Gazelle helicopters that none of us could fly. I imagined a quick march to the capital of Kigali, but to our surprise the enemy regrouped and counterattacked. They were exceedingly well-armed—most of their weapons supplied by the French, Egyptian, and South African governments. With comparative ease their much larger force pushed us back to the Ugandan border, which we crossed at night into volcano country.

For several months, dejected by our miscalculation, we wandered through the vast, cold, mist-heavy jungle. I will never forget the hot steam rising from ground almost cold enough to freeze. We strayed into valleys where hippopotamus herds swung their sharp-edged lips through hippo lawns in swathes two-feet wide, cropping the grass too short for buffalo and bushbuck. We climbed steep hills from which we could see lake flies hovering in swarms so thick that they seemed like surging rain clouds. We came down into a savannah and cleaned our rifles while topi gathered to mate, the delicate-faced females trotting shyly toward the center of the rutting ground where long-horned males awaited them, heads held rigidly high, tails swishing, black hooves pawing the dust. They made me think of my vow of bachelorhood. We moved from place to place like nomads, not soldiers, watching chimps near Tongo eat the fruit of giant fig trees and at Bukima hearing an old silverback gorilla thump his chest and order his females to break down foliage for the nightly nest. We passed near an area of Gahinga volcano, where pure carbon dioxide sometimes settled into depressions and killed small animals that took a few breaths of it. After midday, when the gas dispersed, lizards came out to sun themselves. They avoided us while we stepped among hundreds of dead birds and rodents.

It seemed that our dream of returning home would end in this icy jungle, with each of us dying slowly of exposure and disease. But because most of us were seasoned veterans, we got hold of ourselves and began to replan our strategy. Instead of waging a conventional campaign, we would split up into small groups and make forays into the Rwandan countryside without holding positions. Strike and run, strike and run. Instead of trying to end the war our plan was to drag it out. Until something unforeseen enabled us to win, our goal was to undermine the morale of the enemy. If we caught one of their units in a trap, we left open a corridor of escape so they could flee. That way we'd get equipment without sustaining casualties. We developed a code of conduct. If a soldier committed a crime, his commanding officer was demoted. Grave offenses were drinking on duty, failing to carry out an order, abuse of civilians, stealing. The crime of cowardice meant death by firing squad in the field.

Armed with our renewed enthusiasm, we left volcano country and put our new strategy into practice. Of more importance than our military success, it soon became clear, was our constant presence on Rwandan soil. This so enraged Hutu officials that in many areas they carried out reprisals against Tutsi inhabitants. Every night we slept with that knowledge while every day we inflicted damage that helped to undermine government morale.

Perhaps a cease-fire might have been negotiated, but the Hutu extremists didn't want it, the French took sides by acting more like Hutu advocates than mediators, and the Belgians—facing a hostile public at home on the African question—announced its intention to withdraw from Rwanda's problems altogether.

The little civil war continued for three years until Habyarimana's plane crashed on the sixth of April, so close to his palace that the engine fell into his favorite garden.

What the Hutu extremists had long sought was an excuse for exterminating every Tutsi in the country. Once again we revised our strategy when it became clear that the Hutu were practicing genocide and that the rest of the world meant to stand by and let it happen.

We swept into the Interahamwe stronghold of Byumba préfecture in late April, then eastern Ruhengeri, northern Kigali, and Kibungo préfectures, carrying all before us.

Now, in May, our objective is to take the capital, then turn south and swing in a circular path to the west, north, and east. We won't stop until the country is ours.

The unit I command is camped thirty miles north of Kigali today. A group of recruits are sitting in a field waiting to be interviewed by an NCO. When we first engaged FAR troops in 1990, they were a disciplined force, but lax recruiting has transformed FAR into a noisy pack of ill-trained thugs. To avoid that mistake ourselves, we turn away as many recruits as we keep. Today I leave my tent and take a look at the thirty or so who are waiting. One fellow seems very tall, so I tell him to stand up. He really is tall. I am six-feet-two and he towers over me at six-feet-ten or -eleven.

I speak to him in Kinyarwanda, the language of our motherland, in order to practice it, for I'm better at English, French, and German than Kinyarwanda. "Why do you want to enlist?"

"To fight."

"To fight, *sir*."

"Yes," he adds stiffly. "Sir."

"Where are you from?"

"From around Gitarama. Sir."

"Where's your family?"

He hesitates. "Gone, sir."

"I see. What can you do besides fight?"

"I'm a herder, sir."

Indeed, he looks it. Put him in a knee-length ocher-colored gown, with a long staff in his hand, and he might have stepped out of a photograph taken in the old days by a Belgian colonial. As a boy, I used to have such a splendid photo pinned on my wall to remind me of Tutsi glory. I ask him for his name.

"Emmanuel Rubagunga, sir."

"Your clan?"

"Abasinga, sir."

He comes from a good clan. "Age?"

"Twenty-seven, sir."

I study his high cheekbones, long nose, thin lips, round forehead, the skin of it as brown and smooth and shiny as a nut in the sunlight, and the broad chest tapering to a slim waist, and I tell myself such a tall, fine-looking man is worthy of our Tutsi reputation for breeding warriors. "You say your family's gone. Does that mean wife and children?"

"Yes, sir."

"Recently?"

He hesitates as if remembering. "Yes, sir."

"Go to that NCO over there and tell him we want you." Watching his lean figure lope away at the gait of someone accustomed to covering long distances each day, I suddenly feel a moment of intense sadness, for I am thinking of all the men like Emmanuel Rubagunga who have lost their families recently. Of women and children who have lost theirs. Thousands, many thousands. And I lose any sense of objectivity I might otherwise possess. At this moment, God willing, I can murder eighty-five percent of the people of this country. Eighty-five percent. That's how many are Hutu.

Augustin

I GOT WHAT I wanted, yeah, I'm a soldier in the Forces Armées Rwandaises, and I wear a beret with a button of the dead president's face on it, and on roadblock duty I've already killed my share of Tutsi cockroaches and Hutu traitors. I have a pair of mirrored sunglasses taken off one of them. My boots are called "Wellingtons" and I wear combat fatigues of a sand color with blobs of green for camouflage. I like my job. We drink banana beer at the checkpoints from bottles, not pots, and sometimes sweat-bee honey that's very sweet. The way I am now I'm somebody my sister and her nurse friends in Butare ought to look up to. If only Laurent and Gaspard could see me carrying this Kalashnikov automatic rifle that was made in China or Japan. The French gave it or the Egyptians, I forget which. And I wish the bourgmestre could see me, because if he saw me like this, maybe he'd get rid of Denis and make me his helper. There are all sorts of things out here, like 81-millimeter mortars and 57-millimeter tank guns and 83-millimeter Blindicide rocket launchers, and AML-60 armored cars. I can identify them. It hasn't taken me long to become a real soldier. People know who I am at the roadblocks because I do my work.

Everything seems to be happening at once. Things really happen when people are taken back into the woods. When I asked to go back there and watch, I was told, "You better wait until you're ready." I said, "I'm ready now," because they mustn't think of me as just another recruit. At nineteen, I'm older than most. So the next time some Tutsi were caught at the roadblock, I went along with the three veterans who took them back in the woods somewhere. The man was shot. The woman was told if she killed her little boy, we'd set her free. When she refused and started crying, the three veterans ripped off her skirt while I held the squirming boy. They raped her in front of the boy, who made a noise like a hurt dog the whole time and tried to get loose, but I held him. Finished with her, they slit her throat and came over while I was holding the boy and slit his throat. They didn't ask me if I wanted to do it—I suppose because I was new—and I don't know if I could have done it anyway. Not then, not right away.

But two days later a Hutu offered me money so he wouldn't have to kill his Tutsi wife himself. I took the money and just walked over and did it for him. I shot her. And the next day something like it happened again, which surprised me. This Tutsi gave me money to kill him quickly with a bullet, but after I had the money I thought, What could he do about it if I used a panga instead and hacked away at him for a while like any cockroach deserved? But I gave him a bullet to the head like I promised, even if he didn't deserve it.

Sometimes it seemed almost too much for me, although I didn't say so. The worst things happened around dusk, after we'd been drinking beer most of the day and getting bored playing checkers with bottle caps and singing old regimental songs to rhythms beat out on jerricans. When the sun got low, I figured something might happen, but whatever happened I saw it through. Like watching while a Hutu teacher was tied to a tree and made to look at his pregnant Tutsi wife being killed. They scooped out the unborn baby and held it dripping in front of his face and yelled, "Why don't you eat it, if you like the Tutsi so much?" before killing him. Someone who was grinning said to me afterwards, "You didn't look ready for that." I said I was ready for it, but he gave me a look that meant he knew from my face that I wasn't ready to watch it, much less do it.

I told myself to do what the others did. Next time I was at the checkpoint a man came through with a Hutu identity card and I pulled him out of the line. I knew my comrades were watching.

"Your skin is light. You have a long nose," I told the man, who shook his head and put his hand against his nose as if to push it back in. "Come on with me," I said and led him away. About twenty yards into the bush, I had him stop and turn. He couldn't look at me, he was crying, and I saw from a widening spot on his shorts that he had pissed in them. What should I do? I wondered. Hit him with my panga or shoot him? I could get it done at a greater distance if I shot him, so I decided to shoot him. Lifting the recoilless rifle, I could see the barrel swaying, which meant I was trembling, and I wondered if he saw it too and might laugh. The idea made me really mad, so I walked up and held the barrel against his chest and shot him three times fast, *zing zing zing*, which made him jump like an impala.

When I went back to the checkpoint, a veteran handed me a calabash of beer. It was the first time for that.

"The identity card wasn't his," I explained.

"Just another Tutsi liar." He patted me on the back, which I didn't like. It meant he didn't think I was sure of myself, but yeah, I was, and proved it.

After that I welcomed roadblock duty, and as I say, I killed my share. We buried them sometimes and sometimes not. Once, when we made a half-dozen Tutsi dig a mass grave for themselves, I noticed an old Hutu watching from the roadside. He wore a white shirt and brown pants and sandals like someone who didn't belong around there. "What are you, a doctor, a teacher?" I asked him angrily.

He said teacher.

Then I asked him in the same voice, "What are you looking at?"

"I'm looking at what you're making these people do."

Just to show the old man who was in charge, I turned away from the diggers and pointed my rifle at him. "You don't look happy about what's happening here," I said.

"I'm not." He didn't even smile to put me in a good humor.

"We can't have cockroaches crawling around our new country," I told him and swung the barrel back at the diggers.

"What new country?" he asked.

"The new country we're making."

He said, "I wouldn't want to live in that country."

"Maybe," I said, turning the barrel in his direction again, "you don't want to live at all."

He said nothing, but I have to say he looked right at me without flinching.

Maybe I should have shot him then and there, but he was so old and frail that a strong wind could have toppled him. He wasn't worth the cost of a bullet. I turned the barrel back to the diggers and never looked around to see if he was still watching when they toppled over when we shot them.

I would have liked to stay on checkpoint duty because so many things happened. We got to see a lot of foreigners come down the road for one reason or another. There were Americans who came down from Somalia wearing brown desert uniforms that stood out against our green hills. Then we saw the identity papers of Englishmen and Frenchmen and Germans and Italians and even some people from the East, but we couldn't figure out from their passport scratchings what they really were. We had fun with the whites. Sometimes if we were drunk, we'd pound on the roof of a foreign car with grenades and demand money to let them pass. I liked to see their red faces pouring sweat like a river and their eyes bulging in fear and the way they shoved francs at us to save their silly lives. One thing we were on the lookout for was Belgians. We'd kill Belgians because of what RTLMC was telling us about them. The radio said that Belgians had caused all the trouble in the first place. They supported peace treaties that would give the country back to the Tutsi and they refused to sell us weapons, not like the French. So I was always ready for Belgians when I saw a vehicle pull up and some whites climb out of it. That's what I mean by things happening at roadblocks.

Then one day our squad was transferred to the south. My comrades didn't like that, because the southern roads were heavily mined. A few years back some northern Hutu militia went down and mined the southern roads, even though most of the people using them were Hutu. They did it to blame the Tutsi army for killing civilians. Many Hutu died, and a lot of those land mines were still there, waiting for Hutu boys from the north to come step on them. When we were trucked south it was to join a fighting unit. I liked the idea, because it was different. But one of my comrades said, "Listen, Augustin, some of these troops down here are rough."

"I've seen everything already," I said.

"Oh, no you haven't," he said with a grin.

Our new sergeant was a former member of the presidential guard. He still wore the black beret, and I told myself such a man was a lot more important than the bourgmestre. When he asked me where I was from I told him, and I also told him my sister was a nurse at the Butare hospital because why not, and anyway he just might like the idea of my sister being a little important too. But it turned out he didn't like it. Once he had been in a firefight with the RPF and the wounded were left to die in the battlefield because buses carrying them to the hospital in Gisenyi were too full. It didn't make any difference when I told him she was a nurse in Butare, not Gisenyi, and it wasn't the hospital that was to blame, but the bus drivers. We didn't get along after that, so I wanted to prove my worth. That chance came soon, because we were going into a Tutsi town to clean it up.

Our sergeant from the presidential guard gave us whistles, like we were Interahamwe militiamen instead of real soldiers. It was like an insult. Then he told us to blow them hard when we entered the town. It would terrify them, he said. He said it's better to kill them when they're terrified than when they're surprised. Our unit, about forty of us, got there just after dawn and started blowing from every direction. People burst out of their huts and began running, so we cut them down. It was easy. I had hoped for RPF soldiers in town and a real firefight. I think my comrades felt the same way. They were angry and brooding. The sergeant had us make two piles in the middle of town—one pile for the dead and one pile for the dying. After that we went from house to house and made sure no one was left. Seeing four men yank a young woman from a house, I figured they were going to rape her, but they had another idea. Two of them held her while a third reached out and took hold of her hand and the fourth cut it off at the wrist. When they let her go, she fell down jerking around, screaming. Then one of them, after lighting a cigarette, held one of her legs steady by pressing his foot down on the ankle and with three big swings of his panga he severed her leg below the knee. He asked his comrades to help out, so they helped him toss her on the piles of corpses, where she jerked around awhile, then calmed down slowly. We all listened to her breath get quicker and quieter, and a strange thing happened to me then. I felt a joy as if I were with a woman, and it seemed that the joy was ready to burst out of my throat like a song.

The one smoking the cigarette came up and asked me if I had liked what I saw.

I told him yes.

"You felt something?"

"Yes, I did. I felt good."

"You're nothing but a kid," he said, spitting so I'd know he meant it. "You're not supposed to feel anything. Me, I don't. Do you?" he asked his comrades, who shook their heads. "See? You're still a kid," he told me and walked over to the woman who was still breathing and yanked her off that pile and dragged her to the other pile of the still living and threw her on it. Then, standing on other bodies, he leaned over and hacked away at her with his panga, so did his comrades, until there were just parts of her. They had proved enough to me, but they weren't done. Using their pangas like brooms, they swept her parts off the pile and scattered them in the dirt. Then they stripped off their bloody clothes and walked down to a nearby stream to take a bath. I rushed into the bushes and started to retch, but somehow I kept it down; I did, yeah, and in a few minutes I walked back to the middle of town and stood there, looking at the two piles as hard as I could, so the next time something happened I'd be all right.

That made me ready for Rusumo Bridge.

The two-lane cement bridge, yellow-looking in sunlight, is built over the Kagera River. It's a fast river with waterfalls and separates us from Tanzania. We've been sent here for what reason I don't know, but a lot of people are crossing the bridge, a lot of Hutus. We hear from them that the RPF has already taken much of the country and the capital is under attack. People call the Tutsi soldiers *incontanyi*— the invincibles— because nothing can stop them. I don't believe it because RTLMC tells us we're winning and they say the RPF carry guns but have no bullets. Even so, these farmers are leaving the country. The fools are becoming refugees.

I grab one man who carries a wicker basket full of pots and pans on his head. "Where are you going?" I ask him.

He tells me across the border.

"Across the border for what?"

"To escape the Tutsi."

"Why escape dead people? We're killing them all."

He gives me a look. "Not their army. They'll kill us for killing their people."

I shove him back into the line of refugees leading goats and carrying suitcases and wheeling their bicycles along loaded with goods. "Go on over and die there!" I yell at them. Then I turn away from those fools and cowards and look down at the water going fast under the bridge.

What I see down there just isn't water. Bloated white shapes are coming along, tossing in the current. I see bodies roll over the waterfall and get caught in eddies below, bobbing and swirling in the basin along with grass and silt. Some of them touch against the bank lined with hardwood trees and big ferns. The bodies, not all of them in one piece, are white from being in water so long. I ask one of my comrades where they come from. He's heard the Tutsi in the south were marched to the riverbanks and executed there and toppled into the water. Some were forced to jump in. Sometimes they were tied together and tossed in.

Looking down at the current, I can't believe I'm seeing so many corpses. Hundreds, thousands, many thousands, bobbing and twisting and turning in the fast Kagera River that goes all the way north to Lake Victoria. Some of them disappear in the foam to bob up again, their stiff arms seeming to reach out as if swimming. But they don't look human. I tell my comrade that, and he nods. This is the way Tutsi really are—white, mealy things a lot like insects dead on the surface of a river.

"Have you noticed the dogs yet?" he asks with a smile. When I say no I haven't noticed, he tells me all the dogs around here are very fat. "They drag the bodies out and eat them. Some of these dogs can hardly crawl, they're so full."

"I wonder why Tutsi flesh doesn't make them sick," I say and he laughs.

We stand there looking at the bleached corpses spinning in

little whirlpools. "I wonder how many are down there," he says.

"Thousands."

He nods. "Thousands and thousands. It won't be long now before they're all gone." He reaches out and pats my arm. But then he turns his full face around and squints at me. "They're not winning, are they?"

"No. That's just a Tutsi lie." I look away from the river to the opposite side, the Tanzanian side, where thousands of yellow flowers dot the field. I can see white butterflies swooping down on them, so many white shapes dipping, swirling around, so many white shapes.

Emmanuel Rubagunga

I AM ONLY a recruit, but Captain Mazimpaka has made me one of his four bodyguards. He knows, of course, that coming from the Abasinga clan I will give my life to protect him. We Abasingas believe in honoring contracts, especially the most sacred of contracts: *buhake*, the agreement between an owner and a user of cattle. Captain Mazimpaka is as much my overlord, my shebuja, as if my family had been serving his for generations. Now that I know how to fire this gun, he's safe when I am with him.

This morning we went to check mortar positions on a hilltop overlooking the capital. It won't be long before we go down into the streets of Kigali and take the city. I have little interest in doing that. I want revenge against the Hutu, but aside from the pleasure of seeing them die in battle, I'd be better off going home. Even though I belong to a victorious army, my thoughts are not on this war but on my family. Or my thoughts would be on my family if I could close my eyes and let it happen, but every time I start to think of them I open my eyes wide so that I don't think of them. I think instead of cattle.

I think of cattle, because thoughts of them are soothing. Few things are more beautiful than a herd of Inyambo going out to pasture. In the herd, their long, curved horns rise from their swaying bodies like a forest of trees. Sometimes their horns, when crowded together, click like branches touching, and sometimes their long wattles ripple like banana leaves in a storm. I like to watch my dogs weaving between hocks and tails, never getting trampled, although much of the time they are inches away from death.

I had twenty head, but in a few more years I would have had three times that many. Every day I took them to the river, an hour or so each way, and then let them graze in the pasture, and then brought them back to the kraal at dusk. Each of them had a name—Little Hump, Fat Nose, Sharp Ribs—and I was so proud of them that sometimes I did something foolish. I burned more grassland than necessary, then let my cattle graze on the shoots before they had grown tall and strong. I couldn't deny my herd the pleasure of feeding on young grass, even though it weakened the soil of my ibikingi.

Only my family mattered to me more than cattle did, although perhaps I was gentler with the cattle. I have always tried to follow my father and be a strict master of the household. In my father's youth he was not allowed to speak his father's name. This was out of respect. My father never felt free to live until his father died. It's true that I never demanded such obedience, but I have never dishonored Tutsi tradition either.

Perhaps I demanded too much obedience. That day I told my family to stay inside the rugo unless I told them otherwise. There was no exception to this command. My wife bowed her head to show that my order was understood, and so did my three children, even Pacifique, the youngest at five years old. It was not my intention to leave them very long, because we knew from the radio that the Habyarimana plane crash meant trouble. But

I had learned on that day of an outbreak of east coast fever in nearby hills. I had to go and spray my five calves to rid them of ticks. They were penned in another kraal on a neighboring hill. How long was I away from the rugo? Three hours, maybe four at the most.

I haven't been able to think about it.

Every time I try to think about my family by closing my eyes tight I open them again so I don't think about my family at all. I know only what I saw. My wife and two oldest were battered with stones and clubs under the acacia tree in the yard, then beheaded with pangas. I never found Pacifique. I understand that children in other Tutsi compounds ran into the bush and were murdered there. But Pacifique would not run because I ordered him to stay, just as I told the others they must stay in our compound, and they did. They were slaughtered where I told them to stay. The killers must have carried Pacifique off, thrown him in a truck, and murdered him elsewhere. I have heard since then that the militia took people away—especially children—and hid their bodies so that surviving Tutsi would not have the chance to bury their own.

My cattle in the main kraal were gone, all except two that had been hastily butchered and the choice bits taken away.

I dug a grave large enough for my family, alongside the graves of my parents and my sister who died when I was a boy. Under the acacia tree I washed the bodies of my wife and children and dressed them carefully in their best clothes. Each head I wrapped in the fine cloth my wife used for sewing. The bodies were placed side by side, a child on each side of my wife. Then I covered the grave, pounding the earth as flat as I could. I did not mark

it, fearing the militia might return and see the cross as a challenge and out of anger dig up everything for the dogs to eat.

Returning to the house, I opened an old trunk and took out
leopard skins, a plumed necklace, a feathered headband, belled
anklets, and two strands of beaded chest cloth. In my youth I
danced for a local dance troupe. In the old days, when there
was a court at Nyanza, when there were magicians and hunts-
men and guardians of tradition, I might have earned a place
among the royal dancers. That's what people tell me. My grandfather claimed our clan was high enough and my talent fine
enough. He loved to watch me dip and prance like a crested
crane.

Dressing in my dance costume, I moved my arms to resemble
the bird's flight, just as I used to do while practicing. I left the
short Intore spear in the trunk, because it belonged only to the
dance. From high up on a wall I took down a long wide-bladed
war knife that my father had given me as a gift long ago. The
blade was dull, so I took it out to the shed and honed it against
a grinding stone until keen.

Then I walked to the next rugo, where a Hutu family lived.
The man of the house was an outspoken member of CDR. In
the past I used to hear his boastful voice from inside beer shops,
calling for an end "to the Tutsi problem."

Dressed in my Intore costume and holding the war knife, I
opened the gate to his rugo and walked into the yard. His family
must have seen me coming. I am only a few inches under seven
feet tall, and the plumed white headdress made me taller. I saw
children scattering across the yard. When I approached the
house, the man appeared in the doorway with an old rifle. I did

not stop coming, but loped forward in the light, skipping, proud manner of a crane. He pulled the trigger, but it misfired just as I was reaching the house. Running inside, howling that he had done nothing wrong, he tried to get under a table. His wife cowered in the corner. Because he was too big for the table, I could see about half of his bunched-up body. Walking up, I swung at his leg with such force that it was nearly severed. The blood pumped out in a rhythm like drumbeats while he screamed.

Turning, I looked at the wife, wondering if I should kill her too before leaving. Our eyes met, then I left. As I walked across the dusty yard, two of the children peered at me around a shed. One of them was Pacifique's age. I took a couple of angry strides in their direction, shaking the war knife over my plumed headdress, but then I turned and left the rugo and went back home.

Removing the Intore costume, I packed it again in the old trunk, put on my herding robe, took what money I kept in an old beer pot, and left the rugo. But before leaving, I went to the grave, where I did what I had forgotten to do earlier. I scooped out some of the earth and placed my favorite and most sacred amulet in the hole, then covered it.

The war knife hung in a heavy scabbard from my belt, and I was ready to use it—and I would have used it on any man who came my way—but the road was empty except for Hutu women returning from their bean fields. Coming toward me I saw a heavyset woman who often sold us cassava and beans. She had a reputation for telling the future. I knew that her husband, by the name of Sylvestre, was a loudmouth teacher who also belonged to the CDR. Pauline—I think her name was

Pauline—began to slow down when she saw me approaching. Fury must have shown in my eyes and of course she saw the knife, because her hand went to her throat as if ready to catch the blow.

Standing in her path, I asked where Sylvestre was.

She shook her head, too frightened to speak.

"You killed my family," I said.

Pauline shook her head, still gripping her throat.

"Where is Sylvestre?" I asked again, and when she said nothing, I told her, "If I see him I'm going to kill him."

Then I went on. Somehow I traveled sixty miles over the next few days without getting caught, even though on most roads, at short intervals, were checkpoints manned by FAR soldiers. Sometimes I heard screams and gunfire from their direction. Villages were empty, silent except for the sound of insects buzzing in the dark huts. Until then I had never been in a village so quiet. Not even a dog was barking. Walking through such a village, I could hear the rustling of banana leaves from nearby groves. It was better to avoid villages, however, so I traveled through forests when possible or at night. Once two men surprised me on a forest path. We stared across the twenty feet that separated us, then I lunged forward and after a short chase through the bush I got them both down, almost at the same time, using only one swing of the war knife on each. I might have been a lion and they impala. Once I saw a lioness do something like that. She brought down one impala with a single swipe of a paw, then veered off and got another by the neck.

Of the rest of that journey, I remember little aside from birds pecking at green bananas and wood pigeons sitting in a tree and the scent of wild pine. And I kept trying to think of my family, but every time I did I opened my eyes too soon so I could not think of them.

Then I reached country held by the RPF just north of Kigali. I saw a roadblock where tall, thin men like myself were leaning against trees, waiting and smoking. They smiled in recognition as I went toward them, holding my arms high and asking them to let me join. Later, in a field, Captain Mazimpaka ordered me to stand up, and after some questions allowed me to join his unit.

In a short while I have learned to fire a gun correctly and bandage wounds. We soldiers talk among ourselves about the war, but not about our families. Many of us have no families to talk about. We talk about the Hutu and their desire to kill us all. We have always known that the Hutu don't want us here or anywhere for that matter, even though, like them, we've lived on this land for centuries. We came from beyond Lake Victoria in the northeast and some people say we were divinely ordained to rule. Our height and looks proclaim it, my father used to say. But the Hutu insist that we're evil spirits in the shape of humans, that we're nothing more or less than demons. If they believe such a thing, we ask ourselves, how can they ever live next to us again? To have peace you must negotiate, but everyone knows you can't negotiate with demons. So for the Hutu there's no way out but to kill us all.

That, of course, they'll never do because we are Tutsi. We will defeat them and after we defeat them, what then? They can do nothing but flee. Surely they don't expect mercy, knowing as they do that they fail to show us mercy.

I drink beer with my comrades at the end of each day and we talk such talk, but in truth I can't think about war when I want to think about my family, even though I can't think about them. All I can really think about is cattle.

INNOCENT

I WISH MY nose was broader and my body heavier so I looked more like a Hutu when coming to a roadblock. Roadblocks are bad. If I'm not careful, one of these days the soldiers won't believe I'm like them. Along the road I took an amarozi off a corpse and wear it now around my neck for good luck. Hutu believe that amulets like this will cure sick cows, but that's because they don't know better. They would know better if they were Tutsi, who know more about curing sick cows than they do. They make better bakoma, though. My mother always called in one of the Hutu bakoma when she was sick. I remember being sick once and one of them put a paste of some kind on my head and waved a smoking branch of something smelly back and forth across my face. The next day I was better. Hutu understand such things, my father used to say, because they're closer to animals.

I learned all about roadblocks from the first one I came to after leaving the hill. There was a line of people there, waiting to have their cards checked. Most of the soldiers were lounging at the side of the road, drinking beer from calabashes and bottles. A few stood at the roadblock, which was just a stack of boxes stretched across the road. I watched a man and his family hauled out of the line. Pleading, he knelt down and begged for their lives, but a couple of soldiers pulled him up and hauled him away, his sobbing wife and children clinging to him. They were taken into the bush and after a short time I heard the *rat-tat, rat-tat-tat*. I felt nothing. Why should I? I'd felt enough already. Then the soldiers returned alone. People were crying and yelling in the line when they saw this, but soldiers controlled them by holding gun barrels to their heads. A dozen people with identity cards passed through. Then a tall woman and two children were stopped at the checkpoint, led away, and from within the bush came the *rat-tat* again. I felt nothing. I'm too young to have an identity card, so when my turn came for inspection, I could say anything about myself.

The soldier was not much older than I am, but red-eyed from drinking, and wore a checkered shirt and sunglasses and on his belt a string of grenades.

When he asked me where I came from, I told him.

"Where is your family?"

"Back there." I was not afraid. I was like a stone in a stream. I felt nothing.

He smiled, which was a bad sign. "Is your family alive?"

"Yes, they are."

"Why are you here?"

"What?"

He scowled at me. "I said, why are you here? On this road?"

"I'm going to visit." I couldn't think farther for the moment.

"What are you talking about?" he said. Another young soldier, very drunk, heard the angry tone of voice and staggered over, interested in what his comrade was doing.

"I'm going," I said, "to visit my uncle in Kigali."

The other drunken soldier was looking me over. "Do you believe him? This is a cockroach. Can't you see that?"

I knew that I was taller and thinner than almost any Hutu boy my age, but Imana told me what to say. I said, "People sometimes think I'm a Tutsi. But I'm Hutu like you."

Both soldiers smiled, letting me know they didn't believe it, so I said, "Give me a gun, show me a Tutsi, and I'll kill him." Just like Imana told me to say.

They laughed. The very drunken one said, "Let's give him a gun and try him."

But the other shook his head. "We don't want gun-crazy kids around here. We got enough of them in you."

So I passed through the checkpoint, and I learned from that. The countryside was almost empty. Where were people? Then I caught the drifting odor of bodies hidden somewhere in the bush off the red-clay road. I smelled it now and then as I walked. The smell of death got into my shirt, so I smelled of death all the time. It was a heavy smell. I felt it like rot against my skin. Along the way I slept in tall weeds, among scratchy cornstalks, and sometimes in a nice bed of ferns. There were many road-blocks, but I stayed clear of most of them by using fields and woods. Even so, I wanted peace of mind like a stone has. I wanted that silence.

At the next roadblock, before the soldiers questioned me, I asked to join up. One said, "You can't even lift a gun." A few grinned and another said, "Listen, boy, why don't you become my garagu?"

The others laughed. They thought it was funny of him to

bring up the old buhake contract between Tutsi master and Hutu servant. But I didn't care, even though this would be the other way around, with a Hutu shebuja and Tutsi garagu—not that they knew I was really a Tutsi. I told him I would like him for my shebuja. He had an ugly smile because two front teeth had grown very big, crowding out others, while at the edge of his smile, there were gaps without teeth. But I didn't care as long as I could be safe awhile. I was tired, hungry, and cold from the rain.

So I was glad when he took me in. There I was, an orphaned Tutsi boy in a Hutu army. Best thing about it was eating twice a day and living in a tent. I learned how to cook for my shebuja. I carried his gun and his friends' guns and their ammo. When not doing that, I gathered firewood, washed clothes, and ran errands for my patron. One day he took me out into the woods and used me, so I knew that such a thing was going to be part of the buhake. But I didn't care, not too much anyway, because of the food and tent and safety. I didn't like what he did but I closed my eyes and let him.

We went from roadblock duty to the inspection of villages. *Inspection* was what they called it, but what they did, they killed every Tutsi they could find and anyone who might be a Tutsi. I trailed behind my master and his friends as they went from hut to hut. I saw it but felt nothing, because if I felt something I might be caught off guard and make a mistake. I don't know whether Imana told me that or I told myself.

I learned things during those days with the army. For example, I learned that children are the easiest prey. They yell out when seeing their parents hacked to death instead of staying hidden or they crawl up to the corpses and sit there crying or they whimper from the bushes and get caught. Some of them were older, almost my age, nearly twelve.

I figured out a way to stop feeling when it seemed that I was beginning to feel. What I did then was look very carefully at what was happening until it was something out there beyond me, not at all close.

For example, one time we were coming along the road and found a dozen of our troops dead and two burned-out trucks. One truck had hit a mine. According to my shebuja, who liked to think he knew everything, the other truck had been hit by a mortar. It must have happened some time ago, because the bodies were getting bloated. Seeing them lie around in clusters, I thought of the schoolroom in the church and for a few moments I almost cried. That's when I studied one of the trucks as hard as I could. A body was hanging from the windshield, feet first, head inside. The swollen legs in long pants reminded me of hippo legs. How had the man got into this position? Perhaps he had tried to crawl back into the cab through the broken windshield. That must be it. And was shot while trying to wiggle back in. It is hard sometimes to figure out how dead people get into such strange positions. It's like trying to remember how something happens in a dream. But thinking about such a thing helps me not to feel. I can think but not feel, and that's good. I look at the dead person carefully and wonder why a leg got this way or an arm that way and I just stop feeling. And I never cry.

But I can't stop feeling angry at my shebuja because now he takes me into the woods every day to use me. What I don't like is the way he is using me. Sometimes he's so eager he leaves me bleeding, and we come from the woods with the seat of my pants in blood. Then his friends howl like hyenas and point at me and laugh. But he doesn't just use me, he expects something more. Sometimes, afterwards, he gets up and paces around angrily. I asked him once what he wanted and he told me he wanted me to like him. I told him I liked him, but I didn't. I don't. And I know he'll become more angry each day. One of these days he'll take me into the woods and shoot me instead of use me and no one will care. I can see his friends telling him they never believed I was a Hutu like them. That will comfort him. I hate him and hate them and so much feeling frightens me, because I fear it will put me off guard and I'll make a mistake that kills me.

If only Imana tells me what to do, I'll be safe. Except I no longer believe that Imana is guiding me or that I'm his favorite. From the first time that my shebuja used me after I prayed for Imana to stop him, I knew that I was not a favorite. I was guiding myself and nobody was protecting me.

So I know there's nothing left to do but escape or die while escaping.

This is what I do. My shebuja and three of his friends are going to bathe in a forest stream and when they're out of sight, I don't hesitate another moment but without another thought I rummage through the thigh pockets of his fatigues and take his francs. I steal those of his friends too and his wristwatch that comes from France. Earlier, when we were coming down here, I noticed another path going off to the east, so that's where I'll head as fast as I can. Lucky for me it's late in the day, so by the time they come out of the water it'll be almost dark. Crashing forward, I cut myself on thorns and sharp leaves, but there's nothing else to do except to keep going because nothing is going to stop me, because I want to live, not because Imana wants it, but because I want it. And I'm going to keep going until I reach Kigali and buy Agnès Mujawanaliya a dress made in France, because she is the only one who cares about me, who saved my life and thinks of me as a favorite.

STEPHEN

IT IS TRUE that I became a military man as a way of entering
government service. Because of our recent success against FAR,
I see the day coming when we might turn from war to peace.
General Paul Kagame managed to shift his attention from battlefield tactics to matters of policy, so perhaps I can too. More
than we realized in the last few years, the deteriorating Habyarimana regime was undermining the morale of FAR's general
staff. According to our latest information, top officers have deserted their posts and some are leaving the country. Without
leaders, the FAR troops fight a day or two, then retreat after
sustaining mild casualties. Our own troops, after years of guerrilla
warfare, are enjoying full-scale assaults on towns and entrenched
positions. Over the years we've captured enough of FAR's heavy
artillery to smash them with their own guns. Perhaps if they
believed in their cause, we might have tougher going, but some-
time at the first sound of combat many of them scatter, remove
their uniforms, and wander home.

We should take Kigali within a few days. And the provisional
Hutu government has shifted its headquarters from Gitarama to
Gisenyi farther west, as if preparing to launch itself across the
border into Zaire and escape further pursuit.

General Kagame thinks we shall take the entire country

within a month. He has been the focus of foreign-press interest in recent weeks. As well he should be. From the early days of RPF, through the creation of our rebel army within Uganda and our initial assault across the border, his intelligence and will-power have led the way. It was Paul Kagame who figured out a clever way of getting medicine, ammunition, and military supplies from Europe into Uganda. After matériel arrived in the port of Mombasa, it was smuggled a thousand miles westward in trucks marked "auto spares." Because of so much traffic in auto parts throughout Africa, truck convoys bearing such equipment moved between checkpoints without incident.

Sometimes when I look at him, a man of my height, six-feet-two, but weighing only 125 pounds, I wonder at his energy and toughness.

Recently, to lessen his public burden, he asked me to handle interviews with the foreign press. Yesterday I sat over tea with a dozen journalists in a jungle shed. Steady rain pounded on the corrugated roof as I announced my intention to answer their questions in a forthright and candid way. An American, surprised by my command of English, complimented me publicly. He didn't seem to know that Ugandans speak English as fluently as Rwandans speak French. Annoyed by his ignorance, I nearly asked him why the American government has argued so fiercely over the price of leasing armored cars to UN peacekeeping forces. For the most part, however, I replied to questions in a vague, you might say, deceptive manner. Over the centuries we Tutsi have earned a well-deserved reputation for guile. When asked where our RPF weapons were coming from, I claimed that nearly all of them were captured from the FAR. I did not mention rocket-propelled grenades, mortars, and cannons from

Uganda and small arms brought in from Tanzania and from Kenya. But when a German reporter wanted to know if the Hutu attacks could be described as genocidal, I gave him a full and honest answer. What was genocide? A plan to remove an entire people from this earth. That was genocide, I said. The Nazi attempt at it had made the Western world quite familiar with the concept. I was not, however, done with the question. I then turned to the international community's response to the genocide occurring in Rwanda. During recent proceedings in the United Nations, diplomats had condemned the killing but omitted the word *genocide* from their discussions. In line with its charter, if genocide correctly described what was happening in Rwanda, the UN would be legally obliged to "prevent and punish" the perpetrators. Therefore, no official "genocide." I also mentioned the American president, whose use of "civil war in Rwanda" was another way of avoiding the moral obligation to do something.

The journalists were ready after that to change the subject. I was asked if we were in contact with the exiled Tutsi king, Kigeli, who now lived in America. I said we were not in contact, but we knew that the UN continued to ignore his efforts to speak in the Security Council on Rwanda's behalf. For centuries his ancestors ruled, but today, we're told here, he lives off the gifts of former subjects.

They asked me was it true that we had planted land mines along the northern border. I said it was not true. In fact, we have planted many types there, ranging from nonmetallic antipersonnel mines to those of World War II vintage.

They asked me to comment on the reported movement of people out of the country. I refused to comment on the grounds that I knew nothing about that. Everyone in the shed was aware, of course, that thousands of Hutu were on the move, afraid of the impending Tutsi victory.

The dissatisfied journalists were restless and ready to leave. I had been either banal or accusatory but rarely informative. Good.

After they trooped out of the shed into the driving rain, I held back one of them whom I had once met in Uganda. He was a blunt, pipe-smoking, red-faced Englishman of a cynical turn of mind, so I trusted him more than most of the others. "No more tea," I said. "Let's have wine."

An aide was standing nearby and when I nodded to him, he went into another room and came back with a bottle of French wine and two glasses.

"You planned this," said the Englishman with a smile.

"Yes, I did. I'm curious. In the last few weeks a dozen aid organizations have showed up. Is the world that interested in us?"

"It's television," he said, pulling on his pipe. "When television comes, so do the aid people. As for television coming here, I can think of two reasons. One is Rwanda's accessibility."

"What do you mean?"

"Killing fields are easy to find in such a small country. It's not too expensive to get the cameras in. And then there's the timing."

"Is that the second reason?"

The aide poured us wine.

"You see, the journalists and their cameras are already on the continent because of Somalia and the election in South Africa.

So the equipment's in place. When the cameras roll, they demand a response from the UN and when that UN lot gets into it, the aid lads follow. Have I satisfied your curiosity?"

I thanked him and we continued to drink.

"Now let me ask you something," he said after refilling his pipe and lighting it. "What do you think goes through the mind of someone who does this sort of genocidal killing?"

I had often thought about it, so my answer was ready. "The call of blood is powerful, but most people free themselves from the craziness after awhile. They see the world as it really is again. Not all but most do, I think. There's hope in that."

He drank off his glass and watched me pour him another. "You're an idealist," he said gruffly. "Here's how I look at it. I think you can get past the killing, but you don't see the world as it really is. You give yourself all sorts of excuses for having done what you did. You never see the world as it really is again. You simply can't. What you did is irrevocable."

"I hope you're wrong."

He nodded glumly. "And I hope you're right."

That was the best conversation I have ever had with a white man. Often I recall it while attempting to assess myself. Do I expect too much of humanity? Can what has happened be put right in the future?

Since crossing the border, the composition and collective thinking of the RPF has changed. Many of our Rwandan officers are unbending in their traditional belief in Tutsi superiority. Most of our recruits, like my tall new bodyguard Emmanuel, want revenge more than justice. In Uganda, removed from the immediate effect of Hutu dominance, we had dreamed not only of a return to the motherland but also of a new life for everyone in Rwanda. Now our recruits have lost entire families and see only as far as the end of their gun barrels.

Perhaps in anticipation of victory, many of us are recounting terrible stories of the genocide. The other day I joined half-a-dozen officers who gathered informally after a briefing on the progress of units around Kibungo. One officer claimed that he had passed through a region once occupied by four hundred Tutsi. When the region was liberated, only five Tutsi still lived.

Next, someone related a story told to him by a survivor in a village near Cyangugu. The FAR troops hacked the breasts off a woman and forced the dismembered flesh down the throats of her children, then turned her head so she had to watch it while dying.

All of us were silent. It is said that the Hutu call us demons from hell. What, then, are they? Are any of us human? Or do we all pretend to that state of being? Only if we're truly human can anything good come out of this. And so I struggle against the hard truth expressed by the Englishman. I can only hope that his truth, which I find I cannot honestly refute, is incomplete and leaves room for something beyond it, something more human. Today I also hope to crush a unit of FAR still holding a hill above Kigali in the southwest sector. If every single one of them die, that will not displease the soldier in me.

AGNÈS

I TOOK THE road for Butare through a countryside almost deserted except for women who let nothing, not even massacres, stop them from weeding their fields. That was a few weeks ago. Now I'm walking on another road jammed with trucks, bicycles, goatherds, and great crowds of people. How quickly things have changed since I left home with a suitcase balanced on my head.

On the way to Butare, I kept seeing the bourgmestre in my mind. His big white teeth kept floating through the heat into memory. His goatee, his thick body, his sweat. How could I have done it with him on my own bed? He would have killed the boy otherwise, that was why, yet it was not possible that I did it. What if I carried his child? It was not possible. It was not possible either that my brother ran away or my mother was shot down for no reason. Our people, both Hutu and Tutsi, believe in what is possible. It allows us to live peacefully on our crowded hills. I have always believed that. Order and restraint show us how to survive, even when bad things happen.

When very bad things happened, my father used to say, "That is not possible." Our hills ruined by men like Silas Bagambiki? I told myself, "It is not possible, it is not possible," while putting sandals on because of the midday heat.

Then hearing of slaughter in every village along the way, I thought, oh yes, such a thing was possible. And it was possible that I carried his child.

Arriving in Butare, I learned that every Tutsi doctor and nurse, more than half of the hospital staff, had been murdered along with all the Tutsi patients. The killing spree had lasted a whole day. I felt shame, anger, sorrow.

Training through books and lectures was no longer possible at the hospital. Anything more I learned about nursing must come through doing. So I went to work. The remaining staff tried harder than ever, as if to show the world that all Hutu were not murderers. Surely, I felt that way. None of us slept more than four hours a night. We began taking in Tutsi victims of knifings and shootings, although when the militia came around they warned us not to help cockroaches. Hoping somehow to get away with it, four of us put Tutsi patients on mattresses in storerooms and supply buildings. The militia still came around, but they inspected only the main part of the hospital, as if to make sure they found nothing. This relieved as well as puzzled us, until we learned what the militia already knew: the government was swiftly losing the war. That meant local Hutu did not want the blame for killing Tutsi in hospital beds.

Militiamen and authorities, packing up what goods they could carry, left town. So did people who had done nothing wrong but left because others were leaving. Day after day, looking from a hospital window, I noticed the crowds grow thicker on the road outside. Then one day our director was missing. Soon after that three Hutu doctors failed to show up. That left the hospital with only one doctor, an old Belgian who had been practicing in Butare for nearly forty years. Hutu nurses disappeared next.

One afternoon Julius Kibaki asked me to walk with him in the courtyard. A Kikuyu from Kenya, he spoke poor French but had won respect among us for his good judgment. It was Julius who had worked out the plan for treating wounded Tutsi in the back rooms.

"Go," he told me as we walked in the yard. "Don't stay here longer."

"I've done nothing wrong. I'll stay."

Julius, no taller than I am, touched my wrist. "The RPF could be here in a week. Do you know how many Tutsi your people have killed? Hundreds of thousands. Do you think their army will forgive?"

"Do you think they'll stop a nurse from working?"

He shook his head. "Don't stay and find out. Go with the refugees. Anyway, they'll need nurses in the camps."

"Is that what we're all becoming? Refugees?"

Julius looked at me in a way that left no doubt in my mind. So I said, "All right then. Where should I go?"

"I hear of camps east and north."

"Every day I see people going north."

"Then go there."

So I'm going north, with the suitcase once again on my head. When I left the hospital, only a few veteran Hutu nurses remained—they would never leave except in a coffin—along with Julius Kibaki, the old Belgian doctor, and a pygmy whose name I never knew. He was simply called "the Twa." I did learn, however, that he was an Impunyu pygmy from a clan of potmakers near Ruhengeri. No taller than a child but muscular and hairy, the Twa liked to wear a security guard's pistol, although his nature was very gentle. Soldiers would surely not harm the

Twa or the old white man or a Kikuyu from far away. It was not possible.

But at this moment, as I trudge down the road, I wonder if everything is possible. I think only of getting somewhere, without knowing what the somewhere will look like. On this road all of us together make a broad river rolling northward. We flee from an unseen enemy who might do us no harm at all. That's possible. But the other thing is also possible. They might come along in trucks and machine-gun us down as they pass. Everything is possible.

As we walk northward, more and more people join us. They wear all sorts of clothing. Western track suits, business suits, tattered jeans, khangas, T-shirts, bright kerchiefs, shoes without laces, rain hats. Men smoke corncob pipes. Crucifixes sway on chests. Loaded down with pots and mattresses and window frames, people carry yellow plastic jugs of water on their shoulders, branches of eucalyptus for firewood, and kitchen sinks balanced on bicycle seats. An old woman comes along in a wheelbarrow pushed by a man who must be her son. Then an old man comes along on a bike, holding a portable radio against one ear, the wheels wiggling crazily. Everyone seems to have a radio of some kind. Most of them are tuned to RTLMC, which broadcasts nothing but hatred and fear. The air is filled with hatred of Tutsi demons and fear of Tutsi demons.

That's not all I hear. I hear stories along the way, as people talk and walk and talk and walk because they still have energy enough for both. I hear that FAR soldiers have been forcing children to kill wounded Tutsi. That way no one escapes blame, not even children scarcely big enough to hold a panga. I hear of White Fathers who hid some Tutsi orphans in their mission.

The Interahamwe wouldn't search while the Fathers were there, but wouldn't let food be brought into the mission either. Starved out at last, the Fathers had to leave. There was nothing they could do for the children except lock them in a dormitory. Everyone, including the children, knew that once the Fathers were out of sight, the door would be pushed in and the slaughter begin.

I hear many such stories. I wish I could wash my memory clean like a bowl, but the stories are stuck there forever.

Everything is possible. I even saw him again. Yes, Silas Bagambiki. I saw him, I saw him.

As our column moved north, we came to a road that stretched east and west. A column of refugees as large as our own was heading eastward, so our paths crossed. Three Hutu were driving about twenty Inyambo cattle ahead of them, a herd that recently must have belonged to a Tutsi cattleman. Some FAR deserters, still wearing uniforms and carrying weapons, were scattered through the column. Then a truck passed by. Standing at the front, just behind the cab, was the bourgmestre. Luckily, he didn't look my way. Nearby stood his henchmen, among them the thin little Denis, who also failed to see me. Their faces showed no panic, no fear, but seemed determined and strong, unlike those of refugees. They looked more like soldiers than the FAR deserters did. They even seemed proud. The bourgmestre had a contemptuous smile on his goateed face. Maybe he was trying for the arrogance of a Tutsi mwami in the old days. What must his thoughts be? A pile of rotting corpses in a dark room.

Spewing exhaust and raising dust, his truck passed alongside the eastward-moving column. After a few hundred yards farther on, it vanished behind a hillside curve and took away the man whose child I could be carrying.

As we move closer to the town of Goma on the Zairian border, I begin counting the days to see if it is possible. I am always regular so I'll know soon. Such a terrible worry gives me more to think about than the long, hot journey filled with noises. Blaring radios, bleating goats, coughing, sobbing, the heavy click of truck engines—the noises of a refugee column. It is not possible that I am pregnant, I tell myself, and take another step forward.

I take these steps until they take me to the border. It is marked by a roadblock. A line of soldiers in Zairian uniform regard us lazily as we pass. Confiscating weapons, they pile them on a small hill made of grenades and assault rifles and ammunition belts taken from FAR troops as well as the pangas, hoes, and studded clubs belonging to militiamen. Most of the militia weapons must have been hidden in stacks of goods, but they appear now from nowhere and are flung on the pile. I hear a FAR soldier say that the Zairians don't care if refugees murder one another, but just want the weapons so they can sell them. They threaten to kill anyone who doesn't turn weapons in.

So now I'm on the other side. I have never been north before, never to the Zairian border, but now I stand on foreign soil. What soil? It's nothing but cooled lava from the volcanoes that ring this land. Ahead of us lies a brown, treeless plain with a gray road winding forward. People add a touch of color from their bags and clothing as they plod along the dead-looking ground.

We walk perhaps an hour before seeing where we will come to. Tents of blue sheeting are spread across valley and hillside, partly obscured by mists. I have seen the back of a cape buffalo wading through the muck of a swamp; the hills are just that color.

Smoke rises from the camp, vast billowing quantities of it, and with the gray smoke drifts the odor of excrement and urine and food cooking and something undefinable, perhaps the smell of thousands of sweaty bodies. At the first shock of this mixture of smells, I breathe in shallow gusts, but by the time we reach the edge of camp, I breathe normally like everyone else.

And I have something to be thankful for. I feel cramps and soon a wetness between my legs, which means I'm not pregnant. I can face this future with a clear mind.

In the distance, above the jumble of tents, I see a tall flag flying a red cross. As I head in the direction of the flag, I tell myself that nothing can prevent me from doing what I must do. Politics and war can't stop me from doing my work. It is not possible.

SILAS

OUR PROVISIONAL GOVERNMENT has fled, but I won't run away even though it might seem that I have. What I have done is that I have moved my base of operations eastward to Camp Benaco in Tanzania. Not that I like this countryside. The land is too flat, a wide, brown savannah that lacks the beauty of my own green hills. But I am happy here. Everyone in camp knows me for what I am, a strict and courageous Hutu bourgmestre who won't stop fighting until the cockroaches are squashed.

I could have gone elsewhere. Goma in the north was no good because of my distrust of Zairians, especially their unpaid soldiers, who do nothing but prey upon civilians. I thought of crossing into Burundi because of its proximity to Butare. But the Tutsi control of Burundi's army ruled out that possibility. For that matter, during the last year many Hutu Burundians have fled over into our country to escape persecution. Ask a Hutu from Burundi about the sweet-natured, lovable Tutsi.

To anyone who believes Tutsi propaganda that they're willing to negotiate, I say this is how they negotiate—during 1972 they killed nearly 200,000 of our people in Burundi. Hutu men were taken to the police station at night and held for execution the following day. Then, if the quota were filled before nightfall on the next day, prisoners were sent home and ordered to return in the morning. And they did. They really did. I am asked by curious people, How could those Burundians meekly return to face certain death the next day? Because they felt it was hopeless to fight against Tutsi power, is what I answer. I tell my listeners if they can find me Tutsi created of pure souls like the Christians talk about, the tender souls of merciful saints, then I'll love the Tutsi like brothers, but as long as they kill us, I'm going to kill them.

After I tell people such things, which are true, they look at me from different eyes. Their eyes turn hard and glinting. It's absolutely true. Glinting. From hatred and courage.

As a Hutu official, I had no choice but to leave our hills and go elsewhere to continue the fight. Collecting my assistants, I took a journey by truck through Nyakizu, Gisamvu, Kigembe, and Runyinya, and finally crossed the Tanzanian border to Benaco.

Now that truck.

A few weeks before Butare préfecture joined the rest of the country in squashing cockroaches, a UN truck parked on Avenue du Commerce near the Butare market so that the three white aid workers could eat at the Restaurant Chez Nous. A couple of university students, quite drunk, decided it would be fun to steal that truck while the white men ate barbecued goat. Since the fool driver had left the key inside, it was easy enough. They drove the truck until it ran out of gas and left it on the outskirts of a village with the keys inside. I heard about it and told Denis to go get it for us. But the timid fool shook his head and didn't budge.

"You better go," I warned him.

His lips were trembling so much he couldn't even refuse.

"It's only a truck," I said, "it's not a Tutsi."

"The United Nations has power."

I knew, of course, what he meant by that. One of his many uncles had been a witch doctor and taught him to look for power everywhere. That meant hidden demons, furies, ghosts.

"We're modern men, you fool," I told him. "Get that truck. Paint it brown and black and bring it here." He still didn't move. "Take a militia squad with you, so they can shoot down any demons that might be hiding in the cab." That gave him confidence. A day later the truck was parked in front of the commune headquarters. Identification markings and white UN paint were hidden under the colors of camouflage.

"What do you think now?" I asked Denis. "Are there demons in the truck?"

He smiled a little, but I don't believe he can ever climb into it without fear.

And I don't ever climb into it without satisfaction. I have contempt for the UN who do nothing except talk. But I also like them around because they have what I want and do what I say.

Arriving at Benaco, the first thing I did was speak to the UN people there. I explained that no one else should distribute food to people from my part of Rwanda. Otherwise there would be fighting, disorder, thievery.

A white man said, "Is that a threat?"

"That's the truth," I insisted.

His eyes met mine then turned away. And so the UN, who had no idea who we were, did as they were told. They gave me control of my own people.

Refugees were already helping the aid workers organize the

camp by seeking out their own local clans and marking out
home areas for themselves. Without being told to do it, they
separated naturally into ten sectors, which corresponded to
regions of the country, because it's the way of Rwandans, even
Tutsi Rwandans, to establish order in their lives.

The sector I control represents Butare. A storehouse is mine,
a stockade with the top protected by a row of broken glass, a
half-dozen trucks, and lots of UN blue sheeting for tents. Our
sector is deep within a camp of 200,000 people, off the main
road, down curving lanes too narrow for more than one person
to walk on, through a maze of tents and around and over sick
people and sleeping people, perhaps an hour into the heart of a
busy, smoky, trackless place. It's no wonder that without my
prior knowledge and consent I can't be found. I might as well
be in the midst of the Serengeti or the Congo's deepest jungle.
If anything, I possess more power here than at home. I have
twenty young bodyguards who have nothing to do but carry
weapons and think of my welfare. They go with me everywhere,
even to the latrine. I have more than enough food and water
for people near me, and a bullhorn and a man who presses my
pants every day with a hot iron filled with live coals.

I tell the people of my sector to stay put. You are better off
here, where you can organize your lives. If you try to leave, I'll
see that you die. Then I laugh and run a finger across my throat.
It always works. They slink back to their tents and keep their
mouths shut. I tell them anyone returning to his village will
have his balls cut off by the Tutsi. Every woman will be raped
until she dies and every child skewered on a spear. Tutsi will
infect them with tuberculosis and cholera. I slash the air with
my hand. Tutsi gouge out eyes with their bare fingers and pull

out intestines on a stick through a slit in the belly. They also like to kill by fire. Everyone knows this, I say. It's happening throughout the country. And I sweep the air with my hand again.

Perhaps much of what I warn them of is not true, but I consider the truth to be whatever is good for my people. So I frighten them for their own good. When they want to eat, they line up in front of the stockade gate and wait until my men let them enter, one by one, silently, with their hands out.

Then of course I have women, although none like Agnès Mujawanaliya, who finally submitted herself to my satisfaction and, I think, to hers as well. I was disappointed to learn that she ran off. Like some foolish people, she must have feared the Tutsi because of their exploits in battle a century ago. I had expected more of someone who seemed calm and reasonable and perhaps even brave enough to hide cockroaches in her house. Perhaps something was wrong with her family. Her mother was shot for failing to obey a simple command. And her foolish brother paid good money to join the army. By now he must certainly be dead in a ditch somewhere.

I have a new friend in camp, a bourgmestre from Kamonyi who joins me in going to the UN people and demanding supplies, food, privileges, all of which we get. Nightly we drink together and exchange stories.

He too is a man of sophistication and knowledge. He too has an eye for business, although he has yet to run one. His opinions are strong, For example, he'll have nothing to do with coffee plantations because the price of beans depends too much on the foreign market. More cautious than I am, perhaps he lacks my vision. We plan, however, to grow pyrethrum together when things calm down. It was my idea. He knew almost nothing about pyrethrum when we began talking. I explained that the extracts of those daisylike flowers are processed into insecticides in Kenya. We have only to grow them in high altitudes such as Ruhengeri and Gisenyi préfectures and truck them eastward. We'll apply to some of the foreign aid organizations for money to begin, and I have every expectation of getting it.

My new friend is not only intelligent but hardworking. He told me of going to the Ndera Psychiatric Center about eight miles from Kigali, a place run by Belgian Brothers of Charity. After the Belgians left, my friend came along in an armored car and had his men toss grenades over the wall. The crazies inside didn't understand what was happening, but started to sing Christian hymns and wave their hands in the air. I tried to imagine it and bent over laughing. Of course, the Tutsi in there were all harvested, but all other crazies were taken care of too because it was possible that they were only pretending to be crazy, said my friend, and I agreed. Then my friend allowed his boys to steal all the medicine and furniture and the iron gate too. He took half of the profit that they made by selling the stuff later in Kigali.

So nightly we drink and swap stories. During the day I prepare lists to deal with disloyal Hutu here in Benaco, people who tell lies about a coming peace and a return home.

Meanwhile, I go around the camp and stand at fires where people gather to eat their food. I tell them about our final goal, which is to remove all Tutsi from the face of the earth. Kill even the innocent if they're Tutsi, because if they're Tutsi they can't be innocent, not even infants. Don't try to frighten them into submission, I say. We don't want them to submit, we want them dead. Never think of negotiating. There is nothing to ne-gotiate. There's only one thing to do and that's to kill each and every cockroach. Do you hear me? I ask. If they simply nod, I yell it out. "Do you hear me! *Do you hear me!*" And I don't stop screaming at them until they open their own mouths and cry out, "Yes, yes, yes! Kill the cockroaches!" And I stand there and wait until satisfied that their eyes look hard enough and glinting.

PAULINE MUKANDINA

ON A SMALL piece of land my husband Sylvestre grows coffee as a cash crop and for extra money teaches at a local school. What I do only brings in money if people want to give it. I don't ask for it because that would destroy my powers.

When a woman becomes pregnant, she comes to me and I give her an ibiheko, a special amulet to protect the unborn spirit from evil. I say what and what not to eat. I tell her that her husband should blow tobacco smoke in her face to keep the unborn healthy, as the smoke does that. I go to birthings and see that the newborn is washed in cold water and rubbed with butter. The birth cord is kept as an amulet for the child, and the afterbirth is buried in a hole under the infant's bed to ward off evil spirits. These are only a few of the things I know about birth.

People knock on my door and come in to learn. I explain to them that all living things possess spirit. Spirits disappear when animals die, but in us at our death they become abazimu, spirits of the dead. After a certain time this spirit sheds the memory of being human like a snake sheds its skin. It then becomes a strong wind and mingles with other such winds in the spirit world. They blow around into whirlpools of cloud and spark off lightning and give the human world life-giving rain.

That's when things go right. When things go wrong, the aba-zimu bring crop failure and cattle disease. Why does this happen? People come to me for consultation when a spirit—perhaps a long-dead grandfather or a deceased uncle—brings them mis-fortune. By opening the gut of a chicken and inspecting it carefully, I can often discover what made the spirit angry enough to hurt its own clan and family. I don't succeed if the spirit deliberately hides from me. But often I find out what a family did to bring down such wrath. Perhaps someone cheated or spoke unkindly of another. When this is admitted, the whole family prays for mercy and the spirit grants it. Sometimes, not always.

We Hutu try to please the abazimu far more than do the Tutsi, whose arrogance lets them think they can defy the dead and get away with it. I know better. My father was a famous umufumu of the Bankano clan, who taught me what dreams mean and how to predict the future by chicken divining. He was a handsome man in his leopard skin and cow-tail headdress. No one ever shook a gourd-rattle faster than he did. No one. Everyone who saw him do it has told me this is true.

I listen on the radio to Simon Bikindi sing. I dance alone to the music. Sway and sway. There is nothing I love more than music except my children. I like to listen to the bass and the guitar and the singer weave their sounds together in benga, a style of Luo music. I like the bass pulsing slowly and then chang-ing into rapid-fire bursts of sound. I like to hear D. O. Misiani and his Shirate Jazz Group play "Benga Blast." And I like ca-vacha, a fast rhythm on snare drum or high hat. Then there's a Tanzanian band I like called Simba Wanyika. I like the rumba when it's played with congas and claves and a very soft-sounding lead guitar. Once I heard the royal drummers when I was a little child. There were nine of them. The smallest or soprano drum set the rhythm for each tune, and then it was backed by a tenor, an alto, two baritones, two basses, and two double-bass drums. But my favorite instrument is the eight-stringed luhinga that I think must sound like the strumming of a big, black god who sits in the clouds.

When my family reaches the horizon, I see nothing beyond it. They are my world. My oldest boy has taken work in Kenya, my oldest girl is married in Tanzania. My other four are still with me.

Then there is my husband, Sylvestre, who I sometimes think exists only to have political opinions. According to him, a teacher must have bold ideas. He likes to make speeches. "We Hutu must show leadership that people will obey and if we fail in our plans the enemy will crush us like insects." That sort of thing. He comes in shouting slogans, most of them against the Tutsi. Before the massacre began, he went around telling his friends that they must send the Tutsi back to Ethiopia by river. He meant dead bodies by river. I have since learned that this is a commonplace thing to say.

This morning he was up early, said nothing to me, and left, carrying a hoe and with a panga slid inside his belt. He had done the same thing yesterday.

My three girls were playing rock and sticks next to a sorghum field near our rugo. I was baking sweet potatoes and wondering what Sylvestre and his friends were doing. I knew what they were doing and didn't want to think about it, but sometimes I let myself and then I made myself stop. I was thinking such things when Odette, my youngest, ran into the house and pulled at my skirt. "There's a boy out there!"

Because she was so excited, I went with her. The other two girls were playing by themselves. Odette, only six years old, was too young for them. She must have wandered off into the field of half-grown sorghum.

"He's awake but he won't move," she told me breathlessly. "There!"

A boy about her age was lying on his side in the sorghum. His thumb was in his mouth. He wore a pair of shorts, nothing else. There was caked blood on his hands and forearms.

I knelt beside him and looked into large eyes, clear as spring water, but with an expression of fear in them that took my breath away.

"Boy, are you hurt?"

When he just looked at me, I asked again. He shook his head slightly, then took his thumb from his mouth.

"Can you sit up, boy?"

He looked at me again with those large, pained eyes and struggled, with my help, to sit up. His arms and legs were gangly, and he had the long, thin neck and large, round forehead so typical of a Tutsi.

"Who are you, boy?"

He didn't answer.

"Who is your father?" I wasn't yet sure that he could speak. Finally he said, "Emmanuel . . ."

I waited.

Then he said, "Rubagunga."

"Emmanuel Rubagunga." Well, I knew who that was. His

father was a seven-foot-tall cattle herder. In his younger days he had been an Intore dancer who pranced through festival dust, a short spear in his hand raised to the sky. I had seen him dance many times. He had been a beautiful dancer.

"Where is your father, boy?"

Again he looked at me as if unable to speak, but finally he said, "gone."

"Where's your mother?"

The large eyes widened, then he began to cry.

I stroked his blood-caked arm.

"Where's your mother, boy?"

He said something, but in such a low voice, I couldn't hear.

"Where?"

He said it again and this time I heard him say "dead."

I took both of his hands in mine. "Were there others?"

He nodded.

I held the sobbing boy close. "What's your name, son?" At first he didn't seem to know that either, so I waited patiently and rocked him.

After a while he said, "Pacifique."

"Come inside, Pacifique, and eat." Helping him to his feet, I took one of his hands and Odette took the other and we led the shaky boy toward the rugo.

As we walked, I said, "When your father danced, the arch of his back was royal. That's the most important thing for an Intore dancer, the back. If there was still a court, your father would have been a royal dancer. Both Hutu and Tutsi said that."

Just as we reached the house, he mumbled something. Bending down, I asked, "What was that?"

"Didn't put the heads back."

I wasn't sure what he meant, but I pulled his shaking body close and passed my hand across his nubby hair. "It's all right. It's all right."

That's how Pacifique came into our family.

After I had fed and put him to sleep in the shed, I waited for my husband to come home. He came in with his shirt and pants splashed with blood. He was grinning, his eyes wild. I didn't want to know what he and his friends had been doing, because I knew. Saying nothing, I brought him a large bowl of water to wash his hands and face. He was breathing heavily, as if still in the midst of the terrible things he must have been doing.

Because of his proud and happy mood, I thought this was the best time to tell him what had happened here. So while he washed, I said, "I've put a Tutsi boy in the shed."

Turning, he looked at me in surprise, then in anger.

"I did it for you," I told him calmly. "What if the Tutsi win?" He shook his head. "They can't win."

"What if they do? Think of the past. Think of the warriors they were." I let him think about that. "What if they come through our hills and do to us what you did to their people here?" I had him thinking. "By feeding one of theirs, we protect ourselves if they win. We should keep the boy for your sake."

I knew Sylvestre would do as I asked if he felt it was to his advantage. He's that way. So in spite of his hatred of Tutsi, he let Pacifique remain with us. Soon I had the boy eating at our table with the other children, and although Sylvestre gave him nasty looks, Pacifique stayed.

When I had told my husband that rumor about the Tutsi winning, I had not really believed it. So I was just as surprised as Sylvestre when the rumor proved true. Tutsi troops were here, there, here, there. I wondered if our troops were even trying.

I don't know about war, but I think maybe the victories of the past influence the present. A hundred years ago the tall Tutsi leaped up and down in rhythm, then yelling a call that chilled to the bone, they ran forward with their long spears level at the chest. That's the picture of them we all have. Our boys out in the bush must think of it when preparing to meet the RPF.

Sylvestre and his militia held a meeting and decided that our entire hill and some neighboring hills should leave together for the border town of Goma in the northeast. Sylvestre tells me we have waited long enough. Many of his friends have already gone, and the only reason he remained this long was his elevation to superintendent of the school, because both the superintendent and the deputy superintendent had already vanished, leaving only Sylvestre and two young teachers in the school.

As we got into the line of people, my husband and I shouldered a huge load of goods. We're both heavy people and carry a lot. On the march I spent my time watching the children, like a hen watching her chicks. Pacifique was never a bother. Someone came alongside me and said, "Isn't that a Tutsi?"

It was a wrinkled old farmer by the name of Prosper Ndabateze. Sometimes we talked in the market about crops. They say nobody knows more about farming than Prosper. He's a good man, so I said, "Yes, the boy's Tutsi."

"You're saving his life," Prosper said with an approving nod. Then he added, "But if it's between your life and his, give him up."

Would the militia make me choose? I wondered. Would they say either give up the boy or die? Would Sylvestre do that? I wasn't sure. But I was sure of one thing. I would protect Pacifique's life with my own.

On the second day we came to an RPF checkpoint on the forest-lined road. All of us were surprised and frightened that the Tutsi had come this far.

One of the Tutsi soldiers carried a clipboard. When each man came along with an identity card, the soldier wrote it down. The other soldiers were listening to the radio. They were tuned to a government station that never stopped broadcasting an encouragement to massacre the Tutsi, so everyone knew it as The Radio That Kills. A voice yelled from the sound box, "Every Hutu who can hear me, I tell you the basket is only half-full; go out and fill it to the brim with Tutsi heads!" Why did the Tutsi soldiers listen? I wondered. To inflame themselves? To laugh when they held in their hands the lives of Hutu who came along this road?

Then I saw a man standing back among the soldiers. He was a cassava farmer from our commune who liked to gossip in the beer shops. When men came to the head of the line, the soldiers looked at him and if he nodded, the man was pulled out. When it was Sylvestre's turn, the man nodded.

"You," the soldier beckoned at Sylvestre with his gun.

My husband, lowering his eyes, stepped out of the line. I had never seen him so heavyhearted. Gathering the children, I followed behind until we came to a tent in the woods, where they had put a table. The man who sat in front of it must have been an officer.

He asked my husband questions almost as fast as he could say

them: name, clan, commune. Was he a member of the Interahamwe? Had he been murdering people? My husband answered
in a flat way, as if tired. I think he felt there wasn't a chance.
Then the cassava farmer came up and accused Sylvestre of being
a militiaman.

At last my husband showed spirit. "Yes, I was," he said, "and
so were you."

I tried to speak, but the soldiers told me to shut up and sent
me away with the children following.

Sylvestre would go to prison if lucky. That's what I was thinking. By nightfall my husband could be dead and there was nothing to be done about it. Not one of my amulets could make a
difference. I remembered him coming home splattered in blood,
wild-eyed from the joy of killing. I didn't know if he and his
bunch had killed Pacifique's family. If the Tutsi executed him,
I could understand why.

What I had to do then was think of my four children and
the Tutsi boy.

A soldier walked over and looked at all of us, then bent down
to Pacifique and felt his arms and legs as if judging a calf.

"This is your child?" he asked me.

I said it was.

"He's got a long neck and thin lips. And what about this long
nose? You say he's yours?"

"That's my child." I turned to Pacifique. "Are you my child?"

He nodded vigorously. Good boy. I didn't want these Tutsi
to have him.

Another soldier came along and looked Pacifique up and
down. "Your husband says you brought along this Tutsi child
out of kindness and mercy. Is that true?"

I said nothing.

The second soldier took Pacifique by the arm. "He goes with us. We don't want Hutu raising our children."

Pacifique began whimpering, so I took a step forward and the soldier pushed me hard enough in the chest to knock me down. I got up and pleaded with the soldiers to wait. Pacifique was wailing now. I'll never forget those large eyes opened so wide, when he turned to me.

"Wait! Please! Wait!" I yelled at the soldiers taking him away. Removing an amulet from around my neck, I asked them if I could put it on the boy.

"Please," I begged. "To protect him from snakebite and diarrhea."

After studying me a moment, they allowed me to put it around Pacifique's neck. Great sobs came out of him as he reached out and gripped my hand hard.

"Let go of my hand," I told him harshly. "Let go now. Good, that's a good boy. Keep this around your neck, because it'll protect you. You understand? Do you?"

Pacifique nodded, his eyes full of tears.

Then I turned away, mine full too, and I never looked back, although I heard him wail again. Collecting the other children, I walked past the roadblock, wondering if the soldiers would be kind too and let Sylvestre go. But they didn't.

A few hundred paces beyond the roadblock, with my boy of eleven and my girls of ten and eight and five all following single file in my footsteps, I glanced back once more, but Sylvestre never came. They weren't going to let him go, even though I'm sure he worked hard to convince them he was a good man and merciful to a Tutsi child.

I'm going on alone with four children to somewhere near Goma, a place I haven't seen since girlhood. My children are quiet. All of them are loaded down with things their father had dropped in the road. I didn't need to tell them they must pick things up. They are good children. I wear eleven amulets and touch each of them in sequence.

PACIFIQUE NTAWINIGA

I WAS PLAYING behind a shed when the whistles began blowing. I looked around and saw men in the yard running with clubs. They hit my mother when she got up and she fell over. They hit my brother when he started to run. They caught and hit my sister too. Then they cut off the heads. I got out the back door of the rugo and ran into the bush past the kraal and stayed there a long time until my heart stopped going so fast and they were gone. All curled up, I didn't want to go back to the yard, but I did to make sure. When I saw it I heard a sound and wondered where it came from until I knew it came from me. I fell to my knees and crawled over to my mother's head. I lifted it, but it felt so heavy I dropped it. I heard the sound again. Then I went to my sister and lifted her head and put it near the pool of blood where her neck was. This was as much as I could do. I heard the sound again, louder. Then I got up but almost fell. If I fell then I would never get up again so I ran as fast as I could.

I ran out of the rugo, then ran back in the house. I was looking for something, but couldn't remember what. Then I did. It was a Tutsi warrior, as tall as a hand, that my father carved from wood. He made it for me. Looking around, I couldn't find it. So then I ran out of the rugo again and ran until I fell from being tired. I was lying on the ground beside the road when a truck came by with men in it, waving bottles. I heard a couple of thuds near my feet. Someone from the truck was shooting bullets at me. I heard laughter from the truck get smaller and then go away. I got up and began walking and walked a long time, putting down one foot and then the other and saying to myself, "Mother used to sing to me, now she has no head, Mother used to sing to me, now she has no head." I felt dizzy. I was talking out loud. I was yelling. I was calling the names of my sisters. I wanted my mother, and my father was gone forever. When people came along the road, I ran into the ditch and into woods or fields. They were looking for me to kill me too.

I walked until the darkness came, then longer. When I couldn't walk anymore, I went into a field and slept. But in the night I woke up and looked at the round, white moon that looked like a head staring down at me. I couldn't see the eyes but they were watching me. I felt my body get cold. I was shaking and shaking and couldn't stop. Turning over, I shut my eyes tight and pushed my face hard into the ground so I couldn't see the head up there. That wasn't my mother and sisters back there.

I said to myself, I'll wake up in the morning and be with them. I'll wake up in the morning and be with them. I fell asleep again.

When I woke up from a bad dream, I was sitting up straight. My eyes were open and they saw moonlight in the stalks. I wouldn't look up at the head of the moon. I felt more and more fear because something was happening. Something was happening to me. It was like a storm blowing over me, a wind and rain, but worse. They were angry at me. They were back there without heads so they couldn't see where to go. They were angry at me for not putting their heads back on. If they had their heads back on, they could rise and fly away. But they couldn't fly away headless. I called out to them. "I tried, but now I'm lost," I told them. I said it until the night seemed calm again like a storm passing. "I tried but now I'm lost." Sitting there straight, I fell asleep sitting up, I think.

When I opened my eyes again, a girl was squatting nearby, looking at me.

"What's wrong with you?" she asked, but I couldn't say anything. I just put my thumb in my mouth.

"If you don't tell me, I'll go get my mother," she said.

I looked at her.

The girl got up. "I'm going to get my mother."

She went away. I lay there with my thumb in my mouth, looking at a stalk of sorghum.

Then I heard a sound, the swish of someone coming through the sorghum. They'll kill me, I thought, but I couldn't move.

Then the girl was there and with her a big, thick woman who was her mother, I thought. She knelt beside me to ask questions. When she bent close, I smelled baked sweet potatoes in her clothes.

I don't know how, but somehow I told her about the heads and what happened. While telling her I knew it was all true, and even though my father says I'm a Tutsi of a good clan, I started to cry. She held me in her warm arms. Then she asked me to come inside for something to eat. I could already smell what it was going to be, baked sweet potatoes, my favorite. So I went inside and ate hot sweet potatoes in the skin. She was watching me all the time while I ate, and when I finished she told me to stay. That's what I wanted more than anything, so I did.

The next day I met the man, who looked at me like I was a newborn calf that wouldn't make it. He had a broad face, a broad nose. He said to the woman, "Well, he won't eat much." Then he said to me, "Boy, we're going to help you. Do you understand what I mean?"

I nodded.

"I don't want you eating more than one sweet potato at a time."

I had three yesterday. I nodded.

He looked at me so long that I thought he was going to change his mind. But then he just gave me a look and walked away.

I played with Odette. "Who is your father?" I asked.

"Him." She pointed to him in the field, raising a hoe.

"Does he kill people?"

Odette squinted at me. "I think so."

"Who?"

"I don't know, but he comes home bloody."

So every night when I went to sleep in the shed, I wondered if he was going to come in with a panga and cut off my head too. That would keep me awake a long time, but that was all right because I didn't like sleeping. When I slept I saw things happen that made me wake up shaking. If I saw moonlight come through the window, I waited for the blow to come. Sometimes I called out to my family. I asked them where they were. Why didn't they say something? What happened to their heads?

Then there was a lot of noise and running around. People

were packing up and leaving for the road. They were going somewhere. So were we, she told me, Pauline Mukandina told me.

Where Pauline Mukandina went, I went. When Pauline Mukandina stopped, I stopped. She was my life. I hoped it would last forever, if only I could keep up with them on the road. I knew the man was watching me. He was always calling my people cockroaches and demons and foreign invaders, so if I did anything wrong he'd just get rid of me. I used to think of him bending over and shouting at me, "Get away from us, cockroach!"

Then there were soldiers. They took the man from the line of waiting people and asked questions. The more they asked, the more he was sweating. My father used to say that a Tutsi must never be cowardly. I don't think a Tutsi would sweat like that. I didn't understand much of what the soldiers were saying, but I could tell he wasn't going on with us and I liked that.

A soldier came over and looked at us, then squatted near me and felt my arms and legs.

"This is your child?" he asked her.

Pauline Mukandina said I was, and that made me feel good.

Then another soldier came over and other things were said and everyone was looking hard at me until I grew afraid. One soldier gripped my arm so hard it hurt. But I didn't wince, I just looked at him. I don't think I was sweating.

"He goes with us," said the soldier. "We don't want Hutu raising our children."

And he shoved me forward out of reach of my mother. When I began whimpering, Pauline Mukandina took a step and a soldier pushed her down. But she got right up and started pulling on the amulets around her neck. The soldiers watched her take one off.

"Let me put it on him," she told them, holding it out.

They let her put the amulet around my neck. Then I knew that they were taking her away from me. They were taking all I had. I tried to stay quiet, but the sound came out of me, running out of me. I could feel sweat pouring down into my eyes. "I want you, I want you!"

"What's wrong with you, boy!" A soldier began shaking me roughly. "Are you a Tutsi or not?"

I looked at him through sweat.

"Tutsi boys don't cry," he said, shoving me away from the road toward a truck. "Do you want to be a Hutu?" he asked angrily.

I shook my head.

"Then get in that truck. And be glad you're with your own kind." He lifted me over the back of it and let me go. I fell beside someone else. It was a girl not as old as I am. She was all bandaged around her chest and her eyes stared ahead, even when I got close and looked into them. She was scared, she was hurt. When I asked her name, she didn't look at me then either. So I got closer and we curled together and waited.

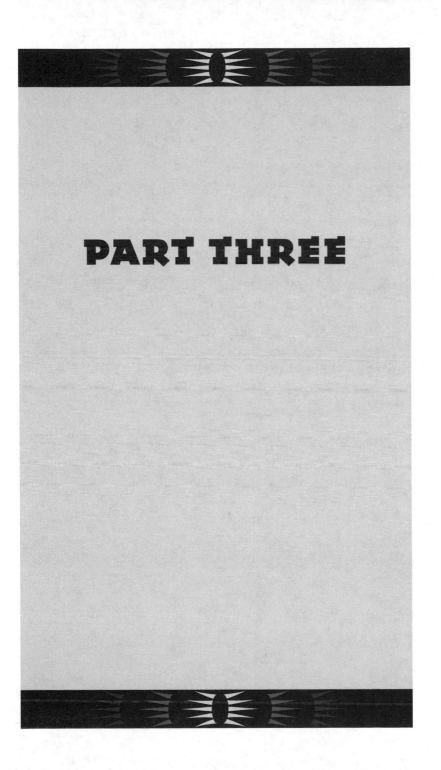

PART THREE

STEPHEN

AS THE ONLY city of real size, Kigali has always been Rwanda's heart, if not its soul. Where was the soul? My father used to say the soul of his beloved country was in the hills.

His beloved country was now becoming mine, and I found myself poised to help with its renewal. With the battle for Kigali won, Rwanda was nearly ours. Last month we took the Kigali airport. Two weeks ago our 105-millimeter howitzers were pouring fire from the heights down into the center of the capital. Skirmishes with government troops took place for ten days in backstreets, but FAR invariably retreated because our determination was greater. Then a few days ago our tanks and mobile cannon and armored cars moved unopposed down the main thoroughfares.

War has little to recommend it. But sometimes it provides the chance to watch shifts in fortune that excite a man while humbling him. Our RPF revolutionary army, for example, will soon be known as "government troops" and FAR as "rebels." We have weapons from Egypt, France, and South Africa that a few months ago were carried by our enemies.

For our troops from Uganda it took nearly forty years to reach Kigali, which they had imagined was a flower-strewn paradise. Waving rifles overhead, laughing and cheering, our Ugandan men waded through shell casings, hunks of plaster, the scattered debris of a dismal city bombarded for days. They were too happy even to smell the death around them. They had reached their goal. I had reached the same goal, although perhaps with less sense of completion. I was already wondering about the next phase of this adventure.

So was General Kagame. He didn't let me join the victory celebration, but sent me on what seemed at the moment a strange mission. I was ordered to inspect a national park.

So, accompanied by a small detachment, I have come here to Akagera, a vast reserve of two thousand square miles, in the northeast sector of the country. At the entrance of the park, now officially closed, stands a battered billboard announcing that here the animals come first.

As our personnel carrier moves down the road, I hope to spot zebras and giraffes, but instead I see large herds of long-horned cattle grazing on the brown savannah. Ordering the driver to pull over, I wave to some herders until one of them finally lopes toward our car. He's a Tutsi from Uganda and that connection brings a smile to my face. But then I say, "Do you know this is a national park? You're pasturing here illegally."

He gives me a faint, cool, unyielding smile.

I explain that grazing cattle here will displace the topi, impala, bushbuck, hyenas, elephants, and even lions whose land this is. Cattle will force wildlife to cross over into the sanctuary of Tanzania.

The herdsman has heard one thing, the word *lion*. He says bitterly, "One of them killed my best bull two nights ago."

I learn that these herders, perhaps a thousand of them, have penetrated only ten or twenty miles into the park. Unless measures are taken, however, I suspect that many thousands more will soon follow with hundreds of thousands of cattle. Next year they could wash over the savannah of Akagera like a tumbling flood. It's sadly possible that the herds of my Ugandan compatriots could destroy the ancient hunting grounds of our ancestors.

I was speculating on this grim irony when we arrived at the hilltop setting of the Akagera Hotel. This fancy safari lodge had been abandoned by its Hutu caretakers to a possessive troop of sharp-toothed baboons. They were strutting near the swimming pool, where dusty, empty wine bottles still lay beside tennis rackets and bathrobes. For a few moments I imagined blue eyes and red faces and pith helmets and commands shouted at black servants. Shooing the baboons away with a pistol shot, I sat beside the pool and looked out over the immense green landscape of central Africa. I saw it glittering through a veil of countless white butterflies. This belonged to me, not to men nostalgic for Paris and London.

I called for Emmanuel, my bodyguard. While drinking a warm bottle of beer, I asked the tall fellow what he thought of herding cattle in the park.

"A bad thing, sir," the former cattleman said.

I asked him why.

"Dry season's coming. Some grass is already withering. I've seen tsetse flies too, and that means nagana. Besides nagana you'll probably find tapeworm and east coast fever. This isn't cattle country."

"I think the herders know that but come anyway," I said. "They look at it as their home."

"Then home will destroy their cattle." He squinted across the plain before continuing. "I wonder how many you could lose in one season."

I could imagine Emmanuel in the trackless silence of ancient pastureland. With one foot cupping the knee of his standing leg, he'd find rest in the posture of a crane. As our herdsmen had done for centuries.

"I think you might lose four out of ten," he estimated. "Maybe not so many this year, sir. But more next year. Five or six out of ten."

"What about culling the herds?"

He thought about that. "You'd have to slaughter plenty of them. You'd have a lot of beef on your hands. You'd need a station to freeze it."

"Yes. And a means of transporting it. Could that work, Emmanuel?"

The tall man shook his head. "Most cattlemen won't cull. They rather let a herd waste away than sell a single cow for meat."

"I'm a military man," I said. "What you say about cattlemen I've heard before. But it's difficult to believe."

Emmanuel's expression became hard, like a face gets when a man talks to someone ignorant of his life. "Difficult, sir, but true. A cattleman prefers ten sick cows to seven healthy ones." He pulled himself up proudly to his full six-feet-ten or -eleven. "I'm like that, sir," he said with a broad smile. "I want as big a herd as I can get."

I smiled back in acknowledgement of his honesty and to end our conversation. But he remained, looking down at me in an expectant way.

"Do you want to ask something, Emmanuel?"

"Yes, sir. Will there be more fighting when we get back to Kigali?"

"Oh, yes. FAR still holds some hills south of the capital. We'll have to get them out."

"Could I go to one of those combat units, sir?"

I studied Emmanuel. He had stood beside me like a tall, black tree during the recent campaign. In serving as a staff officer's bodyguard he'd seen little combat. That had denied him the pleasure of killing his enemies. For a Tutsi steeped in tradition this was an embarrassment.

"When we get back to Kigali, I'll have you reassigned," I promised him.

Sitting beside the deserted swimming pool, I thought of Ugandan cattlemen leading their herds into Rwanda. I imagined them coming next year to Akagera, searching for pasture in their sought-for homeland. None would have time for ancient beauty, for the sight of leopards draped liked spotted scarves in the spindly trees. They'd herd their cattle and take no notice of hippos in the mud flats. They'd ignore those dark little containers of sleeping sickness that buzz across the parched grasses. Not even vultures would get their attention—the great winged birds soaring overhead in anticipation of man's ultimate folly. In the Ugandan herdsmen's case, that folly would be to live in such an inhospitable place. Yet they will probably cross over into Akagera and not only Ugandans, but thousands from Tanzania and Burundi as well, each of them looking for home. Yes, I thought, thousands of Tutsi and all eager to enjoy a birthright long denied. Ten or twenty times the number of people such land could possibly sustain. I saw them returning in my mind, a host of naive immigrants who knew nothing of survival in the harsh savannah. But here they would come, the old Tutsi nurturing the dream of a final return and the young Tutsi driven to recklessness by the chance to prove themselves. All of them crossing into Akagera, following the ancient need to go home.

I must have dozed off then, because I saw them coming in a dream from every direction, in huge groups, lines of white-robed tall people, smiling and happy, coming farther in and farther in, moving to the rhythmic rise and fall of their walking sticks. They were looking everywhere, momentarily awestruck by the beauty of their fathers' country. I saw them streaming across the plain, their white-clad figures spreading into every foot of land until they were bumping into one another, shoving and stumbling and lurching along. One after another they fell out of the milling crowd to the burning ground. Their tongues clung to the roofs of their mouths, their eyes bulged in the glare. A horde of tsetse flies walked on their lips, and their bodies writhed in the heat as far as the eye could see.

I awoke from the terrible vision but it never really left me. Where in this little space called Rwanda might we put so many returnees? Not only would animals suffer because of them, but the immigrants themselves would become victims of their own hope. By the latest estimate nearly 800,000 people have died here in a few months. In reclaiming their homeland, more thousands might die too. We were only at the start of this adventure. I felt that victory was no closer than it had been four years ago when we first crossed the border.

These gloomy thoughts were written in a report. Then I returned to Kigali, where already some of my comrades-in-arms were changing into the Western business suits of politicians. At meetings, if asked to speak, I usually said something about the problem of returning immigrants and refugees.

A week ago a general summoned me to his office. Thin, gaunt, he stared at me through thick glasses. Mine were thick too. I once heard someone mutter that together we looked like two professors dissecting a frog. He affirmed what we both knew.

"Your military duties are coming to an end, Stephen. You know what your new job is."

I must have looked at him in surprise, because he smiled and said, "Or you should know. You talk about it all the time."

That's how I learned of my assignment in the newly created Ministry of Rehabilitation.

Combat again, but of a different sort. I can expect almost daily encounters with the UN and Western embassies. Choosing not to defend us from genocide, they now feel obligated to control our future. I can expect aid organizations of every kind to appear at my door, clamoring to be recognized as saviors who will rescue Rwanda from hunger and disease.

Throughout recent African history other men in my position have succumbed to such appeals. They have given up their power, their confidence, and finally their pride, and in the process have sacrificed the self-determining will of their people. They have done this for money. Even so, it would be folly to refuse the sort of material aid that keeps our people alive. I dread facing such a dilemma, yet for years I've been preparing for it.

In the last week I dreamt the following dream three times. Across a large map of Rwanda, huge masses of people are sliding back and forth like living mud, first this way, then that way, endlessly to the east and endlessly to the west and back again, endlessly to the north and endlessly to the south and back again, until I wake.

AUGUSTIN

I AM PROUD of killing cockroaches, even though people say we're losing the war. Like the bourgmestre told us, "The only way to defend yourselves is to kill them all."

But I don't think I should have paid money to join the army. The army should have paid me. Maybe someday if I find my sister again, I'll give back the money I stole from her, although I stole it for a good cause, and I'm not ashamed of buying my way into the army because it meant I wanted to defend my people against the cockroaches. That hasn't changed, in spite of so many things happening.

I have seen everything. Right now a friend of mine lies ten feet away, dying over there, with a hole in his stomach that I can see from where I lie hidden in the bush. I see it oozing, pulsing. I hear him groaning and calling for someone I don't know to come get him and take him home. I'd show him some mercy and finish him myself except for the noise of shooting him that could bring them in on us. They're waiting there, and when the morning light clears everything enough for them to see, I know they'll come out of those trees firing.

I've seen men surrender. They stand up with their hands high, but they better drop the gun first or otherwise they'll be taken out. Sometimes they're taken out anyway. Sometimes I've seen from a hill what happens when a few of us stand with hands high and the Tutsi come out of the bush. One of those cockroaches will go right up to a man and put the barrel of his gun under the throat and pump just a single shot in and that's that. But sometimes the Tutsi accept the surrender, they do, and the last we see of a comrade, he's alive and being escorted back into the bush, maybe even to prison. I hear people talk about prison and they say it's not so bad, yeah, why not, because you get food and somewhere to sleep and they don't know what to do with you so you stay on there and get as fat as a goat.

But it's taking a chance, and I think that's why, when a man feels he can't fight anymore, he probably runs instead of surrenders. Right now they're running to the west because that's where the big camps are and you can get lost in them because they accept you as a refugee and so you get inside and squat down in the camp along with the mothers and babies and you just wait there until it's time to start killing cockroaches again. But the problem is getting to one of those camps. You can easily get killed on the way. Tutsi like to set up checkpoints and if they get hold of one of us they shoot him on the spot. That's what I hear. They torture him first. It's more than we usually did at our checkpoints. We just killed them. But we're dealing now with cockroach checkpoints.

So it's hard to know what you ought to do.

So I wait for someone to tell me. I think of my old friends Gaspard and Laurent and how we used to hunch around the beer pot and dream of good meals in Kigali and hot women. Well, I've been in Kigali dodging mortar fire and I never once tasted barbecued goat although, well, yeah, I did drink a few bottles of Primus beer. The only woman I've had since leaving home was a Tutsi that four of us raped. Now the mist is breaking apart into big, loose bags of gray and when they roll away, they'll let the light in. I don't want the light in. I mustn't think of the light coming.

Someday I'll go home and reclaim my land and pay Agnès what I owe her so we can be friends again. I'll say, "Here, sister, take this for yourself." And she'll take the money and give me a smile of gratitude in return and that will be that. We are all each other has left. I'll be a nice, quiet farmer and grow cassava. That's what I'm thinking now.

The light is coming in. It's already as light-colored as a river, no deeper than ankle-to-foot. It's that light of a blue. Soon they'll be coming through the bush. I wish he'd shut up. Maybe I should take a chance and crawl over there and cut his throat, but then I might be spotted. The light is now light enough. They could spot me and take me out if I went out there. I wonder what it's like when you've been taken out and you're lying there dying and there's nothing to do about it. You just lie there waiting for something to happen, for it to go black and give you some relief, I suppose. I think it must be what he's hoping for now, while he's feeling the pain. It's the pain that makes him make that sound. I'd be ashamed to have it coming out of me, but I guess he doesn't even know he's making it. He can't help it. The pain makes him do it no matter how hard he tries not to make that sound. Maybe I should crawl out there and give him relief, but they could spot me in the light the way it is now, and I'd go down too, right next to him, and who would come out and cut my throat for me? Nobody, because I can't trust anybody still left in our unit.

I heard on the radio that we're counterattacking, but he

didn't say where, so I don't believe it. I don't believe the radio anymore. I used to take orders from the radio, but they say the radio people who used to give those orders have run off to Nairobi and Kinshasa and even Europe. That's the way it is. If I had one of those voices right here right now I'd shoot him full of holes, I'd put my pistol barrel down his throat and pull the trigger, I'd cut his balls off and believe me, these are things I have learned how to do.

What I hear is it's not only the radio people that got away. The other important people who give the orders won't be caught either. They're all playing with girls in Nairobi, Paris, and Cairo. That's what they tell me. I remember what they told me at the beginning. They said the RPF carried guns but lacked bullets to shoot. They wouldn't be able to shoot back, I was told. I believed it only a little while, but others really believed it. The first they knew of the enemy having bullets was when the bullets entered their own bodies and killed them. The RPF are trained. They know what they're doing. Whenever I see a dead one he's usually older than me.

The thing is I admire the Hutu who come from Burundi, because they're the toughest soldiers I ever saw. They don't care about anything but killing. They enjoy killing Tutsi because in their own country the Tutsi enjoy killing them. What they like to do is prolong a killing. They make jokes and prod the fellow with spears and rifle butts before starting to slice into arms and legs real slowly, oh yeah, with their pangas. While the fellow twists and screams, they keep telling jokes about his mother and sisters. They scare even me.

I look around. There are about a dozen of us unwounded here

at the edge of this clearing. The light is rising and clear like water in a stream. They'll come soon. We'll see the bursts coming through the leaves and then they'll be right here. I look at myself. What will they see? Most of my uniform is gone, torn away by thorns and brambles. I'm wearing a dirty T-shirt that someone tells me says in English *Nintendo*. That's a kind of Western game. I wear rubber sandals, and my trousers got so shredded I cut them off at the knee. I don't look like a soldier anymore. But then my sister never liked me in a uniform. We had a fight about that the last time I saw her. I asked her, did she want me to wear rags like a bean picker. Well, that's what I look like now. I wonder if she's living with the bourgmestre, who really wanted her. Or maybe he's dead. Or maybe she's dead too, although she never did anything wrong.

My sergeant says the French will soon be coming to our aid. As they did earlier in the war, they'll do plenty of work, so he says. They'll position the artillery units and truck in supplies and fly the helos that we can't fly and supervise the questioning of prisoners and man the roadblocks. So I'm expecting any day to see them marching in, singing their French songs. I expect them. I hope they come. I hope they come right now because it's almost morning and the RPF can see everything they want to see.

And they do. I see bursts coming through the leaves and hear the sound of those bursts right afterwards and hear someone screaming nearby. Without thinking about it I just stand up, just like that, dropping my gun as I do it. There I am, huh, as naked to death as the day I was born. They're coming out of the bush with rifles held at waist level so they can spray. They give some bursts. I look to the side and see my friend bounce up from the ground twice, so at last he's out of it. I see another man standing with his hands up and then he goes hurling back from the blow of bullets entering him.

A very tall Tutsi, maybe seven feet tall, is coming at me, and I see my death in his eyes. I can't move. It's like my raised hands are chained to the air. I want to tell him that I'm a defender of justice, not a killer like him. I want him to know I'm human too.

He's taller when I fall to my knees.

I just do it without thinking. Maybe I lost feeling in my legs, because they won't hold me up. The bursts are telling me that some of my comrades have run. I'm kneeling with my hands high over my head, when the Tutsi reaches me.

I wait for him to push the gun barrel under my chin. I think I can almost feel the heat of it. But when nothing happens, I look up at him, way up there, and see his terrible eyes looking down at me, and I'm so, so afraid because I don't know how he's going to do it. I'm all ready for one way, for the gun-under-the-chin way, but I don't think he's going to do it that way.

Then he bends over like a tree and the big, flat palm of his left hand swings around in the air and smacks me on the cheek. It's a terrific blow and knocks me over. I feel the stinging and the dizziness while he grabs my shirt, tearing it as he pulls me to my feet. He's not going to kill me, but he has . . . he has done something . . . he has humiliated me. He has cuffed me like I'm a dog. He has slapped me like I'm a small boy. He doesn't even think I'm worth killing. I see that he's got a big war knife strapped to his belt that he could slit my throat with. But he doesn't draw it out. He leaves it there on his belt.

And what do I do, I just get my body close together, glad to be alive, and follow behind some comrades who have also been captured. This is not good. This is not what I joined the army for. Something small has taken hold of me inside.

I remember hearing this. You can outrun whatever runs after you, but you can't outrun whatever is running inside you. I remember where I heard it. That's an old saying my father used to say. I'm ashamed.

They keep us in a ruined church, which reminds me of the one at home where we finished off the local cockroaches. So it will be a joke if they kill me in such a place. Only they don't know about the other church, so they haven't put me here on purpose and it's not really a joke. But it's a long night. I keep wondering if ghosts slimy from blood are going to squeeze out of the stones and slide across my face. The idea keeps me awake. But I'd be awake anyway because maybe it's my last night alive. Tomorrow they'll take me out and stand me against a wall and shoot.

So I look through the little window of this church for my last look at life, and what do I see in the yard but the tall Tutsi standing with his back against a wall. He doesn't carry a gun, so he's not one of the guards.

He has come to see me.

He's looking right at me and once again I see in his eyes my own death. Yet he let me live. I don't think I ever killed anyone with as much feeling as he must feel in wanting to kill me. So, yeah, I was right. He let me live to test himself.

What I can see from here is the war knife. He has taken it off his belt and holds it. I think he wants to slit my throat, but now it's too late. He didn't kill me, and why? Because he was testing himself. It's what I hear the Tutsi do. They test themselves. They have been that way for as long as our people remember. In the old days they went out alone in the desert to do this testing. They stood on one leg like a bird, as motionless as a rock, no matter how hot the sun got or how cold the rain. They nearly died before going back.

Now look at that Tutsi with his war knife drawn. He dreams of using it, of having that pleasure, but coming out of the bush he was testing himself by not using it on me. That's the Tutsi way. They want control more than anything and test themselves to get it. I hate them.

INNOCENT

WHEN I SNIFF it I can't walk straight. At times I feel like someone is stuffing cotton in my nose and mouth, so it's hard to breathe. I think about breathing a lot. I think about it because when you don't, you're dying. Once I got dizzy from not breathing and went out, so I suppose I was almost gone, but someone brought me back, and when I woke up I was panting hard like a dog.

My breath smells like thick paint for hours.

I sniff from a plastic bag. I vomit a lot. I saw a friend get up all of a sudden and start running and then fall over. Ran, fell, died just like that. His airway wouldn't open, somebody told me. I imagine the airway is like a tunnel that if you fill it with dirt instead of air, you die. The air going down my friend's throat wouldn't go down. Maybe it felt like a hand in there pushing the air back out. You think you're coming in, says the hand to the air, but you can't because I won't let you. Sometimes I think things are in my body that don't belong. Sometimes I know things are living in me, squirming like scared dogs, or a snake winding in and out, or mice poking around, hoping not to get caught, which is my hope too when I'm stealing. I feel things crawling on my skin, but when I look they aren't there, the crawly legs aren't there but I feel them ticking along anyway, one small leg after another going *tick tick tick.*

We smoke bhang, but that's not like the other. The other is what does it. The other is something we know the name of and it is *toluene.* Someone said it's a word in English, *toluene.* We say "tooleen." I don't know what it is. But I know it's the thing that does it in glue or paint spray or gasoline or nail-polish remover, this remover a thing that foreign women in the embassies like to use, so we wait patiently to go through their garbage in the dump for it and once in a while we find some left in a small bottle. Cigarette-lighter fluid is good and aerosol containers and contact cement. Foreigners think we like to steal money but what we like much better is things with toluene in them. It's good sniffed through saturated rags or from a bag. Right away, when you get a good bag of it pulled into your lungs, you feel like a bird flapping its wings and starting to get some height and then going way high over the hills. You feel dizzy and if you walk you can't walk you stagger and you're giggling and what you say is all *ga ga goo goo* and funny and you want to make a friend of everyone on earth because they all belong to you, every one of them, and you to them, because you're stuck to one another like glue, and sometimes you can see your fingers stretch out long like soft glue when you touch someone. They say sniffing is bad, but I never saw anyone die with a rag of it against his face. When you start to get sick or dizzy or tired, you let your hand just fall away and that's it. You come out of it again. You're alive again. So I don't believe them when they say glue can kill you.

I can take it or leave it until I need a sniff bad and even then I can take it or leave it but usually I take it. When I get it, the light starts blaring like a horn in my eyes, I shut them and the light still comes flashing at me until sometimes everything dances up and down and up and down the way pieces of glass glitter in sunshine and then it's not light anymore but something like bright water, a swishing of water back and forth in front of my eyes that makes me sick enough to throw up. I like to vomit because everything always clears for a while afterward. I come out of the water and look around. Vomiting lets me get up and go on or otherwise I might lay back in the garbage like some do and die.

I know how to break elbow bones so I can take a shirt off a stiff corpse. I've changed shirts a dozen times, although only once was a shirt small enough to be my right size. Usually I'm wearing something that makes me look wet-looking or starving I don't look my age of thirteen.

People call us *abanyali*, young city bandits, and we like that. We know things no one else knows. We see things in the back alleys no one else sees. We live like no one else does, and we're proud of it. It doesn't matter if we're Hutu or Tutsi because we like who we are whatever we are. Unless one of us tries stealing glue. Then we kill him. I have helped kill two of us for doing that. I have hit them while they were lying there in the head with a shovel once and the other time with a brick. No one tries to take my glue, and I don't try to take anyone else's glue, which is why I get along with both Hutu and Tutsi.

Here come the wazungu. We love the whites if we see them and we knock each other out of the way in order to get there first to those red faces and watery eyes and fat guts of Les Ricains because the USA is where the money is. I know how to smile and thrust my hand out when I see a white face coming out the door. I run up, shoving my guys away, and scream as loud as I can, "Money, sir! Argent, monsieur! Gelt, mein herr!" Because all kinds of people are coming back here to Kigali from everywhere and I am here too and speak their language.

I don't usually ask money of my own people, I ask for things. A woman comes along carrying a wicker basket on her head—I ask for sweets. But if a man has a little suitcase in his hand and wears Western clothes, I ask for money. When people ignore me, I don't care and tell them so. I yell at their backs, "I don't care! I don't care!"

We like living in the shadows. Anyway, it's safer that way when one bunch of soldiers or other comes bumping along in a truck, spraying walls with enough bullets to kill an army. They say now the new soldiers want to help us. They say the new soldiers come through with food and things for children, but then the ones who say it are Tutsi boys and most of the new soldiers are supposed to be Tutsi.

None of this matters. Only toluene matters.

Give me sweets or what do I care. We're the shadow children. We don't trust the world and don't like it. Some of us don't even talk. They can't. They haven't talked since watching somebody get killed, like their mother or sister or brother or someone else. They lost their voices when they lost their families, and that's the way it is. But I'm not like them. I'm special, even though I'm not God's chosen, a favorite of Imana. This is what makes me special, and it can't be taken away. I lived while everyone else died. I know what pain is too. I've been a soldier's boy and know what pain feels like up the ass. This is me. I want to live and to live. I know how to talk, and I do talk, I ask for sweets and money, and I can say the word *tooleen*.

Sometimes we stand in a row and watch the workers in orange overalls take bodies from houses and toss them into trucks that go out somewhere and dump it all in a hole. It gets me down, until sometimes I want to go somewhere and sniff by myself.

Some kids, they die of sadness. You know it's going to happen from the already-gone look in their eyes. They sit and stare and not even their lips move any and their hands rest like little stones in their lap and the next thing you know they slide over on their side with their eyes closed and their knees tucked up to their belly and later, when you touch them, they're stiff, cold, they're as dead as brick, but their eyes sometimes have opened wide, I guess at the last, so they look like they're looking at something terrible.

But the strangest thing that you see sometimes is a dead one smiling. That kind of shadow boy won't be me, though. I want to know what's happening. I won't die smiling and I won't die at all.

Sometimes I go up the steep hill to the Centre d'Acceuil, where in this old hut the Catholics teach carpentry and prayer. A couple times each week they offer lunch. All of it doesn't matter except the lunch, which I'm always around to get.

I heard of kids murdered in the Saint Andre Mission and of kids taken from the Saint Paul Centre and murdered. I think they were Tutsi. We shadow children stick together like glue so it won't happen to us. What we do, we sell eggs on the street or sometimes pick through garbage for something to sell, anything like empty bottles and scraps of metal, or sometimes we sell nuts if we can steal them.

When I'm quiet and think to myself I know that I want the

peace and silence of a stone. But not now. That's someday. Now I just want food and glue and maybe some bhang. If I must live like a rat, I will live like a rat. I want to breathe and eat and sniff stuff, so I do what I can for that. I stay quiet in the dark breathing as quiet as I can and when others move away from where they are, I slip out and eat what they leave. That's enough. That's what matters. That and the funny voice in my head. There is this voice in my head. It says *ka ka ka* all the time in the way of water moving. It's soft, soft. It says *ka ka ka ka ka* as I walk along or sit somewhere and look at the sun making a cut of light on a tin roof. It says *ka ka ka ka* it says *ka ka* for so long I don't know how long it is saying *ka ka ka ka ka ka ka ka*, it says *ka ka* while I smile at something, at something or anything because it doesn't matter, because I feel my mouth curving up and staying that way anyway, because what is always there is the sound like water lapping in my head, a soft *ka ka ka* lapping in my head all the time that makes me smile at everything, a soft *ka ka ka ka* all the time.

This was what I was hearing when he touched me. I looked up and through the water I saw someone moving. I saw his face coming closer. I felt something touch me and I knew he was doing that to my arm. He was pulling me to my feet and out of the garbage heap. I tried to see him through the water. Finally I saw his eyes shaped like the almonds I steal and sell and his straight nose and his round, shining forehead.

"Tutsi." I was giggling.

"You too?" I think he said.

I giggled more. Looking up I wasn't sure I was seeing him because he was up there like a tree in the water, no flat-topped acacia, but like a tall, narrow tree coming out of the water and cutting through the air of a high hill.

"Tall," I said.

He smiled at me. "Come along."

Although he had me in his grip and there was no chance of my getting free of it, I said as clearly as I could, "Give me money."

He told me something. I think it was he said he would give me money later, but I don't know because I was lolling then, listening to the *ka ka* in my head, and trying to keep my eyelids from shutting before the water came flooding in and drowned them. Then I was lifted into the air and put down where I think I knew it was the boards of a truck, warm wood under me, but I don't know because in the next *ka ka ka* I was gone, I was out, I was given mercy.

When I opened my eyes again, a long time later I think, the water was gone and the tall man was looking from sad eyes at me where I was lying down. I sat up and saw we were in a building with bunks in it. He was a soldier in a uniform. I was drooling and wiped it away. There were other soldiers around and a few boys like me carrying wood or ammo belts or helmets. He told me I could stay there with him and be his kadago. He told me it meant running errands like the other boys. It meant getting fed, which meant I said yes.

So I'm with the tall Tutsi soldier and right now I'm happy to be his errand boy. I'm grateful he has never once used me. That isn't his way. He's using me another way, though. He's using me to remember his dead family and I know it. At first it was all right, because he'd tell me about them and look at me a long time with tears in his eyes, so long that I'd start to remember certain things myself, like the church and being under my dead mother, soaked in her blood, and I would hate that. Even so I knew that he saw his dead son in me and I used that feeling in him to get privileges that another kadago wouldn't get. I got sweets and money and new shoes and pants for not doing anything.

I ride with him in a truck through the streets of Kigali like I never did before. I feel the wind going by. Now and then I see someone from the old bunch in the shadows, but I don't wave at him. That would make him feel bad. Sometimes I have a big need for sniffing, but I eat all the sweet potatoes I want and smoke bhang with other boys when we can get by ourselves. I'm thirteen and if I keep eating so much I'll look it. I've got the tallest master in the brigade. Once, for just a little while, I saw him go through the motions of an Intore dancer. I once saw that Intore kind of dancing back home at the church when a troupe came through and stopped at our hill. That was before the church. I remember the dancers looked like strutting birds. That's what my master, who they call Emmanuel, looked like when he danced. The other boys told me I was lucky to have a master who could dance, but I don't know. I don't see myself as lucky. Someday I'll get tired of being here. The barracks are outside of the city and there's nothing to do but play stick and hoop and watch the soldiers practicing with their guns or watch them when they sit outside the barracks and smoke. If they were going to fight again, I'd go along, I guess to watch. Otherwise, I'll want to go somewhere by myself and be alone again. From the moment I climbed out of that mountain of dead bodies I've been alone and nothing but myself. Even Agnès hiding me in

the rafters didn't change that. Nothing will ever change that.
I'm alone and like it that way and I don't want to remember
when I wasn't like this. I don't want memories. Just give me
freedom is what I want. Just point me in the direction of a road.

PAULINE

I REMEMBER COMING to Goma with my parents when I was a little girl. There were white villas along the shore of Lake Kivu and volcanoes in the distance and flowers planted everywhere. Now the refugees have come, dying of disease in the streets and chopping down trees for firewood and trampling the flowers and leaving garbage everywhere and my four children and I have come with them.

Ever since the Tutsi checkpoint guards took my husband away, we have moved with other refugees along the road. In the streets of Gisenyi there was fighting. We all raced for the border. Some of the old and the young were trampled underfoot. Fifty, sixty. The sound of mortars exploded in our ears. Government troops, fleeing too, came by in their trucks, waving at us as if on holiday, while tracer bullets raced across the evening sky.

When we crossed the Zairian border over to Goma, men were supposed to leave their weapons behind. They made big piles of spears and hoes and clubs along the roadside, but everyone, including the Zairian border guards, knew that most of the pangas remained where they were—stuck in belts, hidden by shirttails.

Now we must leave Goma. We're being herded beyond city limits into a huge volcanic field. The ground is almost too hard to drive tent pegs into it. Who has herded us here? We don't know. People in trucks, UN people, whites from Europe in their trucks painted various colors, our own Hutu men who have torn off their uniforms and threaten us with clubs.

I think this is what's happening. No one knows why we're here or where we'll go next or what we can do about it, but the outside world feels it must help us get through each day. I stroke my amulets for good luck and keep a close watch on the children so they don't get lost.

Someone has joined us and that's good. Prosper Ndabateze, the old farmer from our hill, is traveling with us these days and looks after the two youngest. He must be sixty, old for a Rwandan, but Prosper is still vigorous even if sometimes he mumbles to himself. He shares what he has with us and never withholds. He keeps saying it's too bad that the Tutsi guards took away that little boy I had with us, and I agree. Oh, of course, I agree. I miss Pacifique and the way he looked at me from his big, wide eyes. But of course the Tutsi have won, so they don't want their children raised by us. I know that, but I miss the boy.

And I miss Sylvestre too, though what he did was very bad. Every morning, his eyes as clear as spring water, he went out in a clean white shirt. Every night, his eyes still clear, he returned in a shirt red from the blood of people murdered that day. I fear for him, but if the Tutsi kill him I understand why. I understand the need for blood. There must be justice. The men who led the slaughter must be slaughtered too, and the killers who went along and did what they did without thinking, some of them must be killed too for any of the rest of them to be pardoned. Sylvestre was a teacher and should have known better. Yet every morning I rub one of my amulets and say a prayer to Imana in his behalf.

For the last week we've been settling into this camp, which sits under the gaze of a great volcano. Smoke from so many cooking fires has made our eyes red and itchy. People walk to and fro with big loads of firewood balanced on their heads, while they carry suitcases and wicker baskets filled with squawking chickens. It's difficult to relieve yourself here. We hear there are only five hundred latrines for 300,000 people. They say the aid workers say there should be twenty thousand latrines. Some people are using the spaces between tents, and that, of course, is bad. There's enough sickness already. You hear coughing everywhere, just everywhere. It reminds me of the ugly sound of crows settling in a tree. There's so much other noise too, the roar of bulldozers, the crying of lost children, all that yelling in food lines, the crackling of firewood. The ground is littered with rags, torn boxes, broken pots, all sorts of unrecognizable things. It's as if a huge wind had collected the ruin of a hundred miles and deposited it all in this black-rock camp of hell.

Every day I go out with the two older children while Prosper looks after the younger ones. We go for water ten miles away. People wait in line with buckets, pots, and plastic bags for many hours to get to the water pump. Then after returning with water, we go to the UN feeding stations for another long wait. Sometimes we go out for firewood. My little ones carry only twigs, but they want to carry something. And all the while we're inhaling the rancid smoke and the smell of excrement and sweat and the worst odor of all, that of rotting flesh.

I believe fully half of the people in this camp are children. They die first, even before the old people. Sometimes they wander alone through the camp, even though they have parents somewhere. The parents can't stand to watch them starve or get

sick, so they put their children on the road and hope that someone stronger will come along and care for them. Some refugees
here are Tutsi who have no other place to go either. Their
children play with ours unless militiamen come along and
stop it.

The militiamen run things, even though the white aid workers seem to think they have control. Because of the militiamen
certain things aimed at the refugees don't always get there. The
militiamen and former FAR troops sit beside piles of relief
goods—bags of flour and blankets and cans of cooking oil—
grinning and selling and holding up fistfuls of Rwandan francs.
Plastic sheeting was supposed to be freely distributed, but it's
sold. Prosper bought what we have. And salt is sold too or you
stand for many hours in a line to get half a handful.

The militiamen set up a beer crate and one of them stands
on it while the others round us up to come and listen whether
we like it or not. In our local Kinyarwanda, instead of French
that the whites might understand, they tell us that foreigners
are our enemies. They claim that foreigners support the Tutsi
government and give us aid so we won't return home. That way
the Tutsi keep the country. That's what I heard one day. The
next day they changed their story because it might encourage
people to cross over the border and return home. One of them
got on the box and said, "Foreigners give us aid now, but they'll
take it away soon. They'll force us to go back home where we'll
be slaughtered. The foreigners work for the Tutsi. Don't trust
them. They give us food only to trap us. What we demand of
the big powers is this: They must give Rwanda back to democracy, back to the majority, to the Hutu majority, to us."

The militiamen seemed to like that story better, because we

heard it every day afterwards. I was surprised that Prosper seemed to agree with it.

I have picked up another stray. That makes five children with me, but of course I have Prosper helping too. We get rice and beans from thirty-gallon barrels at the food station. Prosper somehow managed to find himself a corncob pipe and tobacco. I like to watch him smoke while he wears an old rain hat. Underneath it his face reminds me of my father when he wasn't performing rituals and felt relaxed.

Each day I crawl out of our tent and look at the rising sun and think today I'll wait for many hours in a line for food and then hours more to get water and in these lines I'll hear the same things, exchange the same rumors, express the same hopes and fears. Then the sun goes down in the smoke and I lie awake with the stench of many odors in my nostrils until finally I sleep a little and waken to go outside and look again at the rising sun.

How do the children do it? They play, they wait patiently, they keep their own worlds safe within the roundness of their pure eyes. Right now I have seven children with me—two I never saw until last night, when they suddenly appeared and sat down without a word alongside mine. I forget the name of the littler one, but maybe he forgot it too and never told me. Anyway, he rarely speaks, just holds on to the older boy. His hand is always somewhere on the older one's body, on elbow or hand or waist or shoulder or cheek or thigh—somewhere, always touching.

We have been grouped in camp according to communes. Therefore, we come under the control of people who had controlled us most of our lives back home. Some of these people led the massacres. Do the whites know that? Or care? They have enough to do just in keeping us alive, I suppose. So I don't think about such things. I just mix water with maize flour and make a porridge over an open fire in a clay pot, and what comes out hot I feed to the children.

Sometimes a pregnant woman will come around to see me, because I am known. I carve a little ibiheko out of a piece of wood and give it to her to protect the spirit of her unborn from evil. There's plenty of evil to watch for in this camp. The militiamen sneak around and tell gruesome stories about the Tutsi and what they'll do if we go home. The aid people and UN say nothing. They don't use radio or bullhorns or sound trucks to go around and talk the way the militia do. They don't assure us it's all right to go home. You have to ask these white people, tug at their sleeves, and ask if it's all right to go home. Then they look surprised and have that white contempt on their faces and say of course it's all right. Go home if you want to.

If you want to? Who among my people ever do what they want to? If only we could take care of ourselves and not depend on whites who have no idea who we are. All the whites think of is keeping us breathing. That we have thoughts too doesn't seem to interest them.

Have your husband blow smoke in your face, I tell a girl. That will keep your unborn healthy. But she doesn't have a husband. She doesn't know who the father is. I tell her never mind. I'll come and wash her newborn in cold water and rub it in butter if I can get some. At least I'll see to it that the birth cord is kept for the baby's amulet. Women give birth every day around here, within the distance of a few-dozen steps. I hear this heavy breathing and the grunts and the screams and then the wonderful sound of a child filling its lungs for the first time, announcing it has started to live this life.

Prosper likes to sit and smoke while I tell him what I know about spirits. I tell him that all living things possess spirit. It's something he already believed because of a lifetime of farming. A farmer knows as much as a witch doctor, he claims.

I believe, as the White Fathers do and as my people have believed for as along as time has been, that there is something living after death that goes back to the supreme being. Does the farmer in you believe that? I asked Prosper, and he smiled happily. We've become good friends.

But when I listen to music on the radio, he goes outside and waits until it's over. That's all right. He's too old for rhumba and benga. Cavacha gives him a headache, so I listen alone or with some of my seven children, who all seem to like music. It's better than listening to radio news that tells you how many daily rations you're supposed to be getting when you know you never get that many. What they don't say on the radio is that children under sixteen aren't counted as a full unit, so you never get enough maize flour to feed a whole family—surely not a family of seven—and including me and Prosper, nine. So to enjoy the radio, it's better to tune in music and let it take you into dreams. I like the old songs too. Sometimes if I sing one of them, Prosper listens. The Hutu sing at harvesttime and for weddings, whereas the Tutsi sing about war and the beauty of their cattle. But I like the Twa songs best. They're about hunting and love. In the old days they entertained the Tutsi mwami at court with such wonderful songs.

Maybe it wouldn't be so bad in this camp if the trouble stopped. There is always trouble. Most of it begins near the road, not in the heart of camp. That's because drunken soldiers and looting thieves and young toughs know they can't escape from deep within camp so easily. If you're going to do something bad, you stay near the road where you have a chance to escape. That's the idea. I hear at Kibumba camp a dozen soldiers wearing the uniforms of Zaire went through the camp and took blankets, radios, cooking pots, and six-gallon jugs of banana beer and stalks of green bananas probably bought with someone's last savings. When the refugees surrounded them with pangas, the frightened Zairian boys shot their way out, killing a few dozen on their way, but they never reached the road. People cut them down when they ran out of ammunition, and I heard there wasn't anything bigger than a forearm or a thighbone left of any of them. I'm sure their severed feet didn't wear shoes. When someone dies in camp, the shoes are taken and sold either to a hawker or a shoemaker, who cleans them up and resells them from a mat spread by the side of the road. Nothing is wasted. Crosses on graves are removed overnight for firewood. What can people do when their children are cold?

This morning when I awoke to go outside and watch the sun come up, I noticed something. Counting, I found eight of them. Counting Prosper and me, that makes ten of us.

PROSPER NDABATEZE

MOST OF THESE people here have little to remember. None of them can recall the riots of 1959 when we Hutu rose up and burned thousands of Tutsi homes. I was young then and part of it. We set off singing in bands of ten, armed with matches and the paraffin used for lamps. We pillaged Tutsi huts and set them afire and laughed at the occupants who ran away. We enlisted others who took our places when we were exhausted and had to trudge home. Day after day the fires spread. Many of the Tutsi fled to Uganda in those days. That was almost forty years ago when we rose up because of an incident. As I recall, a Tutsi chief had threatened a Hutu crowd that was angry over the death of a popular Hutu leader who had been assaulted by Tutsi youths. Something like that.

We were stronger then than now. But we weren't out to kill every last Tutsi, just the worst of them, and destroy their houses. The important thing was that we felt the mwami, the Tutsi king, was on our side because our complaint was warranted. When a military plane flew overhead, I remember us cheering because we thought that the mwami was in the aircraft, directing our operation against his own offending tribe. By the course flown he was showing us which direction we were to take in starting more fires. And so we headed in that direction and set more fires.

It was so different then. A belief in justice kept us going. I don't find any justice in what has happened recently. No one even knows why the president's plane crashed. I don't mind the killing of thousands of Tutsi. I mind doing it without knowing why.

So here I am, right or wrong, in this camp. If I'm not busy with the children or talking to Pauline, I sit by myself with a pipe and think of farming. I'm a conservative man. I believe you must lessen the risk of failure rather than seek maximum reward. I believe you should diversify your crops rather than concentrate on one, even though it might be the best suited to soil and climate. I have always planted what experience has shown to be the safest, not necessarily the most profitable. I have always put one fourth of my land in banana groves because they bear fruit all year around. It's a food reserve at the end of the dry season, a guarantee against famine. That's what my father taught me. Then, too, we Rwandans love beer and nothing ferments easier than bananas. This is the cautious and sensible way I approach life at sixty years of age.

When the camp around me is pulsing with the sounds of pain and of machines roaring and of radios crackling and people screaming at each other, I close it all out by remembering my bean fields. In one of my higher fields I plant beans, in my lowest I plant peas. My main crop is always sweet potatoes because they require little acreage and have a high yield. Also, although sweet potatoes taste good when fresh, they can be stored for months if sliced and sun dried. I also like a field of cassava because it's something that can be stored underground for a couple years. That's to fight drought. I like maize too, although the yield is low. Sorghum is steady but its taste becomes dull after a while and the beer it makes turns bitter. These are the things I think about when the world outside our tent is whirling like a windstorm. Someday I want to grow peanuts, rice, and soybeans. I have already tried sugarcane, but with little success. I'd plant rice except our climate won't allow a second yearly crop. Soybeans are difficult to cook. My soil isn't dry enough for peanuts. During the long, useless, stinking hours in this camp, I work out plans for my future. I discard one, consider another.

When we don't have enough to eat here, I work hard at recalling how my rugo looked. I can see the banana grove from the front north window. I see the tethered goats and that old rooster, scarred from many fights, puffing himself up and strutting among the hens. I go up and down the hill in memory and inspect my small parcels of land put into beans, peas, sorghum. I have some fallow land for pasturing a half-dozen cows, more for manure than for milk. I have an isolated plot far up the hill for coffee trees. Something else about sweet potatoes I remember. You can take them from the earth without hurting the rest of the plant. What I always say is this: It is best to have a variety of crops, because they're a safeguard against blight, insects, and drought and roving warthogs. That's exactly what I tell young farmers. I remember my hoes with stout handles and shiny black blades that I like to keep well-oiled when not in use. I like to lift and heft them and feel the correct weight in my hands. This time I was too old to use one of my hoes against the Tutsi.

I like the idea that our terraced hills are too steep for ox-drawn plows. We have to use hoes and pruning knives the way our ancestors used them. Bending down like my grandfather did, I like to pull up weeds with him in spirit.

Remembering 1959 is more pleasant than remembering the events of a few months ago. On our hill in April I saw Tutsi being cut down like bananas from a tree—*swish swish swish* with a panga. They came down with the thud of bananas. Some of us Hutu went down too. If someone didn't like you and told the Interahamwe that you were a spy, two things might happen. Either they questioned you and found out the accusation was false or they just believed it and finished you off like you were a Tutsi. This happened to three friends of mine. One shot in a courtyard, the other two hacked to death against a wall. I'm glad my father and his father did not live to see such an irresponsible thing.

Pauline insists we're safe because we did nothing wrong. Yet who's to say that someone—perhaps a returning Tutsi with an eye on my land—won't call me a murderer? I can hear him now, pointing his finger at my chest and yelling, "That's him, that's one of them! I saw him slash open a woman's skull with a hoe." Then he'd ask for my land. Well, I'll never give up my land, even if it means staying here in this camp to avoid it.

I might have killed some of those Tutsi if given the chance. Yes, sure. Perhaps my age saved me from doing it. Those young men raced off with hoes raised above their heads. I won't be dishonest, not an old farmer like me. I hate the Tutsi as much as any Hutu does, and yet I recall the days when the Tutsi mwami was a ruler for everyone, because he dispensed a rough justice to both Hutu and Tutsi. We Hutu took some wrong and gave some wrong, and somehow it worked. The Tutsi lost and gained too, although they cheated more. We knew they cheated and let it go. We smiled at each other in our huts and knew we were better in some ways than the Tutsi. Everything worked, so why did it change? Politics?

I don't know. Politics must have changed it.

What I do know is that I'll stay right here until the hatred and confusion of politics has burned off like elephant grass in a bushfire. Then maybe I'll say to Pauline, "Let's take all these children—how many do we have now? Let's take them back home."

AGNÈS

EACH MORNING AT the clinic the first thing I do is give fluids intravenously to malaria patients, or for children prostrate from dehydration I use a nasal-gastric drip. To replenish the salts lost from diarrhea and malnutrition I deliver a canteenful of a solution containing electrolytic powder. When I begin, the patients are sitting under plastic blue sheeting on three rows of benches. Quietly they take their medicine, then rise and go away, and their places are filled by those waiting outside. Although I see many of the same faces every morning, I can't remember them. They're all gaunt and bony. The eyes seem too big for the heads, the teeth too. Malnutrition has made many of them look more like Tutsi than Hutu—high cheeks, prominent jaws, small chins, balllike skulls. Something they did not teach in the classroom is this—hunger and disease make people look alike. If I had time, I'd try to remember certain faces. What I do now is smile equally at everyone. They must feel bitter at being so sick without anyone knowing who they are.

Our small clinic has been transplanted from Butare Hospital. We have one doctor. He is short, no taller than I am, and wears thick glasses and never stops sweating. He carries nitro for a heart condition and I see him halt now and then to slip a pill under his tongue. He and the chief nurse are both widowed, and they have worked together for so many years that they seem more like an old married couple than colleagues. I envy them their closeness, even when they're not getting along but mumble about each other's poor judgment. When I see them together I think of Jérome, of whether or not we would have married. Now I don't even know if he's alive or dead. Few people know if friends or relatives or lovers are alive or dead. I should have slept with him at least once, but instead I let the bourgmestre have me. I have never lost the picture in my mind of his big white teeth and goatee and the little heaving sound he made while on top of me. Jérome would not have been that way, and yet I don't think I ever loved him.

Every morning I check on the volunteer nurses, who are either too lazy or forgetful to change the drip bottles, which can cause tubing to clog. Almost every day we get babies burned by pots of boiling water knocked over into the crowded paths. Burns look bad and hurt terribly but aren't as lethal as dehydration. Yesterday I squeezed a salt solution through a syringe into a plastic tube leading into a boy's nose. He was five years old but looked two in his torn red shirt. His mother didn't bring him back today, so maybe he failed to make it. That could be another reason why I forget faces. I remembered his today when I should have been studying a wound. Every once in a while I see the back of a boy's head in a crowd and I think it's Innocent. Running forward, I call out, "Innocent! Innocent!" but when the boy turns, I know it isn't he, even though Innocent must have grown since last I saw him. If he's still alive and getting enough to eat, I imagine he's almost as tall as I am. And slim as bamboo. After all, he's a Tutsi.

We are always worried about the latrines. Without proper

disposal of human waste a heavy rain can bring dysentery and malaria. Our doctor warns of that all the time, sweating and putting nitro under his tongue. The chief nurse scoffs at him for repeating himself so often.

When I look across the vast gray sea of tents and humanity, nothing stands out. But when I walk through camp, I see these little flagged huts where people get food and medicine and I think somehow we are all going to live. Yesterday I drove over to Katali camp, thirty-six miles north of Goma, where 200,000 refugees are living. Holland's Doctors Without Borders has a hospital there, which in size and staffing reminds me of a hospital in Kibumba run by Goal, an Irish relief agency, and staffed by the Association of Medical Doctors for Asia. Then there's also a clinic in Katali run by Care Australia and a very fine water system installed by a British organization. A lot of these aid organizations give us some of their extra supplies, so when our truck returns we have enough medicine for another few days.

Our camp has endured many setbacks, but sometimes there are victories as well. We prevented a measles epidemic recently through mass vaccination. Mobile UNICEF units with cold-chain equipment for delivering inoculations came into camp in a squadron of jeeps. By bullhorn they announced that vaccinations would save lives. Children were brought in. We did three thousand a day. The chief nurse and I didn't sleep for fifty hours straight. Weakness makes children vulnerable to measles, which is often fatal under these conditions. When the little fellows get weak, measles cause a high fever in them and painful gum ulcers that make them whimper both day and night. That's a sound I really hate to hear. It's a constant thing, like the sound of wind carrying dust. We bathe a child's mouth every few hours and get him to drink enough to halt dehydration. Given a high-protein diet and liquids, a child with measles can recover in a week. Without these simple measures he'll be dead in less time than that. This is not a complicated thing we do. It's a simple thing.

So much of what we do is simple. Give us a row of thirty six-liter stockpots and we can prepare enough Unimix to feed hundreds of undernourished babies. That's what our grumpy chief nurse says. And she's right. It's that simple—doesn't anyone see how simple it is? I think I'm losing patience. I talk much too fast, I talk at people when I'm moving away from them because there doesn't seem time for standing still and talking. There isn't time for anything.

We're having a lot of lobar pneumonia and isolated cases of TB and whooping cough. We're getting too much kwashiorkor. I hadn't seen kwashiorkor until coming to this camp. I had just read about it. Kwashiorkor occurs at weaning when a baby changes from a protein to a carbohydrate diet. Signs of it are easy to spot: fatigue, loss of muscle, edema, protuberant belly, a blank stare in the eyes. It can all be reversed if protein delivery begins soon enough. It's really so simple.

When a volunteer nurse asks me is there anything she can do for a dying child, I tell her, "Yes, there is."

It happened to me just yesterday with a three-year-old girl. There was nothing else to do for her, so I touched her body. I put the tips of my fingers against her chest and kept them there a while. I would have stayed that way until she died, but there was too much else to do, so I stayed that way only a few minutes. Her breathing didn't race as much. The muscles in her face relaxed a little. She felt my fingertips. She felt the little spots of warmth going from me to her, and I think it helped.

"Touch," I tell the volunteer nurses. "Always touch if you can't think of anything else to do. Touch the child's head or chest or arm or leg. Anything. Touch, always touch. It's what you can always do."

I treated a man who had a festering cut on his hand. He had lost his wife and four children. Within a minute he was asking my age and if I had children and would I like to have some with him. Reaching out, he took my hand in his good one and proposed marriage. He wanted to start life again. He said he wouldn't ask a bride-price. I thanked him for his offer but told him I already had a man.

What he'll probably find in our camp is a plafond—one of the Tutsi girls who survived by hiding in the rafters, just as I hid Innocent. Is he alive? I wonder every day. Ceiling girls are usually very quiet and still scared, and most of them are orphans, so the man might find his new wife among them.

We have learned of something else to worry about. There's a new fever in camp. Doctors think it might be an outbreak of typhus because of lice. We're going to get on the bullhorn again and try to convince people to pick themselves clean and shave off their hair if they're itching.

A few days ago this girl came in and sat down. She was a Tutsi, about sixteen, and very pregnant. She was too heavy-hearted to tell me what was wrong, but I figured the pregnancy was her problem. So I took a chance and asked, "Were you raped?"

She nodded and looked down, sobbing.

"Tell me about it."

"It was the Interahamwe," she said. "These six boys made me travel with them. They took me to Burundi, then Zaire, and yesterday they brought me here to this camp."

"Where are they now?"

"I don't know. They all came here, but I don't know where they are now." She waved her hand vaguely. "I'm too pregnant for them now."

"We'll take care of you," I told her.

The sound of my voice did not reassure her, because she gave me a little smile and said, "Nobody can help me now. I shouldn't be blamed for this. It wasn't my fault."

"No," I said, "it wasn't."

"But I can never go home. I am no good now. I'll have this child with me—" She looked down with disgust at her swollen belly.

"You'll have a fine child."

She gave me the little smile again. "Fine? Why?"

"Healthy."

Getting up slowly, putting one hand on the small of her back, the girl started to leave.

"Come see me tomorrow," I called. When she refused to turn, I walked after her and put my hand on her arm. "Come tomorrow," I told her, but she looked at the ground and said nothing. She didn't return the next day. I don't know what she did. I went next door and looked at the table with gynecological stirrups. Two babies are born in camp for every one that dies. If she goes home with that Hutu child and if there is still family on her hill, she won't be accepted and neither will the child. I have a daydream. In this daydream I climb the hill with her and she's carrying the child in a bright khanga on her back. A crowd of Tutsi assemble at the top of the hill and I tell them, "It wasn't her fault. Don't you see? And the child is healthy." They come around and study the baby and begin to smile. That's my daydream.

I tell volunteer nurses, "If you put a blanket on a sick child, watch closely. People will take it if you're not careful. And we don't have blankets to lose." The very young and very old can't defend themselves, so they suffer most. Young, vigorous men suffer least. If I ever find a man, I won't want him too young— my age or younger. I'll want him to look old enough to suffer. I'll want him older than Jérome.

When I first came to this refugee camp, I heard sounds from the tents. At first it disgusted me. I thought of them doing that in there, while not six feet away someone else was breathing a last breath. Then I began to listen differently. I thought of them in there capable of living outside the sounds of death, of finding something between them, of reaching the ecstasy of a few moments together, and it seemed good to me, a wonderful thing, a recapturing of life, and sometimes when I was listening I wanted to be the woman inside that tent.

What was never taught in the classroom I have learned in camp. I have learned what a strong people we are. I have seen people brought into our clinic with panga gashes right to the bone. These people walked for two or three days without food through woodland and over hills before reaching a relief truck that could take them in. I saw a man given a hard bristle brush and soap and told to clean his own wounded hands because at the time none of us had time to do it for him. He did it without a murmur. I saw a white worker staring in astonishment at such fortitude and I was proud of our people. We survive. A white aid worker told me once, "You people don't cry. I treated a woman about your age this morning. Back in Ireland a wound like hers would have meant screaming. But this woman didn't even cry. Mind you, I didn't have painkiller to give her. You people are unbelievable."

The aid worker meant it as praise, yet in her voice I heard annoyance too, as if she were saying, "You people are not quite human."

Children who don't brush flies off their eyelids have lost hope. Usually they die. That's something I didn't learn in a classroom but it's something I will never forget.

Doctors Without Borders has three clinics here and a three-hundred-bed unit. AmeriCares has a unit almost as big. Spanish nuns run a bigger one than both. Here we have a big city of latrines and warehouses and hospitals and orphanages and food sites. Nearby, I see stacks of aluminum sheeting that will go into an expandable, high-domed field hospital. Our doctor says that people stay where the help is, and I believe it. The more things improve in such a camp the more permanent it becomes. People begin clinging and lose the ability to survive on their own. That's one thing our doctor and chief nurse agree on. But when people become too weak even to walk, what do you do? You feed and care for them if you can. Our doctor and chief nurse agree on that too.

Another thing I have learned outside of the classroom is this: In a bad bout of malaria, the eyes fix in a filmy gaze and the body trembles so hard that the metal-framed cot shakes like a beaten drumhead. I also know the most important question never asked in a classroom. Who should you help first? Those most likely to die or to live? When I first came here I wanted to take the worst cases first in the hope that I might help them live. Then one day the chief nurse asked me to choose between two children. I asked her why. She said I must choose in order to learn something. I chose the one worse off for the trip to a hospital a few miles away. It was a panting little boy with enormous staring eyes. On the trip there he died. Now I always choose the one who has the best chance.

Then something happened that I had been dreading and hoping would not happen. Our doctor brought us together and announced it in a soft, frightened voice. An epidemic of cholera was sweeping through camp. He took his glasses off and cleaned them, while warning us to brace ourselves for seeing a lot more death than we had ever seen before.

It wasn't hard to recognize the symptoms of cholera: voluminous watery diarrhea, dehydration, vomiting, muscle cramps. What we needed most was boiled and treated water. Within a few days we were having eighteen hundred dying in each twenty-four-hour period. There was nowhere to put the corpses in such hard volcanic soil. Cholera dead should be burned for safety, but our people have always disliked the idea of burning. Many fear it will cause trouble in the next life. They want burial, but the ground here has been too unyielding.

Meanwhile, the bodies piled up and swarms of insects circling them were as thick as storm clouds.

Fifteen thousand died of cholera right here around Goma. Relief teams were airlifting water-testing equipment and Ringer lactate into camp. The Finnish people donated tanker trucks of milk. A number of European countries were hauling in high-protein biscuits and oral-rehydration salts.

Suddenly there were more foreigners in camp than I had ever seen before. A Japanese contingent was chlorinating water. Even what we didn't need so much became available. A surgical field hospital appeared almost overnight under the direction of the Australian Red Cross. Its chief surgeon was from Sweden. The operating theater was equipped by the Norwegian Red Cross, and its electricity was supplied by generators donated by the Germans.

I felt something then that I never felt before or since. I felt that truly the world was one place, that we were all linked together by an invisible thread running from one soul to another. But this feeling didn't last. I was too exhausted for it. Once, during the epidemic, I fell asleep while gripping a cup of tea.

I began to know things I never thought were important before. I knew how big the planes were that flew from Europe into Entebbe with water-purification equipment. They were seventy-ton C-5 cargo planes. I knew that the supplies were reloaded in Entebbe on C-130 turboprop planes that could land on unpaved airstrips near Goma. We nurses would rush in to tell one another in breathless English, "Five C-one-thirty turboprop come in!"

Usually a cholera epidemic lasts three weeks. Perhaps five percent of our camp population of 200,000 was going to become infected by cholera and half of those would die. That proved true. But just as predicted, after the first week the number of deaths began to drop off. Following a few more weeks of adequate water supply and medicine, the death rate fell to less than one percent.

Then suddenly the epidemic was over. It had come and gone like a fire sweeping across a savannah. A little boy was brought in with cholera and responded to treatment so quickly that he was up and out in a week. We waved happily at each other when he left.

Two weeks later a wave of dysentery swept through the camp. It was worse than cholera. Even more so than cholera, it was spread by human waste. It killed five times more children than cholera did, even though the dehydration was more rapid in cholera. For both epidemics, our chief need was to replace lost fluids and salts immediately. Dysentery was more resilient, meaner, stubborn.

The same little boy came back to the clinic, only this time he had dysentery and died here. There wasn't much time for such a thing, but I held his hand during the last half hour. I remembered his smile and his happy wave good-bye after the cholera. For the first time since the epidemics began, I wept over a dry, lifeless, little body.

A few days later we faced a new outbreak of meningitis. Three children, all boys, died of it in our clinic.

And not a hundred yards away from our clinic a small boy exploded a grenade he had found, killing six people, including himself.

If I ever have a boy, I know one thing. I'll ask his father to name him Niyonsenga, To God I Pray, in our language of Kinyarwanda. Such a name might protect him a little. That's all I have time for these days, a quick prayer to whatever or whoever it is that has mercy on us, and sometimes I don't even have time for that.

PACIFIQUE

WHEN THE TRUCK stopped, I peeked from the corner of the lifted canvas and saw a huge garbage can steaming with soup. I took a deep breath and got the flavor in my nose of that soup, and I thought it was good they brought me here.

But that was before I knew what it was like in this place. The people who ran it called it an orphanage, but there were too many of us and we couldn't go outside and we didn't always have soup. The people who ran it were grown-ups and a few whites, who ran around looking important, but they didn't pick us up as much as our own people did. Nobody picked me up because any of us who were six or seven were too old unless we looked younger.

A lot of us were rounded up by relief people who drove a truck around looking for wandering kids or they took us away from huddling next to a dead mother or father or walking down a road all alone.

I met Chantal the other day. She was eight. Her family came from Kigali. If you ever see Kigali again, I asked her, what will you do? She told me she would read. Why? I asked. Because I like it, Chantal said. Chantal wore a red shirt and blue-checked skirt and one shoe, a black one, on her right foot. Where's the other shoe? I asked. She said that she didn't have shoes that she

could remember but found this one outside of a village. I wondered if she had taken it from a dead girl, but said nothing.

Chantal said, "How do your arms feel?"

"Okay," I told her.

She held up both of hers high. They were very thin like
bamboo or even thinner, and the chest bones stuck out where
I could see them through her torn shirt. "When I lift them,"
she said, "they don't feel good."

"How do they feel?"

"Heavy." She dropped her arms to her sides. The hands
looked too big for the arms. "And stiff. When I lift them like
that I feel tired." She reached over and touched my arm. "You're
okay. My arms used to look like your arms."

"They will again," I told her. Chantal was nice and I liked
her.

I got to know things. If I saw a kid with a bandage on his
face, I figured it was full of pus and if he looked real tired along
with it, I knew he might die.

They come in and write our names down. Our last names are
different than our parents', which I can see makes the whites
unhappy because they don't have it like that where they come
from. They try to get our parents' names and home district and
when we last saw them. A lot of kids can't tell any of it, not
even their parents' names, and when the whites write this down
they frown. I know my mother doesn't have a name anymore
because she's dead, but I'm not sure about my father, so I tell
them his name and when they say is he still alive I always say
yes and nod my head hard. I tell them he's a dancer and a
cattleman seven feet tall. They always smile because they don't
believe that or that he's alive.

Sometimes we hear of good things happening. Like two boys who lost their parents and three other brothers and a sister. One, about ten years old, went with a Hutu neighbor to a camp in Zaire and found a brother there. Another, thirteen, was in an orphanage in Burundi and then somehow got to Kigali, where he found his cousins and later a brother. But they never found their parents.

We take food in the big hall filled with smoke. Beans and rice cook in big garbage cans over wood fires. We sleep in a building with a big hole in the roof, so when it rains we get wet. In the next room they keep the sick ones who make noises all night. It stinks. Today we had maize porridge. I don't much like maize porridge but eat it anyway. Two others and me play a game with sticks and some wire. I cough and have a runny nose all the time. My mother used to wipe my nose for me when I was sick. No one wipes it now. The flies stick on my lip some-times. I can't remember what it's like not to have a cough and runny nose. We sit around and look at each other and cough. There aren't many mattresses and those they have go to the sick ones, except the sick ones who go all the time have to lay on the boards so it can be cleaned up.

Sometimes grown-ups come in and talk to us. They ask about our families and how they died. A little girl said, "Why did our friends do that to us? My father's friend killed my mother. I saw him do it with a panga while she asked him not to do it."

When we talked about such things, the grown-ups gave us sweets and foreign candy.

Now and then women would come and look in at us to see if any of us belonged to them. We were fifteen in there. I can count. If a woman would pick me out I would hold on to her and never let go. Sometimes a woman peeks around the corner and I think it's Pauline. I feel a chill go through me because I want so much for her to be Pauline. I think I dream of her and her other children, but I'm not sure when I wake up. When people come into the tent, I smile at anyone who looks at me. Whites come around with cameras and I stand in front of them and smile. I smile as much as I can and I talk a lot because some of us can't do that anymore, so maybe I'll be picked out for being able to talk and get taken home in place of a lost boy or maybe they'll find Pauline for me.

I met a new boy. Always the first question we ask when first meeting is what I asked him. "Where are your parents?"

"Bandits killed them because my father had some money. People fed me along the way. Someone took my hand but he went for water and left me and never came back. I don't know my village. I forgot my name."

"This is not a bad place," I told him. "Don't ever leave here."

"Then I won't."

"It's safer here than anywhere. Safer than home."

We played together all afternoon.

When we sat down and held hands, he said, "I was in this camp and they had speakers yelling at mothers to hold on to their children. They told children to hold on to their mothers' clothes. If I knew my village, this white woman said they would take me there. But I forgot the name."

"Anyway," I told him, "you're safe here."

A woman brought in a baby she found in the arms of a dead mother down the road. Today the woman came back to see how her "baby" was. It had died, but the white told her the baby was fine. I liked that. I said, *"Bonjour, Mademoiselle,"* to the white woman, who gave me a smile from her red face.

There were other babies too. There was one I remember who seemed to be dying but they didn't know why. Then they found a lump in her chest. Caught in the bone was a bullet that must have gone through her mother first. When they took it out, she stopped crying and began eating again. So good things happen.

I left that place because they put me in a truck to take me to another place. I got out of the truck, I don't know why, and began walking. On the way I asked for food and someone gave me some. Later I got sick. I was sitting beside the road in my own stuff and feeling sticky, when a white truck came along and whites got out of it and picked me up and put me inside with other children. Three babies lay on a blanket. I could see one of them was already dead. A fly was crawling in and out of her open mouth. She had a little gold chain around her waist that she could take with her to heaven unless someone took it away from her first.

I'm covered with lice and my own stuff, but I've been rescued like I heard could be done if you reached the truck stop in early morning. When it stopped you got in or you let them put you in, which is what happened to me. This white, she had big teeth, but gave me a hug even though my own stuff was sticking to my pants and legs. Then as we sat on benches beneath the canvas in the truck, she came around with a biscuit and a drink of water. I miss hugs like that. I miss Pauline hugging me.

We got out where there were a lot of tents where a lot of children were. Some stayed in special tents because they were too sick to move. And others like me were put into tents with floors of plastic blue sheet. A girl maybe nine or ten helped me get off the stinky, dirty clothes and wash myself clean. She wouldn't touch the stuff, leaving that to me, but she wiped my face with a wet rag. After she shaved my head because of lice, I give her a smile and she gave me one back and we held hands a while.

Later I left there for somewhere else in another truck. We were going to Goma, someone said. I kept saying the words to myself because they sounded like music: "We are going to Goma, we are going to Goma, we are going to Goma."

Then the truck in front of us hit something and blew up in a big explosion. I was scared and started to cry. Some kids got hurt and were screaming. I jumped out. I could walk and so that's what I did, I walked, and pretty soon I saw all of these tents ahead of me as far as I could see, and a big cloud of smoke moved back and forth over them. People were everywhere I looked. They were anywhere that there was a place to sit or stand or move.

Nobody paid attention to me, so I kept going. I figured someone would give me a little something to eat. Sweet potatoes were in my head. I could almost smell them baked. I saw a girl about my age sitting with a torn umbrella held over a smaller girl who lay in her arms. She was holding the umbrella in a way to get shade. I went up and said, "Is that your sister?"

The girl nodded.

"She looks sick. Have you got parents?"

She nodded.

"Both of them?"

She nodded.

I looked at her with a frown. She was a lucky girl. Then I

looked at her sister again, who hadn't moved. She looked stiff like a doll. "I think your sister is dead."

The girl nodded.

Then I went away and sat by myself, feeling hungry, feeling weak, and feeling something in my stomach that felt scratchy and alive, until a man came along and bent under the umbrella that the girl was still holding over her dead sister.

The man sat down and tears rolled down his face. He began rocking back and forth. "Your mother just died in the hospital," he told the girl. "Now I've come back to this." He kept rocking and touching the dead little girl with his hand.

The older girl kept holding the umbrella so it shaded her dead sister. The father kept rocking while holding on to a plastic wash bucket. I think it was all he had left. I looked at the dead girl and wondered about her shoes. If she was bigger, I'd ask for them but she was just a baby.

Waving good-bye at the girl who held the umbrella, I got up and walked away, hoping to get some food in my belly. Food would kill the live thing in there. That's how I thought. So here I was in Goma, but it didn't really seem like music and I stopped saying the words.

EMMANUEL

INNOCENT SLIPPED AWAY in the night without a word. I
knew that someday he would do it and in that way. Whenever
I looked into his eyes I saw a mirror looking back at me. I didn't
see depths in his eyes. If they are there, they don't show. He
has the eyes of a lion waiting in the bush. I always wanted to
trust the boy but never did

Innocent never described what happened to his family. He
just shrugged and told me they were dead. I think the way they
died must have been very bad. I think he saw it happen and it's
with him all the time. I think too that Innocent is more of a
Tutsi than he admits. The boy stands against the world without
flinching. Most boys who sniff glue can't stop the way he did.
Deciding it was time to let go of it, he just did. No sickness, no
moaning, no crying. Only a tightening in his lips that meant he
felt awful. There is a strange and wonderful and terrible power
in that scrawny boy. I have wondered if he prefers the life he
has, one of trouble and testing, to the quiet life of someone who
might grow into a cattle herder. In the old days a boy like that
might have grown up to live at court, perhaps as a ritual adviser
or a war counselor to the king, because this is a boy who has
something special in his mind, even though what it is might
not be helpful to anyone but himself.

Although at first I thought so, he really isn't like my Pacifique, who is much gentler and closer in his heart to others. Of course, Innocent is seven or eight years older, even if he looks only four or five older, so maybe he thinks more like a man. Pacifique is strong but a sweet boy. He's like good banana wine. Sometimes I wonder if he might want to dance later on. He'll have the long, slim body, but what about the heart? Does he have the right heart? Why do I think of him as still alive? Perhaps because I never saw him dead like the others. I carry his living face with me.

I dream too much these days. I am dreaming of cattle. They run through my dreams with their horns curved like slivers of moon. I see their heavy withers and jutting nostrils, their high bony hindquarters, their long tails with black clusters of hair on the end—all of their bodies loping through dusty fields until I'm exhausted when I awake, my heart pounding.

Sometimes in the dream a woman stands at the edge of the pasture, watching as I collect strays, especially Sharp Ribs. The woman is very long-legged with a long, thin neck and high, round forehead and pointed ears and hair like a small, black crown around her skull. I can't see her expression clearly, but the way she stands with her long, slim fingers folded in a dark clump just under her breasts is a way of telling me she is my wife. My wife used to stand that way. But she says nothing and after a while, during the roundup, I look over there and she's gone. She's come to tell me something but leaves before I can get over there and ask her what it is.

If I were home, maybe I'd go see the woman Pauline, who they say can read the guts of a chicken. Her father had been a well-known umufumu who taught her how to tell the future and read dreams. It would be all right to seek help from a Hutu. After all, in the old days they supplied witch doctors for the court. I used to know Pauline's loudmouth husband. Sylvestre was a CDR man and a teacher who liked to make political speeches in the beer shops. That day I left home, when I met Pauline on the road, I would have killed him if he'd been with her. I'm sure of that.

So I'd go to this Pauline and ask, "In the dream, what is my wife trying to tell me?"

And Pauline might know. If she's still alive. I hope her loud-mouth husband is dead. I would have killed him as I killed the other loudmouth who lived in the next rugo. But I'm glad I didn't kill the loudmouth neighbor's wife too, although I was angry enough to do it. Our eyes met, so I stopped. I remember that.

I have seen enough killing. My comrades in the barracks are restless and hope for one last campaign. They'd like to round up a few hundred FAR troops and shoot them just the way our own people, our women and children, were shot at roadblocks. I think of that sometimes. I think of Tutsi families coming to a roadblock where troops who can't read are looking at identity cards, at plastic death sentences. I think of drunkards having the sudden power of life and death. I imagine a family led into a nearby thicket. They stand there pleading a little but not very hard because they know it won't work and then the gun barrels waving around and fixing on their faces and stomachs and the last terrible moment of fear when they know they can't hide before death leaps out at them.

When I think of such things I would like to go out and find more Hutu to murder.

But the other day we had to clear out a dozen of them hiding in a small health clinic just east of the city. Three ran and we shot them. The rest surrendered, but somehow one of our boys killed one while he was just standing there, waiting to get into a truck. We left him for the garbage trucks beside the road along with the three other dead.

What we found in the clinic were children. One little girl had a hand whose fingers had been struck off by a panga when she deflected a blow to her face. That's what someone there told me, saying it was a common injury, if a nasty one, and quite dangerous if infected. The girl said nothing but looked at me from eyes as big and round and more frightened than I have ever seen in a human face. The stumps had become gangrenous. Her right arm was swollen with purplish black rot to the size of a python's belly and would soon kill her. I stood and watched a nurse change the stinking bandages. The girl groaned, but only a little. The pain must have been unbearable. I gave her a sweet from those I carried in my thigh pocket. She put it in her mouth and sucked a little, but then it fell out. I gave her another and she sucked again. She didn't lose it, so this time I got a faint smile. I could feel my eyes filling, even though I'm a Tutsi soldier, so I turned away from her sweet little dying. She was a Hutu girl who had been attacked by our RPF troops, but I was told this by the Hutu nurse, who said it with a mean smile so I don't know if it was true. I don't know who killed her. I can't think of it.

I have had enough of soldiering. My hands are bloody enough at last. If I go home and raise cattle, perhaps my wife will come toward me in a dream and tell me what I need to know. I wait in the barracks and smoke in the evenings and play checkers with bottle caps. Sometimes I see Innocent in my mind, his quick glance around when he thinks no one is watching him, his mouth opening in a laugh that means he's doing just fine, his spindly legs taking him lightly over the ground to go and get something he wants. I hope he lives.

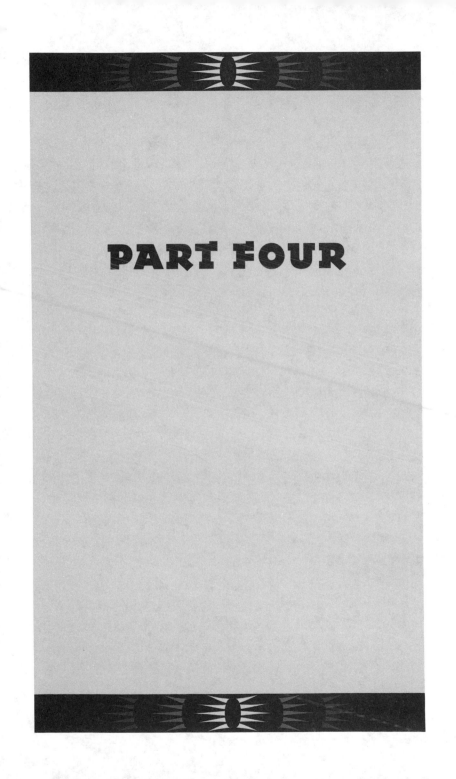

PART FOUR

AUGUSTIN

THERE ARE FOUR of us to a square meter, so two must stand while two sit. None of us can stretch out, but then the courtyard is filled with mud and shit and urine, so stretching out would only let the diseases in quicker.

That's how it is here. That's how strange and terrible it is here. Not even the worst of nightmares can touch this place.

The prison sits on a ridge near some banana groves and potato fields in the southern part of the country. The walls are brick and most of the rooms are roofless, but then most of us live in the courtyard anyway. Built for about four hundred I hear, it holds more than seven thousand right now. We choke and gag on the smoke of fires cooking potato skins. Twenty die each day from suffocation and dysentery, but that doesn't help the over-crowding, because right away the dead are replaced by the living. You hear them coming through the metal gate that squeaks when opened. You hear it *squeak squeak squeak* all day.

Sylvestre, someone I met from Gitarama préfecture, is never discouraged. He tells us that this is nothing but a setback for the Hutu cause. We'll finally exterminate the Tutsi. We're just as human as they are, except we're better because we're the majority. Yeah, yeah, yeah; I've heard it before. But this Syl-vestre says it in a good, strong voice like the teacher he is. He tells us the Tutsi landlords must go, every last one of them, so we majority people can use the pasture for grazing our own cattle or for plantations if we choose. However we choose. Yeah, yeah, yeah; I've heard that. We're the majority, he says, so it's really our land. That's the way of democracy, he says. Yeah, yeah, yeah; but I like the sound of his voice.

Sylvestre laughs at the idea of remorse. According to him, it's what the whites want us to feel. I believe it. He says a Hutu who feels remorse for killing Tutsi is no Hutu at all but a Tutsi in disguise. Sylvestre had four children and a wife who called up spirits. She read chicken guts. Once he wore a professional shirt, white and ironed, but now it's filthy gray. He still has his brown slacks and sandals, even though you can't tell their color from the mud covering them. Sylvestre tells us he was once a superintendent of schools, which makes him an important man. Maybe that's why he talks so much in such a good, strong voice.

I wear my army camouflage fatigues and a pair of Adidas high-top sneakers taken off a fellow who died next to me some weeks back. Twice already I woke up to find someone trying to steal my shoes.

Not only Sylvestre, but other people talk a lot in the yard. It's all they do. Some are soldiers like me. Others are waiting for trial because returning Tutsi have charged them with killing neighbors. I hear they're not charged yet on paper because there's no paper in the prison. And nobody ever saw a judge or a lawyer come in the gate. So no trials.

Even so, we're lucky in a way. We could have been sent to secret detention centers where they tell me people are tortured by men wearing women's clothes and on their faces something called Halloween masks from America. The torturers come from

Somalia. They use the kandoya, which is a way of tying a man's arms just above the elbows behind his back. The pressure of it finally paralyzes the upper arms. Men get smacked across the shoulders with the flat side of a panga. It's a blow that can rip flesh like a hoe ripping earth. If they get angry, they stab a man in the ear with a screwdriver. That's what Sylvestre says and he knows most things. They whack a man's feet with a rifle butt until the soles split open and fester and the festering brings gangrene and gangrene brings death. All of that talk of secret detention centers scares me.

From the courtyard, I can see over the wall to the top half of a rain tree. I used to climb a tree like that when I was a boy. I would tease Agnès for not climbing as high. Now I've taken her money and she'll never get it back. But if she's living with the bourgmestre, my sister won't need it. Maybe she's rich now, living with him in Nairobi or Paris. Maybe the bourgmestre ran there like many leaders did. If I saw him today, I'd ask for my sister's money back and if he wouldn't give it to me I'd slit his throat. Most of us here would kill our leaders because they ordered the genocide, not us. It isn't fair. Just because I'm young and strong, the Tutsi suspect me. I did nothing wrong, but they won't believe it. When the tall one captured me, I was held with others on a hilltop without food or water for three days. Then they put us in groups of ten and asked questions. If someone claimed he was just a farmer and had never been a soldier, they took off his shirt and inspected his back for the strap bruises of a military pack. They beat him if he was lying.

When we got to a prison, they gave those of us who were soldiers pink uniforms to wear. I liked that because it separated us from the militia. It made me feel better about paying to get into the army. We were told to wait in the courtyard. That's what they said: "Wait." I guess it sounded hopeful because we sang religious songs and marching songs, and someone played a wooden flute. We were being treated honorably the way soldiers ought to be. That first day they gave us maize porridge. But it was the last food we saw for two days and the third day we were trucked down here to a sector in southern Kibungo préfecture, I'm not sure where.

So we're waiting in another yard and we've been waiting here, for how long I don't know. Some of us die from being in this yard; both militia and soldiers die. They don't separate us anymore but treat us all the same. The only thing that matters is your strength. A weak man will slide down into the mud and when others know how weak he is, they sit on him because there's no other place to sit. Slowly his chest is pressed down and he suffocates easily. They sit on him until the guards drag him out and another takes his place in the square meter.

Even so, it's better in the yard than inside in the prison. Sylvestre was taken in there a few days ago and I saw him carried out dead this morning. They say they put 150 men in a hot, dark room no bigger than the space for parking a truck. Why they were put in there, I don't know, but I think it was to make room for more men in the yard. A man who came out of that room alive was able to tell me how it was. He found a spot in a corner that he never left. He sat with his knees drawn up and breathed one breath after another without thinking about other things.

Out here in the courtyard, we wait in the rain and share our square meter. Earlier, months ago, men died from the rot of their feet if they stood in rainwater too long. It's been some time since

anyone died because of that, because whites gave us towels to
dry our feet. The whites helped us live during the rainy season,
but the Tutsi won't let them feed us. The whites aren't allowed
to do that, I hear, because of a law. Whose law I don't know.
Often we go a day or two without anything to eat. The Tutsi
government has also refused an offer of tents to house us because
they say it's a security risk. I know what Sylvestre would say.
He would say, How can that be? Most of us can't walk a hundred
meters without falling down.

Now that's true. The idea of walking is what we think of all
the time. The other day a visitor from the Commission on Human Rights tried to walk through the courtyard but couldn't get
through. Everywhere he put his feet he stepped on somebody,
so finally he just shrugged his shoulders and gave up. We
laughed, because at least he knew how we felt when trying to
get to a latrine.

Now and then the Tutsi stand at the entrance to the yard
and study us like one of their herds of cattle. They cull out some
people and take them inside for interrogation. Sylvestre once
said it was the worst thing that could happen to you. How could
it be the worst? I wondered at the time. To me everything was
the worst.

Then one day the Tutsi guards picked me from the crowd.
All of a sudden I was in a dim room and after so much sunlight
it seemed like they had taken me underground. I was told to
kneel on the floor. Someone behind a desk asked me one question after another. They all had to do with killing Tutsi during
the genocide. How many did I kill, when, who, how? Each time
I said I never did that. I swore I never killed one of them,
because lying about what you did to Tutsi was not the same

thing as lying about doing something to other people. Tutsi are the biggest liars on earth, so lying about them is what they ought to expect. Sylvestre used to say those things, and I agree.

I told the man behind the desk, I said that I only followed orders. Lifting my head proudly, I said I paid to get into the Forces Armées Rwandaises. The man asked me to say that again, so I did. You paid? he asked me. I said I paid to defend my country. I heard laughter, but that didn't bother me. For a few moments I felt brave. The man behind the desk asked me what sort of orders did I follow. Why should I tell a Tutsi the truth? I said I didn't know. I forgot.

Someone came along and held my arms tightly behind me while another undid my Adidas high-top sneakers and took them away. I yelled at him to give me my shoes back, but someone hit me in the mouth. Another hit me with something on my bare feet. Oh, it hurt. I lost hold of the bravery then. It got away from me like something slippery, and all I could feel was the hitting. I think they hit me with a club spiked with nails. I was hit on the bottom of both feet maybe three or four times. What I heard was my own screaming, then my own groaning. Finally I heard the man behind the desk shouting at me to tell him about the orders I said I followed.

The words came right out of me, as slippery as fish. I was told to kill people, I said. He asked what people. I said Tutsi. There, the man said. I heard him say I was guilty of murder. Then they lifted me up and dragged me out.

So it was over. When I asked for my shoes, one of the guards laughed. So I wouldn't get my shoes, but I still had my life and though I was guilty of murder I was not charged on paper. At least I never signed anything so it couldn't be legal, could it? I asked myself. Did I tell them my real name? I wondered, but I couldn't remember something like that because of the pain. Oh the pain, the way my feet hurt.

Hauling me out to the yard, the guards tossed me into a sea of bodies. Prisoners were angry at the way I tumbled against them, so they began hitting and shoving me. I put my arms across my face and curled up to wait out their fury.

When I could squirm away and find a little space, I sat up and looked at my throbbing feet. At least a dozen holes were oozing blood in each foot. Both were already coated with the muddy filth of that place. Looking at the two bloody lumps, I began to sob. What was happening was wrong, yeah, because I didn't do anything but follow orders. Now my leader must be living in Paris with my sister, who would never forgive me for stealing from her so I could join the army and do what was right. I didn't want her to curse me after my death, but if I didn't give the money back, maybe she'd do just that. She had some education, so maybe she knew how to curse me. I didn't want to become a ghost wandering the hills forever. I shouldn't have joined the army. I was innocent. That thought made me sob harder. The holes in my feet would never heal in this foulness. They were going to fester, I knew it, I knew it. I had seen gangrene and could remember in my nose the sickening odor of it. I didn't want to die that way. It wasn't fair, because what I did I did because I was told to do it.

I didn't do anything wrong. To die in such a way is wrong. I don't deserve it.

PAULINE

PROSPER SAYS THE whites who work in this refugee camp hate us because we're murderers, while at the same time they pity us for suffering so much. I don't know what the whites feel about anything. I don't know anything about them, but I do know that Prosper is wrong if he thinks we're murderers. Of course, some are. A few. They sit on piles of goods stolen from the white organizations and laugh at the world and at us and sell us things at high prices and get drunk. But they aren't us. They aren't our neighbors, even if Prosper insists on recognizing killers here from his own hill. He claims that he saw them pick up hoes and go out each morning to harvest their share of Tutsi.

He hasn't said so, but I wonder if Prosper ever saw my husband taking a path to such work. Sylvestre went off every morning in a spotless shirt and returned at evening with it smeared red. What I remember most was his look of satisfaction, as if we had just made love and he was turning his eyes upward and smiling. What made my husband happy was the blood of his neighbors on his shirt. I think he would have killed Pacifique had I not been around. We had slept together for many years without talking about killing Tutsi. Now this old man Prosper was reminding me every day of my husband's part in the massacre and justifying it.

"Our men were protecting their own," he told me every day.

"Our family didn't need that kind of protection," I argued back every day. "I protected our family with amulets."

Prosper would look past my shoulder as if I said nothing. "Good men defending their homes. Now Tutsi and foreigners want them to pay for it. If I had to choose between calling them heroes or murderers, I'd call them heroes."

I'd call him a fool, but that would show disrespect to an elder. Surely he was a fool. Sylvestre and his friends had not been thinking of their families, but of their own daily grievances and their manhood. Surely Prosper knew that. Or surely he was a fool. At least he was stubborn. And I could see how much he liked to upset me. In fact, I think he liked me in the way a man likes a woman and said these foolish things to get my attention.

My attention wasn't easy to get when I had eight children wanting it. Today I told them that the soul exists, so does God, and there is life after death. They were most interested in life after death, because death is always so close to them, surrounding them like the air they breathe. Three of them feared becoming ghosts, so I said if they became ghosts it would be for a short time—only until their souls were cleansed. They didn't understand about cleansing souls. I told them it would be easy for them, because their souls were almost clean right now. That seemed to comfort them.

The Radio That Kills is heard every hour of every day on thousands of sets. We're told it is our duty to follow the Hutu government into exile deep into Zaire. We're told it's our only hope because otherwise the Tutsi will murder us all. The RTLMC broadcasts from mobile units nearby, according to Prosper, who makes it his business to know such things.

On the other hand, the new Rwandan government broadcasts from Kigali. That makes tuning it in hard, but I listen when I can. The new government tells us we have nothing to fear by going home. They promise we'll get back whatever we left behind. Persons guilty of murder will be punished by execution, but otherwise the innocent can return in peace.

"Who calls himself innocent?" Prosper asked in a rage when I told him what the new government promised.

"We are," I said. "You are."

"Because I was too old to crush skulls with my hoe. Ten years younger, I'd have been out there with everyone else."

"But you weren't."

"Does that make me innocent? Am I innocent?"

The furious look on his wrinkled face stopped me from saying more. What is innocence? What is guilt? I don't know the answer to such questions. But looking at Prosper when he isn't aware of it, I see a nice old fellow who should be working in a garden patch, enjoying his last years.

Sometimes sick people come to me instead of going to the aid stations. In a few dry leaves I wrap a piece of wood that I've blessed and strap it to the place of illness, like a heaving chest or over a festering sore or on a hot forehead. For others I make amarozi of sticks or human hair to ward off evil, because evil surrounds us here. Doing these things and caring for the children keeps me busy all day, so that at sunset I'm ready to sink from exhaustion. That's good, though. That way I don't think too much about tomorrow.

I look at my children, at my own four and the other four. I see the sun shining on their smooth foreheads and close-cropped hair. They have on torn T-shirts from which their skinny arms come out knobby at the elbows. The same for the shorts—their legs come out knobby at the knees. My children look so delicate, as if a gust of wind could blow them over. Most of the time they're silent like a row of roadside trees. When I look at their eyes, I see the beauty and sadness of life.

Every day we go out for water and some food. That's when we see the camp throbbing like a jungle. This morning I saw a witch doctor sitting in front of dishes filled with grains that he was trying to sell. I studied him. He was not really an umufumu like my father. He could never speak with the dead or tell the future or make rain or call up spirits like my father did. This man was not of the right clan either, not of the Bankano. He could never rattle the gourd with the speed of my father. What was the world coming to? I asked myself. Murderers living next to you on your hill. Witch doctors selling fake potions.

And people eaten up by furies within. I overheard a mild-looking Tutsi woman tell one of the white workers, "I want to see the Hutu die. Look at the pain and suffering they cause. They're not even human. I want them all dead."

She could not have been a Tutsi of a good clan. Otherwise, she would not have permitted herself such an outburst, and to a foreigner. She was from a low family, one of the petits Tutsi. On my hill I would not have nodded in greeting when we crossed paths.

"Do you know what's happening?" I asked Prosper one day in exasperation.

"Of course I know what's happening!"

"Do you know the food coming into camp rarely gets to households? It's going into the hands of killers."

"What killers?" he asked with a little smile.

"What killers? You know what killers. The government killers. The Interahamwe, the soldiers, the officials. Those who forced us to come here."

"I wasn't forced," Prosper insisted. "Unless you say the Tutsi forced me to come here."

He won't listen. How can I get him to listen?

I saw a child longing for milk from a sick and listless mother. The child kept pulling with its little hand at her sweater. If only I had milk of my own, I thought.

A boy caked with dirt was lying beside the road. Flies were swarming in a cloud above his parted mouth. That was a bad sign, so many flies. How long did he have? I wondered. Two days? Three?

Then I looked closer because there was something about him that held me. From the shape of his face he was a Tutsi, although most dying children look like Tutsi with their chins coming to a point and their huge eyes. Someone had stolen his shirt, so his little chest was bare. The bones in it spread out like branches of a tree. He was five, six, maybe seven, maybe even older. Hunger disguises the real age of a child.

I went closer and knelt down.

Was it possible?

I recognized the amulet around the child's neck.

Bending close to his ear, I murmured, "Pacifique." Then I said it again, softly, and again.

One large eye shifted my way and almost immediately a tear formed at the lid and rolled down his cheek.

I grabbed him to me and held him a long time, while the other children gathered around to watch. I felt his body against

mine, the sharp bones, the flesh as dry as animal hide, the rapidly beating heart. The longer I held him the harder he clung
to me and the more he cried, until the crying shook both of our
bodies. I was smiling as I glanced around at the circle of my
children.

"See? It's Pacifique," I said to my own four who knew him.
"He's come back to us."

They began to smile.

"He's one of us. This is Pacifique," I told the other four and
they began smiling too.

Pacifique did not let go of me, not for two days. Wherever I
went, he went, his long, bony fingers clutching my arm, my
breast, my neck. When I looked at him, his big, round eyes met
mine with such a white-and-black look of fear that I caught my
breath. Finally, when I was able to put his feet on the ground
and steady him so he could walk, he held my hand with both
of his own and wouldn't let go. He was like a child learning to
put one foot in front of the other for the first time. My children
watched silently. I knew they'd help him if he wanted, but he
didn't want anyone's touch except mine. Not then.

But on the third day, he allowed my youngest girl, Odette,
to take his hand. They were about the same age, although she
had grown taller and stronger than Pacifique and he looked
much older than Odette. I knew he'd look like a tiny old man
until flesh filled out his face again.

I took him to an aid station, one that was run by our own
Hutu people, not the foreigners. A pretty young nurse looked at
him and gave me pills for "dehydration," is what she called it.

"How many children do you have?" she asked.

I told her nine.

When she gave me a look of surprise, I explained that only four of them were my own.

"I see. He isn't one of them," she said.

"Pacifique is a Tutsi."

"Are you able to feed them all?"

"An old man from my hill is with us and buys food when we can't get enough at the stations. But his money's running out."

Taking up a pencil and a pad of paper, she wrote something down and stuffed it in my hand. "There's a Red Cross down that path," she said. "They're Dutch but speak French. You take that paper to any one of them and wait."

"What will happen?" I asked cautiously.

"They'll feed you." She frowned at me. "Don't you believe me? They'll feed you then and there. They know me. If I send you, they'll give you food. Do you understand?"

I told her I understood.

"That's today, tomorrow, the next day. Maybe for a while. Bring all of your children."

"What is your name?" I asked.

She told me Agnès and where she came from, a hill in the préfecture of Butare.

"Where I come from I am known," I told her. "Every one of my children wears an amulet of protection. Tomorrow I'll bring you your own." I could see in her eyes she didn't believe in the protection of amarozi. So I asked her, "What do you need right now more than anything? Health? A husband? A child?"

The young nurse thought a moment, then smiled. "I suppose what I need right now is a husband."

Taking Pacifique's hand, I turned at the tent's entrance and said, "Wear my amulet and you will see."

One afternoon a week or two later, music came out of a nearby radio instead of a voice telling us who to kill. I heard Simon Bikindi sing. I began swaying to the music, swaying and remembering my girlhood when I danced until nothing else mattered but Simon Bikindi. I swayed to his music and to the sound of my children tittering as they watched me move.

"Come, children," I called out to them and beckoned. "Come dance with me. Come on now. Come on. Dance!" And all of them, the entire nine including Pacifique, began swaying to the music.

INNOCENT

HERE I AM. This is outside of Goma at Kibumba, the biggest of six big refugee camps in the area. More than a quarter of a million people, that's what I hear, are squatting on this hard gray rock that's the color of a gun. All around me people are doing business. There are shoemakers and radio repairmen who are patching up transistors and they let me watch sometimes, and peddlers and tailors and auto mechanics, and banana-wine sellers, and gamblers who slap down their torn cards in the dust and tell me to get out of the way. There are many hairdressers. People are getting their heads shaved close to the scalp because of lice.

I like it here better than in the military camp where Emmanuel and his friends sat outside their barracks every night and dreamed of home. It's not as exciting as Kigali, but not as dangerous either, so I feel my chances are good here for a while, and that's all you can expect.

Here in the camp almost anything is for sale. Refugees who brought their most prized belongings with them are now ready to sell furniture, appliances, clothing, door frames, bricks, toilet fixtures, sinks, anything.

I have tried to make friends of the young militiamen who sit on piles of relief goods, but they're a nasty bunch. They want no part of someone who might steal from them, which is what I'd do if I had the chance. But I did do a little business with them. I hired some women to bring me five liters of water from the well ten miles away. They did it because bargaining with the militiamen frightened them, and they were afraid of getting raped too. So I did the talking for them and gave them half of what I got for the water from the militiamen. Generally, I got two hundred francs for five liters. That meant a hundred for the woman carrier and a hundred for me. Then I took my hundred francs to another militia stockpile and bought ten high-protein biscuits or two tablespoons of sugar. I liked the sugar but the biscuits were better for me, so usually I took the biscuits. This lasted until the militiamen decided to pay boys smaller than me to lug in their water at a cheaper price. I think they resented doing business with a Tutsi boy. But I did well for about a month.

When I first got here what I ate was potatoes only. Those potatoes I paid for by cutting down and selling bunches of leafy branches. People used this foliage to hold down the wooden poles and plastic sheeting of their tents. For me it was too much work for too little food. I might have followed the relief organization way, but that meant standing in line for hours at food sites. Aid workers wouldn't feed me otherwise, because I had grown too tall and looked too healthy.

Searching for a way of getting food, I hung around the Red Cross stations, where sick people got attention. They sat on the verandas out of the rain and let the aid people bring them bowls of gruel. I waited until they were alone, then ran up and snatched a bowl away. They'd be given another bowl when they cried and I got fed too, so this way it worked out for everybody.

There was only one thing wrong. The aid people got to know my face, so when I showed it on a veranda they chased me away.

It's good to be young, because people say in front of you what they wouldn't say near someone older. For example, I hear that Zero Network is organizing new killer squads in camp. They're preparing lists of Hutu who cooperate with the Tutsi. Those Hutu will be executed as traitors someday. Well, someday. When is someday? To me there are only two days, today and tomorrow. I keep my mouth shut about politics. Let them fight it out and leave me to pick up any pieces they leave behind.

I'm thinking of selling porridge by the cup from large pots, but maybe there won't be enough customers who can pay. I wouldn't part with a drop of porridge free.

They can't find people in the camp who will burn bodies. Our Catholic people hate the idea of cremation. But how else to get rid of so many corpses? In this rock you can't dig graves deep enough fast enough. So I went to the UN refugee agency and volunteered for cremation work. Most of what I did was sprinkle lime on corpses. After a week at that miserable job I earned enough money to buy bananas and cooking oil and pots of maize beer for sale. I sold everything and bought more and sold everything again and bought more.

I went into the city of Goma, where I heard they have a restaurant that brings in frog legs by private plane and shrimp from Kenya and you can buy foreign wine and Belgian sugar. I stood outside that place in the rain and watched people go in and come out, the men mostly in uniforms, the women in Western dresses. Everyone arrived and left in automobiles. I gave up hope of going in there, but that was the place to be.

In the rest of Goma things weren't good. Zairian troops were stealing everything that wasn't nailed down. Shop owners kept only a few items on their shelves and hid the rest. You could buy big portable radios on the street, though, and French dictionaries and plastic sheeting stolen from UN trucks. I bought a small radio and hung it around my neck on a wire, so it couldn't be snipped off and taken. The RTLMC is using street words and dirty jokes to get attention these days. A vampire voice is calling for blood every few minutes. It's boring to listen to. I try to get music when it's on.

Today in Goma, from across the street, I watched an army officer doing business with aid workers. He was a captain from his FAR uniform or rather he had been a captain. Now he was a refugee like everyone else, but his former rank continued to give him power. He controlled this business, I could tell that. He gave out some money and shook hands with the aid workers, who might have been Ghanaians or Somalis. Then the aid workers uncovered the tarpaulin on a truck and took off some crates and stacked them on the ground right there on the street where people were walking. Then the officer's own men came out of nowhere and hauled the stuff away. He had the arrogant face of someone in power. Wherever he went, I'm sure he kept that look. I studied him, the way he walked and the expressions on his face until I memorized the look of a man in power.

I hope for the day when, at the end of it, I can throw wads of Rwandan fifty-franc notes on my bed and tell myself that tomorrow I'll make more and the next day even more.

Today I sold dozens of pieces of fried bread, but it was hot work and I won't do it anymore.

I've been paying attention to food distributed by the Non-Governmental Organizations of the world. Usually a family ration consists of ten ounces of corn flour or rice per week per person, but it lasts a family of four only one day. Distribution for each sector is made from NGO semitrailer trucks. It's carried out by leaders who came from that sector back home. That made me realize I couldn't do much business of my own here because every food site was controlled by local chiefs. I wasn't discouraged, though. In such a place you can always get along.

Alphonse is a tailor. He sets out his scissors and tray and a Saudi-made sewing machine by the road every morning, rain or shine. If it's rain, he props up part of a tent under a pole and gets beneath it and works. He makes pants and shirts out of various scraps. He has offered to teach me, but only if I sleep with him. He has bad teeth, so I refused. Anyway, I don't like the work of a tailor, and I don't like to sleep with ugly men.

I thought of becoming a shoemaker too. I have watched them lay out their tool pouches with nails and stitching thread. But where would such work lead to? Only to the next pair of shoes. I can take more shoes off the dead than a shoemaker can fix. I have done that. I have waited alongside the road where bodies are dumped for pickup by garbage trucks. When no soldiers or whites were looking, I slipped up and removed shoes and sandals and ran off with them. Spreading a cloth on the ground, I sold these new shoes to other refugees. Now and then I have to pay Zairian soldiers for the privilege of selling things on the road, but that's all right, because by the end of the day I manage to have enough francs to buy myself something to eat and save enough so the next day I can buy food to sell.

Sometimes I get other clothes at the body dump. Today I could have taken a bright orange tracksuit for myself, but it was too big and torn. And there was the problem of removing it from the body before getting caught. So I took a few T-shirts to sell, that's all.

Around my neck, along with my radio, I still wear a crucifix given to me by my mother. She liked them better than the amulets of witch doctors. I can't remember what she looked like, except that she was tall and wore bright kerchiefs around her head. The crucifix is supposed to mean God, but what does that mean? To me it's the only thing I have of my mother, that's what it means.

I want to sell radio parts and watch parts and wristbands.

Maybe I'll become a witch doctor, like one of those who cure diseases with little grains laid out in wooden bowls on a mat. Or a butcher. There's a hut in camp where they sell cow buttocks and heads with the horns still attached. Whole clans buy them and have feasts and get drunk and fight over things that happened long ago back on their hill. I like the meaty smell of a butcher shop, but the look of blood frightens me—thick and red and oily. I feel it oozing down my face from a body on top of me. It makes me remember the church. I don't want to be a butcher.

In the camp market I saw grenades being sold alongside fruit and pieces of meat. A merchant told me that the French gave grenades to FAR, who are now selling them to civilians who want them for protection. The fruit cost as much and the meat more than the grenades.

I heard about it, so today I went out to see for myself how FAR troops were leaving their past behind them. They were accepting the RPF offer to go home. On their way to the border, they tore up their old identity cards. The road into Rwanda was littered with paper that whirled around like leaves. It made me wonder where I'll go next. Not home, not Uganda or Tanzania, because they're all too near. Maybe I'll go to Kenya or Angola or as far as Zimbabwe. Maybe I'll stay right here in camp. If I want to sniff again, I can get it here and I can make money here and have pretty much what I want. I see boys like me prowling around too. We're like wild dogs trailing a herd of antelope. When wild dogs are hungry, they pick out a weak young antelope and bring it down. I have flesh on my bones these days as I look across the camp and see the cooking fires blowing their smoke toward the volcanoes over there. They say one or more of the volcanoes might erupt. Let them. Nyiragongo and Nyamuragira, just go ahead and erupt. Somehow I'll survive.

I don't mind the camp so much, but many people do. More than anything they want to go home. They sit around a fire and tell stories about how beautiful their own hill is. Of course, they don't go home because they're afraid of being murdered if they do. Today, some whites mounted bullhorns on trucks and drove around telling us it was safe to leave. I suppose it would be safe for me, a Tutsi boy.

Today I noticed an aid station over there that flies the flag of Rwanda. So I wandered over to see what kind of business I could do. Under a tent was a row of benches with sick people sitting on them and nurses busy with one thing or another. I glanced at the adjoining tent. Medical tables were inside there and a lot of shelves with medicines lined up in them. I didn't see anyone in there, so I slipped from the sickroom into the tent with the medicines. I didn't know what they were, but within seconds I was stuffing little plastic bottles into my pockets.

When someone called out sharply, I whirled around to see a nurse at the entrance staring at me.

I knew her immediately for Agnès. It was Agnès all right. Agnès who hid me in the rafters, who let the man have her so I could live. For an instant I nearly rushed forward and threw my arms around her. Agnès! I felt my eyes blur and my whole face lift in joy.

"Innocent?" She was squinting as if she couldn't believe it. "Innocent!"

Plunging bottles into my pockets, I turned to sweep up more bottles from a shelf. Holding a bunch of them, I took a few steps toward Agnès. Watching what I did, she was starting to frown. Yet as I stepped closer, she smiled and suddenly opened her arms wide to take me in. We were almost the same height by then, so I had to duck under her arms. With my elbow I pushed her aside and ran out of there.

Later I placed the bottles along the road and began to sell them. They sold quickly, even though the buyers had little idea what they were. They knew it was white medicine, that's all, so it was important and might cure them of something. I made a big profit on that medicine, and within an hour not one bottle was left. I looked at the ground where they had stood in a row, and for a few moments what I saw was the face of the woman who had saved my life. I might have thanked her for that. Sure, but she might have called for help and taken away the medicine.

Counting my money, I wondered how to use it. That was almost the best part of making money. But for a moment I saw her face again instead of the franc notes. I remembered peering down from the rafters at the bourgmestre's grinning face and her frightened one.

Well, think about it, I told myself.

There was nothing I could have done today. She'd want the

bottles back, whatever I said. I couldn't pass up good fortune even to tell her how grateful I was for what she did. The world can't wait for such things.

With this money I'll buy something to sell and then buy more and sell more and buy and sell until someday I'll find Agnès again and take her to that restaurant in Goma, where we'll eat shrimp from Kenya and Belgian sugar and drink foreign wine together and speak of the old days at home before the bourg-mestre had her, when my family was still alive.

PROSPER

IT WAS GOOD in that camp. More than seventy agencies from around the world brought in food and other supplies by airplane. That's *seventy*. Bulldozers prepared ground for new buildings. Three big Red Cross tents held tons of things, including beans and jerricans filled with cooking oil. And there were nine circular tanks containing 800,000 liters of water, chlorinated. That's 800,000. When I heard this, I tried to imagine how much land you could water with those nine tanks. In that big camp we had hospitals, orphanages, latrines, warehouses, food stations, markets, a few schools, and churches. We had restaurants in huts along the road that served banana beer, sugarcane, and sorghum porridge. I went to one called the Café Ituze run by a fellow named Jean Ndahago and had a beer. There were also small adjoining camps where the government of Zaire allowed us to train our young militiamen and turn them into real soldiers. You could hear guns going off when they practiced their drills. Weapons came from the French through the Goma airport, so I was told. I was also told that our men were in contact with Hutu troops in Burundi, so maybe someday they'd mount a joint attack against the Tutsi. Meanwhile, thousands and thousands of us waited for things to get better.

I knew a lot about that camp. I should. I lived there for more than a year and expected to live there a lot longer. Instead, the camp was closed by the new Tutsi government and their foreign allies. I have heard whites deny they were Tutsi allies, but just like the Tutsi they never tell the truth. We have had enough of foreigners, except when they offer food and water. Otherwise they bring nothing but confusion. Most of the time we have no idea what they mean. We have dealt with Germans and then Belgians and French and now these strange Americans, and who knows what any of them mean? Yet when people say bitter things about the Americans and their lack of help, I wonder if we're being fair to them. What I say is this: The Americans have their own problems. If they can't bring a water-filtration system over here, maybe they have a water problem of their own and that's the reason. Maybe they have epidemics.

When people don't help you, it's not always their fault. That's what I used to tell Pauline. Last time I saw her she wore a striped blouse, a scarf around her head, and carried a woven basket. In the bright sling of a cotton khanga she carried a baby on her back. That was child number ten. She left with ten children.

Not long after she left, we were moved to a smaller, dirtier camp and the Zairian government closed the old one. Our own militiamen herded us into this area about ten miles west of Goma.

They called it Camp Mugunga and from the way they warned us and waved their guns around, we understood we better do as they ordered and stay right there. The other day a fellow was claiming that the new Tutsi government never killed people who returned home, so he asked us why we shouldn't go back. Yesterday he was found dumped in a latrine with his throat cut.

This happened even though the camp is patrolled by all kinds of soldiers. Troops from Zaire walk up and down the paths along with men from Holland and Switzerland, from Benin and Guinea and Cameroon. You can't look anywhere without seeing a rifle slung across someone's back, yet bad things happen anyway. Three days ago in another part of camp some fellows fired guns into the air while they were drinking. It caused a panic and fifty or sixty people, mostly children, were trampled underfoot.

I don't like this Camp Mugunga. We don't get enough to eat because the relief agencies have backed away. They want to force us out of here. They want us to go home so they can go home too. Yesterday I watched some little boys in the hospital courtyard picking through waste in a latrine. They were looking for kernels of undigested corn to collect in plastic bags. When they got enough kernels, they washed them in buckets of rainwater and cooked them in pots. When I saw them doing such a poor thing I thought of Pauline's children, but all of them left with her weeks ago and if I know Pauline they're taken care of.

Only a few meters away from where the boys cooked their corn, just across the border, some relief teams had prepared food in big garbage cans. You could see it steaming, you could smell it. To get that food, however, the boys would have to leave camp and cross over into Rwanda again. The new Tutsi government won't let them go back into Zaire once they cross. They'd have to go home, probably through the Inkamira transit center. I watched the boys watching the UN trucks travel back and forth at the border. I know what they were thinking. They could go over and eat from the big cans, then run back. Only they'd never make it back and they knew it. So they kept picking kernels of corn out of human waste and watching. They were afraid of Tutsi murdering them in the transit center.

The new government radio says that the Red Cross and UN have promised escorts for Hutu who return home. That doesn't convince everyone. Those boys won't budge, and I say good for them. Neither will I. I won't give Tutsi the satisfaction of killing me on the road. I'm a Hutu of a good clan and my land is on a good hill.

I'm not happy with our young militiamen, who seem to forget their family and clan ties. They think only of themselves. Smoking cigarettes, they guard stacks of food that once belonged to the relief organizations. They never take orders from whites, which is something I like, and they won't let the UN write down information about us or register us on paper, which is something I like too. They scare the relief people. They warn if the relief people interfere, the whole camp will go bad, become wild and collapse, and thousands will die. These boys stand up to the world, but they don't do it to help us, they do it to control things for themselves. Most of them are arrogant young fools who bicker among themselves and drink too much because nobody can stop them. I'm embarrassed by them. Their ancestors should not know how they are behaving.

So Pauline left. She's gone, and I miss her. The nurse Agnès who helped us has left too. I heard she went to Kigali. We're told by the new government radio that leaving is the right thing to do. But I say leaving means death at the hands of the RPF. I say what I believe. I won't leave, because you can't believe a thing the Tutsi say. Some families remain here because they claim Jesus tells them they must. They would be willing to leave if Jesus told them they could. Others brag that they're going to leave, but when the day moves out of morning into afternoon, they untie the goods they'd tied at sunrise and start fires under their three-legged pots. That means they'll eat and stay until tomorrow. They don't even know they won't leave tomorrow or the next day or the next. Some people think they'll go home when they don't even have the strength to walk a half mile for a bucket of water. They're too weak, so they drink brown water from little depressions in the mud, and yet they swear that tomorrow they'll leave for home.

If I decided to leave tomorrow, I'd leave tomorrow, because that's who I am, an old farmer from a good clan on a good hill. I'd think only of my crops back home. I'd hope the millet would be nearly seven feet tall at the end of the dry season. I'd think of pineapple, of planting sweet potatoes in a low plot and cassava in a high.

So here I am alone, without Pauline and the children. I see things I never thought I'd see. This morning some of the aid workers—I don't know whether they were white or not—they got lazy or tired and just tossed the corpses of those who died overnight there on the road rather than in a neat pile in the ditch for pickup as usual. Some of the bodies were run over by trucks. A few were run over many times until they didn't even look like dead people. I felt myself shivering from the sight of it. We're not animals, I told myself. This is not the way to treat people. I would not want my father and his father to see such a thing.

Later I felt myself shivering even more, and after that I spent a long time in the latrine. I felt thirsty and sick enough to vomit. By that afternoon I knew I had cholera. All of us know the signs, so if we get it we know right away. I knew where the hospital was and I could go there and get one of those drips in my arm, but I didn't want to go there.

Suddenly my head was as clear as it had been before Pauline left. I wanted to go home. It was the strongest feeling I ever had in my life. After arguing so long with Pauline about going home and standing in the road waving good-bye to her and warning her to be careful because going home was foolish, I realized that what I had wanted all the time was what she was doing. I wanted to go home. And I wanted to see Pauline again. I wanted to invite her to my house and the children too. We'd all be together again, I told myself as I was walking across the border. Once across, I looked back in surprise. I had gone across without being aware of it. At least no one paid any attention to me, so I wouldn't be hauled into the Inkamira transit center. I had just simply crossed over. Then I felt glad because I was going home. After walking a short distance, I sat down because cramps in my stomach took my breath away. Watch out old man, I told myself. To get old is to get robbed. Don't let them rob you of a single thing, not a thing, if you have anything. I couldn't remember if I had money left because my head was whirling and my tongue felt as big as a cooked potato and as hot.

I had to go again, so I got to my feet and went into the weeds, where I stayed a long time. At last, trying to rise, I stumbled and nearly fell. What I wanted more than anything was a drink of water. I had to have it. So I went farther into the bush and pushed through weeds and fronds a long time until coming to a mud hole. Flinging myself down, I drank from it and drank. That was what I needed, a good drink. But cramps made me retch and my sight went in and out so that I couldn't see clearly. Then I vomited up the muddy water.

Even though I feel weak, I'm going to get up and keep walking. But for a while I'll just stay here and rest and think of planting a second crop of beans, maybe some maize. Is that the moon coming out? Then I'll rest longer, even though I have a long way to go. They say if you last three days with the cholera, you live. So I'll stay right here a while longer, because I need my strength to walk all the way home.

AGNÈS

I HAVE COME to Kigali because the Ministry of Rehabilitation wants to know about the state of health in the refugee camps. Our doctor was asked to participate in these sessions but he would never leave his clinic for anything except another clinic, nor would the chief nurse leave him for anything except an argument and without him how could she argue? So they sent me to represent the Goma refugee area.

The capital did not yet have full telephone service or electricity in some neighborhoods, but to me it was a magical place after such a long time in the camps. I walked down the streets in wonder and surprise. Some people carried briefcases, a lot of them wore Western clothes, and most of them looked healthy. Buses honked, policemen blew whistles at intersections, hawkers yelled out the price of fruit and vegetables. Only a hundred kilometers lay between Kigali and Goma, yet it seemed as far as the sun from the earth.

But after a few days, I began to see something else in the city. I noticed the same look in almost every passing face. The more I studied people, the more I saw in their eyes a deep sadness. No matter what the rest of a face told me, the eyes carried a terrible message. Every day, Hutu and Tutsi, we passed one another in the secret knowledge that our thoughts had us wading through the blood of a million bodies.

At night in my dormitory room I lay awake, entangled in memory. I imagined people plodding down an endless road. I saw particular faces coming toward me. Sometimes a family would stop and furiously accuse me of living while they were dead. What I learned in those long nights was the stubborn way that the dead have of holding onto us. They aren't buried in a field or in a ditch, they are buried in the heart.

Sometimes I saw Innocent standing alone under an acacia tree, offering vials of medicine for sale. Perhaps he was lost to the living. Often at night, thinking of him and the dead faces, I cried myself to sleep.

But the mornings belonged to the waking city. I stood at the window and admired the steady pulse of bicycles and cars. I watched people striding along in bright colors, going somewhere important to them, and I told myself to join in and let the past go. I must let memory fall back into the shadows of my mind.

We have a lot of meetings here in the Ministry of Rehabilitation. They are held in a cement-block building with a tin roof and walls still pockmarked from bullet holes. Inside there's a long table, folding chairs, and a watercooler. At first I wondered about attending such meetings. Perhaps I was too young and untrained. Yet looking at people going into other buildings for other meetings, I noticed that many of them were my age. The harvest of death has left us with a young country.

Foreign journalists sometimes come to listen. Sitting along the wall, wiping sweat from their faces with starched handkerchiefs, they scribble notes and stare from the windows as if bored by talk of refugee camps. Sometimes I'm bored too. Many of the participants talk only of themselves or of technical things that show off their knowledge. Yesterday about twenty of us had to discuss inoculation procedures, vaccine refrigerators, liquid crystal monitors, single or double racks, EPI portable steam sterilizers.

Attending this discussion was Stephen Mazimpaka, a deputy minister of the Ministry of Rehabilitation. Although he wore the uniform of an RPF major, the thick lenses of his wire-rimmed eyeglasses and his quiet manner didn't fit his reputation for being a guerrilla fighter of renown. Everyone knew that he had led the Tutsi invasion across the Ugandan border and that his troops had been the first to enter Kigali.

So far the deputy minister had showed more of an interest in camp life than medical equipment. Now he broke impatiently into the technical discussion.

"Do you have any *practical* ideas for improving clinics?" he asked with a glance around the table.

No one volunteered.

"Let me warn you." He put both hands flat on the table. "If we don't learn from one another, we'll do what Africans have done for decades. We'll sit back and let the whites tell us what to do."

So I said, "Lockers."

Everyone looked at me. Fumbling for words, at last I suggested that hospital wards would function better if there were storage lockers for patients. Otherwise, the aisles got clogged with their goods and then there was theft to worry about. Getting their goods off the floor would also release space for more beds.

Deputy Minister Mazimpaka wrote something on a pad.

My suggestion was followed by others until a spirited session was underway. After the meeting ended, the deputy minister came up and invited me to have coffee with him. I noticed two other women frowning and whispering. They had already shown an interest in him by giggling at things he said, although Stephen Mazimpaka was not a funny man. It was common knowledge that years ago he had vowed to remain single until the Tutsi of Uganda returned to Rwanda. Of course, that condition had been met, partly because of his own efforts, so what now? I think the women there were curious about that.

When he took me to a small restaurant and found us a table in the far corner, my cheeks felt warm. I was a little breathless when I spoke. He asked me about the refugee camps, although I suspected that he was quite familiar with them. That didn't matter. The intent way he looked at me made me want to keep talking as long as possible. When he asked if I'd like another cup of coffee, I said yes.

He told me I spoke excellent French and apologized for his. Not only had he been raised on Ugandan English, but he found languages difficult to learn. He smiled after making this confession. I felt myself smile back. Tutsi were supposed to be reticent, detached, arrogant, but Stephen Mazimpaka was none of these. Suddenly, I didn't feel the need to talk so much.

He asked me to describe dengue fever. I gave him a list of symptoms. He asked me was it true that malaria could resist treatment. I told him that in Rwanda a half-dozen strains didn't respond to chloroquine. He asked me to go back with him to his house.

He asked me that in the same tone of voice used for the other questions.

Tutsi cunning. That's what I told myself. So his interest had turned from refugee camps to me. In spite of his deceptive way of asking me, however, I liked him for asking. Had he been a Hutu and just asked me directly, I might have said yes. But I didn't answer his question, and he didn't ask it again. My refusal to answer made me feel bold.

"Let me ask you something," I said. "If the pain felt separately by Hutu and Tutsi was shared, do you think they'd work together without fear?"

Searching his face, I added quickly before he could reply, "I see you don't."

"The fear runs too deep on both sides. And I think it will for a while longer."

"How long is a while longer?"

"Five, maybe ten years."

"It won't take that long," I declared.

We were silent, each looking down at the table. I was shocked by my insolence, shaken by vague feelings.

Finally he said, "I like your hope. I feel it too sometimes, though I'm embarrassed by it."

I looked up. "Embarrassed?"

"Yes. I wonder if hoping is foolish."

No man had ever spoken so openly to me. Then he surprised me with another question. "Do you mind that I'm a Tutsi?"

What did he mean? Did I mind if he felt superior? "Why should I mind?" I asked cautiously.

"It's easy to mind. We're different. Do you mind that we're different, is what I mean."

"Do you mind that I'm a Hutu?"

"No."

"How can you be a Tutsi and not mind?" I asked rather sharply.

"We don't need to let the difference matter."

I wanted to believe him, though he was a cunning Tutsi.

"Even if it did matter," he said, "we could go past it."

"How?"

"I don't know. Somehow. We could go past it. We could let that part of ourselves go to sleep."

Suddenly I just let myself believe him. "We could let that part of ourselves go to sleep," I repeated.

Reaching out, he touched my hand. In the camp I had known a man, an aid worker from Ghana, who used to meet me in the clinic now and then at midnight. We had said little to each other as we used a cot in the supply room. That was the last time I had been with a man. I realized I had just put one hand against my blouse so that my fingers were feeling the amulet that hung from a cord around my neck. The woman who needed food for all her children had given it to me in camp. I wore it for a joke because I knew that such a thing would never get me the right man. Yet I touched it through the cotton before drawing my hand away.

Staring hard at Stephen Mazimpaka, I said, "Yes, I will." Unable to go on while looking at him, I turned slightly as if to watch someone coming into the restaurant. "I mean, yes, I'll come to your house."

So I went to his house with a courtyard lined with flowerpots and a ceiling fan in the bedroom.

Stephen has the high cheekbones and pointed ears and a smooth, rounded forehead that we Hutu as children had been taught were features belonging to evil Tutsi kings. But his eyeglasses have thick, black rims that give him the humble and serious look of a priest. He laughs at the idea of being a priest. Stephen laughs easily and that's when I see in his unguarded face, the sweet expression of a gentle boy.

Stephen is not a gentle lover, though, and for that I am grateful. That first time in bed under the ceiling fan, I was overwhelmed by his need and it pulled me along into a windstorm of need of my own making. I felt the warrior in him. I knew the soldier who led troops into the jungle and without hesitation killed the enemy. Leading me into a wild darkness, he frightened me into forgetting everything, into feeling nothing but desire and more desire and more. When I entered into such a place, he took what he wanted from me and let me take what I wanted from him.

It has been that way ever since.

We go our separate ways in the physical act of love, but sleep in each other's arms. I have not gone back to Goma because of Stephen. Wanting to be close to him, I have found work as a nurse in a Kigali hospital. Nothing is more important in my life than our life together. I no longer lie awake thinking of the dead, but fall asleep and wake up next to him. We make each other free. I love him.

STEPHEN

SOMETIMES I WONDER if Agnès catches me staring at the Hutu with hatred as I recall something horrible that happened during the genocide; if she wonders am I ready to sacrifice her people for the satisfaction of Tutsi honor; if in these moments of doubt she feels there's no way our minds can follow our bodies into a lasting union. I don't know what she is thinking. In the old days a man and a woman knew what each other was thinking. They came from the same hill, the same clan, the same tribe. But Agnès and I come only part way out of the shadows. Somehow we must cross the gap between our traditions, go beyond differences, put the bad thoughts to sleep. That's what I told her and what I believe, yet sometimes I can't even get beyond the daily problems of my work. I hold her in my arms until she falls asleep, but I don't sleep too because one thing after another drifts into my mind like brush clogging a river. When one load breaks free and goes downstream, another follows it, and another.

One of our country's dilemmas is too little land, too many people returning. Ever since going to Akagera, I've been haunted by the idea of resettling immigrants in national parks. Every day more of them encroach on park land because we've not yet resolved the issue. I have not accepted the facile solution offered by some of our politicians, which is to let go of the past to meet the demands of the present. Not when I consider the savage beauty of our fathers' sacred land being overrun by endless herds of cattle. They're now thirty or forty miles within park boundaries. That's the latest report.

I see in my mind the rolling savannahs dotted with thundering herds of topi and troops of zebras. I see lions yawning, giraffes leaning into the tops of trees, wildebeests snorting and bucking, tiny white birds pecking insects off the backs of rhinos. Must the world of our fathers go? I can't imagine such a loss, yet droves of Hutu and Tutsi from neighboring countries are entering Rwanda every day to seek a home. They want their place in the sun, and they're willing to push aside buffalo and leopards to get it.

I understand that since our people have been leaving Uganda with their cattle, the price of beef in Kampala has nearly doubled. They need our meat in Uganda, we need their money. How much better it would be for us to transact business with an African neighbor than accept aid from Europeans.

A white journalist said to me the other day, "I wonder if you know that never in world history have so many people been killed with handheld weapons in such a short period of time than were killed here, right here, old man, in your own country, during a few months in 1994."

"Why did you say that?" I demanded. From the look on his face I knew my tone of voice had frightened him. Although a deputy minister of government, I still wore combat fatigues.

"Come now, old man," he said with a shrug, "I just thought you'd like to know."

"Never again speak to me." I clapped one hand against my

holstered gun. "I've used a handheld weapon many times. I'd have no trouble using it once more. Never again speak to me."

I know why he made such a tactless remark. He was angry. After all, to make sure that Africa behaves, the West has spent a lot of money. Our region of Central Africa has always been chosen for experimental social programs. We fit the requirements. World organizations can rely on a network of good roads, a fairly efficient phone system, adequate utilities. Perhaps most important, our small size allows the impact of aid to be quickly estimated.

Surely we're too dependent on foreign grants and favors. Now we must help ourselves, whether some politicians like it or not. The truth is we're no longer trusted to behave correctly. Because of the last few terrible years, Europeans consider us madmen, or at least troublemakers. Well, I say, let them. Instead of dwelling on our mistakes, profound though they are, I say let us remember that our country is very beautiful, that our children deserve a better life. But as Agnès points out when I talk this way, to do anything for ourselves we Hutu and Tutsi must learn to trust each other. Can we do that? Such a question keeps me awake.

As do other questions. How can we cooperate with foreigners we deeply distrust? I dislike the UN. I will never forget how they stood at the side of the road and looked on, while many thousands of our people were hacked to death at checkpoints. Now they censor us for our poor justice system. It is indeed poor, and we must begin again in the humblest way to reform it. For one thing, we need typewriters and enough paper to prepare legal documents. Along with finding space for courts, we must train both lawyers and judges. To show good faith, we have opened our inadequate prisons to foreign scrutiny by inviting in human-rights monitors. But the UN has reacted by condemning us for the faults we acknowledge. Even so, our government has agreed to support an international war-crimes tribunal and not to take prosecution of genocidal criminals into our own hands. We have promised, furthermore, not to indulge in summary executions. Yet our forbearance is seen by some observers as a deceitful way of holding innocent men in prison.

Meanwhile, critics have declared our new administration inadequate for conducting the business of a real government. Can't that be said of any rebels who have unseated an entrenched regime and started their own? It takes time to shape embryonic resources into mature systems. Rome wasn't built in a day. Neither were Paris and London.

But the world seems as remote and watchful as a vulture, while we try to rehabilitate our country. It's clear what the international community is thinking. How is small, impoverished Rwanda going to provide normal lives for uprooted thousands?

It's true that our Land Dispute Committee has failed to work out a return-and-eviction policy. Both Hutu and Tutsi come home to find squatters on their homesteads. Land-grabbers evade the law by being absent on the day scheduled for their eviction, or crippled old people are left on the property so their removal would be dishonorable, or friends merely stand guard with rifles and halt the dispossession. Only a few evictions actually succeed.

I commit myself to the law at four in the morning. It's such an easy thing to do in the silence and darkness. Equality under the law. But in the light of day, what does it mean?

What happens when a Tutsi refugee comes home to find his land occupied by a Hutu? The Hutu must leave, of course, but by our law he can first harvest his crop. I go over that law in my mind a dozen times a day, because I'm telling people that they must allow a man who may have killed members of their family to enjoy the profits of a harvest on land that's not his but theirs.

On the other hand, Hutu who simply remained on their land throughout the crisis, unfazed by the hatred and violence sur-rounding them, have been arrested on trumped-up charges, or abducted or even murdered.

We should build temporary housing for returnees, but with what money? With what money?

Lying awake, I think of Tutsi screaming "Traitor!" at me. I think of Hutu yelling "Unjust!" Right and wrong come whirling and twisting at me like bats.

Turning to Agnès, I put my fingers on her warm thigh as if to steady myself. I'm careful not to wake her. We're going to marry next month in the Cathedral of Saint Michel here in Kigali. We'll get our clothes at Chezzozo, a wedding shop that recently reopened. I'll wear the uniform of a colonel and Agnès a ruffled white gown of a Brussels design. There will be music, clapping and drums, African rhythms, Catholic hymns. We'll have our reception in a club that has a generator for electricity. A disc jockey I know is going to play Eric Clapton and Ethio-pian dance music. We'll celebrate with Fanta orange and local beer and Moroccan wine.

"Who is satisfied with his own wisdom is not wise" is an old saying. Then I should be very wise. Soldiering in the bush was far easier than governing. I lie awake thinking about an incom-prehensible future, and Agnès must sense it, because sometimes she rolls toward me and lays her hand on my chest for a few moments before rolling away and going back to sleep. I carry the warmth of that hand into long, dark hours of worry.

Last night I dreamed of our upcoming wedding. There are many weddings these days in our country. People hope for a new chance at life. In the old days our two families would negotiate a bride-price and invoke ancestral spirits for good luck. My father would bless a pot of beer. There would be a major sacrifice to Lyangombe, spirit of fecundity, performed by Agnès's family. Her relatives would give utensils, clothes, and beer to my family. In today's chaotic world there's no transfer of bride-price.

I'm not accustomed to the easy communicative way of a Hutu woman in the household. Usually a Tutsi woman is a quiet, superstitious, aloof caretaker. Agnès sings in the morning, walks naked through the house, comes up behind me and throws her arms around my waist. She gives me her thoughts like carelessly picked flowers. What about our children? As in any Rwandan household, of course, I'll have the main responsibility for discipline. But which way, Hutu or Tutsi, will our children lean? I hope neither way. Is that possible? Perhaps hope really is foolish. I think of that at four in the morning. I think of small things and big things. I think that recovery of a nation means health centers and schools, the printing of textbooks, the repair of electrical grids, the introduction of desks and other equipment into offices, health tips on the radio. We must dig up land mines and find a location for cultural events. We must do such things, but with what money?

How many questions are there? They flit through the black air until the world seems to be tilting. Reaching out for balance, I touch Agnès ever so gently. I'm careful not to wake her. The other day she asked me why I still wore a uniform. I had no answer, but I've learned to look into her large, honest eyes and see a sensible answer reflected in them. I must come out of the bush soon and leave the uniform behind.

At four in the morning I stand at a podium and take questions from an audience made up of our own people. I say we must separate génocidaires from other refugees and bring them to trial. I say we need a schedule for refugee camp closures—perhaps one every three or four months. We must set up transit centers for returnees. We must allot them food and supplies for the first months of their return. We must train our RPF troops to help in repatriation. We must set up local boards to deal with land tenure and property disputes, which in the old days had been the function of bourgmestres. We must do this, we must do that.

Long into the night I lecture the shadowy audience, reaching out now and then to touch my beloved Agnès until at last I too fall asleep.

Pauline

PROSPER TOLD ME I was a fool to leave camp. So did the Interahamwe with their bullhorns blaring at us from trucks, "Who leaves this camp is a fool, a maniac!" And so insisted some women I met who had children of their own to protect.

I dreaded meeting them in food lines because of the fear and confusion they brought along with their baskets to fill. One woman claimed that Hutu returnees were being injected with a vaccination that made them lose their minds. A man came back to camp after such a vaccination and he was crazy. These injections were given forcibly at night at the Inkamira transit center or if not there, then back at the home commune. Another woman agreed. A number of children in Goma General Hospital had been injected and every one of them had died.

Another woman swore that the Tutsi government had set up torture houses in the countryside. They were hidden so people didn't know of their existence until taken there.

Another Hutu farm woman, speaking like a grand Tutsi queen, said that she might leave camp, but only after returnees had come back and reported on the situation at home to her satisfaction. Six or seven of these women nodded wisely in agreement. Meanwhile, declared another, prostitution in the camp must stop. There were too many unplanned pregnancies and cases of AIDS. I agreed with that. Food for a week lasted only two days, complained another woman, and I certainly agreed with that too.

But I didn't agree with them about staying. There was too much death in camp for me. When someone died, a great flood of deaths seemed to follow. The contagion of death spread as if it were a disease in itself. I would not let death overtake me and the children, no, not without trying to escape.

So one morning I gathered them together and walked to the main road. Rain had washed out the campfires. Barefoot children wearing adult shirts that fell below their knees were huddling in piles of matted elephant grass for warmth. Poor things.

At the road a woman was selling potatoes she had stacked neatly in a series of pyramids. We exchanged smiles, and she seemed happy that I liked the pretty arrangement.

I led the children along until we came to a roadside barber who was giving haircuts less than fifty meters away from the corpse of a baby left in the ditch. Looking at my children, I figured half of them needed haircuts, along with myself. Taking out what money I had left, I told the barber that if he moved another fifty meters away from the body, he could cut the hair of five children and one adult. So he did. When he had finished, I lined up the children and inspected them. They looked clean and healthy, all except the second-from-youngest, who had a deep cough.

Then I went to see Prosper and told him we were going to the bus stop.

"Are you really leaving?" He had tears in his eyes.

"Come with us."

He shook his head, then gripped my hands and pleaded, "Don't go, please don't go. I'll never see you again."

"If these children die, it will happen on the road or at home. We won't die here."

"You won't get farther than the transit center," he claimed. I had to pry my hands free of his.

"Come with us," I said once again but without hope. Then turning, I collected the children and walked toward the UNHCR bus stop. I knew that UNHCR meant The United Nations High Commission for Refugees. Around here anything you knew could help and sometimes could even save your life. I knew the UNHCR bus was for people who agreed to go through the transit center. That day the UNHCR bus was almost full, not like other days when few had the courage to board. A smiling white woman came up the aisle and encouraged us to go. If we didn't change our minds, she told us, we would have a nice surprise. I gave her a frown. Aid people didn't believe we wanted to go home. They thought we liked it in their camps because we were fed and didn't have to work. They thought that's how we lived our lives. The smiling woman didn't know us at all.

The children laughed and shouted when the bus pulled away. Some of them had never been in a vehicle before. Some had rarely seen a road except the one through camp and the tiny paths between blue tents and cooking fires. It was a short ride. The bus stopped in a dirt courtyard surrounded by wooden poles that supported fluorescent lights. They were turned on because it was almost evening. I recalled what the women said: vaccinations were given only at night.

Leaving the bus, we were told to line up in front of the transit center buildings. Aid workers came around with clipboards and asked for information. A worker had trouble with me because of so many children and my poor knowledge of some of their personal histories. I was promised a one-month allotment of beans, maize, salt, and cooking oil, along with plastic sheeting, blankets, and seeds for planting. One half I would get before leaving here and the other half at home from UN officials in the commune. I wanted more because of so many children, but the aid people had their rules.

"Are you going to give my children vaccinations?" I asked, but none of them spoke Kinyarwanda well enough to understand my question and my French wasn't good enough to ask another way and actually I was afraid to know. I told the children to grasp their amulets and wait.

Inside one of the huts we were told to sit on benches until called up. We were called up and stood in front of a white doctor. He wore a green T-shirt and the thing they listen with around his neck. For a moment I feared he might give us the deadly vaccination, but all he did was put the thing against each of our chests and listen and wave us on. Except I was given medicine for the boy with the deep cough. So this is what they do here? Cut off women's breasts, disembowel children? I wanted to tell Prosper, because maybe he would change his mind, but there was no way of going back.

In a tent within a compound enclosed by razor-barbed wire we waited three days until our turn came to board another bus. I can't remember the trip except for seeing a man yank on the neck of a reluctant goat and a smiling group of children who stood alongside the road and waved at my children, who waved back. Maybe I remembered nothing because I thought only of what we would find at home. I saw in my mind a mess of charred wood and a pile of broken bricks.

My own four children would remember home, but not the others who came from other places. And then there was Pacifique. What would he remember?

I was overjoyed to find our house intact, although someone had taken Sylvestre's tools and most of our furniture. All the livestock was gone, of course. In a short time we'd run out of food, so our fields had to be weeded and planted immediately. I needed help for that, and our first night home I couldn't sleep because of it.

The next morning my cousins and two uncles appeared in the rugo, carrying bowls of food. At last I sat down and cried. I had cried after losing Pacifique on the road more than a year ago and then cried after finding him again. Otherwise I couldn't remember crying. Now I sat against the wall and sobbed until my stomach ached, while my cousins and uncles and all my children waited patiently for the fit to pass.

So we got home without vaccinations or torture and all of us alive. I remember Prosper once saying, "Even if you make it home, just wait until the RPF comes around!" A contingent came around one day a couple of weeks after we returned. I suppose they didn't expect to find contraband items on one woman and ten children, so they glanced at the rugo and went away. Maybe, as the government says, they are watching over us rather than watching us, but I would never say anything that hopeful.

When a woman comes to ask my advice and have me read

chicken guts and predict her future, I do it without mentioning politics.

Nothing on our hill stays the same from one day to the next. Some people return to burned-out farms. Others have lost almost nothing. In passing on the road, they must then decide how to greet one another. Sometimes they stop and embrace. Other times they barely nod or glare, or start to cry.

Some returnees are Hutu who fled from the hill merely because others were fleeing. They are welcomed back as much by Tutsi as by their own clansmen. People seem to understand how easy it is to be fooled into losing everything. The other day I heard in the market that some of the killers have also returned. They walk around as free as they please, even though Tutsi survivors have come back too and notice them in the market. They are not welcomed by anyone. Sooner or later I suspect that something will happen to them. I like to stay clear of the market, because even though buying and selling take place there as usual, the air seems to be waiting, the way it does before a storm. I don't want the children caught up in anything.

It's hard to say what might happen next, even for someone like me who can read a chicken's innards. For example, the other night Pierre Kalimwinjabo, a local Hutu farmer, was badly wounded and his wife and three of his children, ranging in age from five to nine, were murdered by fellows who came around. Pierre claims his family was attacked because he had accused someone of being a génocidaire. His assailants were former Hutu soldiers of FAR. But that's according to Pierre, who admits he's not sure. Now he's going to move with a surviving daughter to a village near a military post.

About a week after our return, I called Pacifique to me and sat him down under the shade tree. I asked him how he was.

As usual, he smiled for an answer.

"Do you remember being here before?" I asked him.

"I think so."

Without pointing to the hill opposite, I looked over there. "Do you remember what happened before?"

He nodded.

I waited for him to say more, but when he didn't, I said, "Come here." When he scooted over, I hugged him. "Do you feel like you're home?"

He nodded, but I didn't see the same answer in his eyes. In his eyes I saw nothing but what I suppose hope looks like.

SILAS

FEAR DRIVES PEOPLE to do foolish things. Fear of Tutsi revenge drove thousands from our Benaco camp into the Tanzanian wilderness north of there. They ran off looking for the safety of the jungle. What a good idea—the safety of the jungle. Except they could hardly shoulder through such a tangled mass of nothing. Paths were obscured by elephant grass so high that drivers couldn't see through the windshields of their trucks and had to turn back. Thousands of fools squatted out there without food, water, or medicine. If epidemics didn't get them, pneumonia from cold winds and rain surely would or starvation would. In Benaco one clinic I know of had a line of a thousand people in front of it by sunup every day. But out there in the jungle? The fools had to shake mambas and adders out of their blankets in the morning. Some of them counted on a little village called Ntobeye, which had one brick building. Its sole purpose was to store tools that no one could use in such muddy, putrid soil. Local people fled from Ntobeye out of fear of those desperate refugees, then died next to them from exhaustion. Instead of wandering through the jungle in search of bananas, all of those people should have stayed in Benaco and let me lead them.

Of course, I'm not allowed to lead anyone now. The bourgmestre from Kamonyi, my dear friend with whom I was going to grow pyrethrum, decided to cooperate with the Tanzanian police and save himself. Accusing his old friend of being a génocidaire, he got me arrested. They sent a whole squad into my private stockade. My bodyguards, twenty fine young men, threw down their AK-47s and ran away.

I was a good bourgmestre at home in Butare préfecture and later in Camp Benaco. People trusted what I told them. At Benaco I spoke to them through a bullhorn. I gave them good advice when I said to stay right there for their own safety and for their country. How could the Tutsi expect to govern in Rwanda when everyone they might govern was over here in Tanzania? It was our duty to stay put.

When my people complained about camp life, I said to them, "What's wrong with you? People arrive at the refugee camps in Zaire sick and wounded. But you've come here well-fed and in one piece. Why? Because of me. I take care of you. I'll see you don't get cholera. If you become separated from your children, I'll find them. If you need anything, I'll get it for you. So stop complaining. Do you know something? The other night a lion wandered into camp and our women scared it off by beating pots and pans. That's the kind of people we Hutu are. No one can stop us."

A Western journalist came into camp and asked me for an interview. "Do you feel bad about what has happened?" That was his first ignorant question.

I smiled at him and said nothing. Why should I feel bad? Do you feel bad when you squash a mosquito, a fly, a cockroach? When he repeated the question, I told him I was not interested in answering the ignorant questions of foreigners.

True, Camp Benaco was not a pretty place. There was a dirty brown lake nearby and latrines gashed into the bare slopes. But I knew how to keep my people happy until new opportunities surfaced. I knew how to lead.

For example, a man confessed to me that he had killed his sister's three children because her husband was a Tutsi. Good for you, I told him, and ordered a straw for him so we could drink beer together from a communal pot. The story was told throughout Benaco and gave Hutu people confidence. The Tutsi in their own camp sectors kept silent and drew their heads in like turtles.

So what did that white journalist think was at stake? Didn't someone tell him that every living and breathing Tutsi was a foreigner and therefore born to collaborate with the RPF army that invaded us from Uganda? Didn't the white fool know that if the RPF won the war, every Hutu would lose his land? Listen to the radio, I told my people, because it tells the truth about the Tutsi. I told them, "Tutsi troops have eyes that glow in the dark because they smoke great quantities of bhang. They worship Satan and despise Jesus. They're sex fiends and drunken demons."

I ruled from within my walled stockade. I controlled a dozen trucks at the end and every day a man came by to press my pants with a hot iron. Surrounding me, as I have said, were devoted young men equipped with walkie-talkies and AK-47s. The week before I was taken prisoner, I had a pleasant experience. An American organization donated a drink called Gatorade to our sector. We liked it so much that we commandeered a truckload of it and drank case after case. It's very sweet, much like sugarcane in season. That's a good memory to have while rats skitter at night across the cement floor of my prison cell.

I'm being tried here in Arusha, Tanzania, under the auspices of the United Nations International Criminal Tribunal for Rwanda—a fancy name for something misguided and inefficient. Last week in the dock I pled not guilty to a score of charges, among them genocide, murder, crimes against humanity, and that sort of thing. What makes me lucky is the tribunal's mandate that excludes the death sentence. Had I been sent back to Rwanda, they could hang me—that is, if they ever got around to trying me. A trial in Rwanda is not so easy to get. I understand that in theory it would take two hundred years to try the number of detainees rotting now in Rwanda jails. They have about fifty judges who can hear criminal cases, but fifty thousand cases are pending and ninety thousand Hutu have been jailed altogether. In Kigali one prosecutor and his four assistants are supposed to deal with nine thousand cases. It's not surprising that the government talks about improving the system. For example, the Ministry of Justice wants to institute a confession and guilty plea whereby self-confession will result in reduced penalties for some. Obviously, that wouldn't apply to me. Rwanda is critical of the tribunal here in Tanzania because it won't impose the death penalty on people like myself. Things go quicker in Rwanda, if they go at all, because witnesses can make their statements in writing and don't have to be called up at trial.

I don't have a defense lawyer nor do I want one. In the West I understand you must have a defense lawyer, but here it isn't necessary and I feel it isn't a good idea. It's better to say what you think right into their faces and see them wince.

Yesterday, I walked into the small, packed courtroom to the noise of loud jeering from standing room. Seated on low benches were human rights monitors, diplomats, lawyers, journalists, civil-damages claimants, and other fools who have suddenly emerged as experts. The tribunal is understaffed, however. There's only one telephone in the pressroom. Yet the judge has announced that defendants in his court are always innocent until proven guilty. He also guarantees security for witnesses. No filming, sketching, or photographing of witnesses is allowed. The judge is proud of himself.

For all the grand pronouncements about universal justice, this tribunal is a measure of Western justice, not of ours. They are trying to prove that the West needs to police us for our own good.

This is what I know. After the Cold War ended and old alliances no longer applied, the West wanted to reshape its African policy. To do that in Rwanda, the old Hutu regime had to accommodate Tutsi politicians, who once again had the backing of Western embassies. At the time we were suffering economic reverses, especially in the coffee market. I know about coffee. I know about economics. I know about the brutality of Western economics. I know what happened to us when the world price of coffee plunged. Both Hutu and Tutsi needed money desperately and were quite ready to fight each other for what little there was.

So it was war, a conflict based on politics and economics. How unusual is that? We Hutu wanted to defeat our enemy utterly. Is that or is that not the objective of war? Yet today the RPF is looked upon as having been a moral force trying to halt genocide, not a military force trying to win a war that it had started in the first place.

I am a small man in size, but in my head I am a giant. I keep clean-shaven except for my goatee and my shirt is always spotless. At least it was until they threw me into this dirty cell. I am innocent except for one thing. I am guilty of protecting my people.

The prosecutor raised his eyebrows and said to me in the courtroom, "You deny killing anyone?"

"I'm saying I protected my people."

"Did you tell your people to kill cockroaches?"

"Of course. Don't you kill cockroaches when they infest your house?"

"But you meant Tutsi."

"I meant cockroaches. You decide for yourself what a cockroach is."

Westerners talk in the courtroom as if Hutu and Tutsi live on different planets. On my hill they lived next to each other. Sometimes a few generations of intermarriage left them looking alike. Yet they really were separate in their minds. I knew them, every one of them. I knew them all like the grooves in an old Chillington hoe.

A witness from my hill took the stand. A dried-up old Tutsi, he claimed that the militia on our hill had left him for dead. "The bourgmestre thought he had killed me."

"Not true," I answered. "If I had been there and tried to kill him, I would have killed him."

It was a bold thing to say, but then I was trying to impress someone among the spectators. Today I saw Agnès Mujawana-liya seated in the third row. She was as pretty as ever, and as

cunning as ever too, because she was with a tall, bespectacled
Tutsi who wore the uniform of an RPF colonel. I bribed a guard
to find out about them. The colonel was a deputy minister in
Kigali and she was his bride. I wondered if the minister knew
that his wife had once spread her legs for me in her own house.
I was thinking of how to get that word to him, but the two
stayed for an afternoon only and then returned to Kigali. During
the session that Agnès did attend, I felt her eyes on me all the
time. When I turned to glance her way, she didn't shift her gaze
but stared hard at me. What did it mean? Clearly, she had come
to see me. Once I smiled at her Tutsi husband and got for it a
look of intense rage. So he already knew what had happened
between his wife and me. Was that hard look of hers murderous
too? Or passionate? Perhaps she was remembering our one time
together.

I choose to believe that she would like to be with me again.
It's a pleasant thought and makes the time pass. All my life I
have been an active man, but now I sit here or there alone and
wait. My only activity is to answer questions.

This morning the prosecutor wanted to know who was re-
sponsible for the massacres. I told him I had no idea. But it's
reasonable to suspect the RPF of killing their own people just
so they could blame it on us.

This afternoon the prosecutor kept using the word *genocide*.

Finally, I interrupted him. "Please don't call what happened
genocide. Call it massacres committed during a war."

The judge admonished me for speaking out of order.

They try ceaselessly to place blame. They say the main or-
ganizer of the genocide was Colonel Théoneste Bagosora of the
Ministry of Defense. Also Joseph Nzirorera, secretary-general of

MRNDD, in charge of Interahamwe operations, was called a major plotter. So what was I? A minor plotter? I consider myself a major force in what happened, and I'm proud of it. At least around here the guards respect me. One of them told me I'm known as the most defiant and cocksure of their prisoners. Good. I still shout daily through the bars, "Send those Tutsi back to Ethiopia by river, floating with their faces down!"

During questioning I tried to introduce the effect on my country of falling coffee prices. Instead of harassing men of principle like myself, I asked, why doesn't the world turn its attention to what we eat and drink? The judge warned that one more outburst would put me out of the courtroom altogether.

"Do you feel remorse?" I was asked during the interminable questioning.

"No."

"Why not?"

"Why should I? For what?"

The prosecutor turned to another of his favorite themes—the cause of the genocide. "Did you like President Habyarimana?"

"No. He failed us."

"Were you glad that he died?"

"Yes, I was. I hated him because he agreed to share power with the Tutsi. He foresaw an army in which half the officers would be Tutsi and a government in which half of the ministers would be Tutsi. I despised him for turning away from the truth. We Hutu were fighting for survival. That's what men of principle have done since history began." I opened out the palms of my hands in a gesture that meant everything was obvious. The prosecutor did not return my smile.

Once in Benaco I went to see the maître d'hôtel of the Hotel

Akagera, whose employees lived in a section of camp exclusively theirs. I presented myself to this representative of the finest hotel in the capital city of Kigali, and in mutual respect we drank a bottle of wine that had been brought from the hotel's cellar. I will never forget that day and the pride I felt and the satisfaction. He was also a Hutu, and we drank to the glorious future of our people.

EMMANUEL

AFTER BEING MUSTERED out of the army, I walked home in
my uniform, wearing a black beret and a starched shirt and a
canvas belt discolored from ammo clips.

It had been a long time since I walked alone and among
civilians. The roads were crowded with refugees going from west
to east or east to west. Most of them were Hutu and jumped out
of my way when they saw the uniform. I caught a skinny little
man staring at me from large round eyes as I walked down the
road. When I stared back, he gave a start like a small animal in
the bush. I wanted to laugh and shout at him at the same time.
Instead, I walked up and glared down at his frightened face.

"What do you think you're looking at?" I asked. "Do you
think because I was a Tutsi soldier I have a tail and hooves and
horns?" When the man blinked in terror, I removed my beret.
"See? No horns." Removing one of my shoes, I said, "See? No
hoof." Exasperated by his look of dumb fear, I dropped my pants
and turned my buttocks toward him. "See? No tail."

Finally, a faint smile crossed his lips. At last I had convinced
him I was truly human. Glancing around, I noticed a crowd of
people had assembled. They were smiling. Then we were all
laughing, and it occurred to me that I had not laughed in a long
time.

As I walked home, I could see that the autumn harvest had gone poorly. Fields had been neglected, banana groves untended. I suspected that beans were planted shallowly because old women, left behind on farms, couldn't break the ground except in soft, shaded places. Before leaving the army, I heard that people in the countryside were eating seeds instead of planting those donated by NGOs. Where were the garden patches of onions and cabbages and tomatoes I should have been seeing from the road?

On my way home, I kept wondering how many of my neighbors were still alive.

And I kept thinking of a comrade in my unit. He came from the town of Nyamata near the Burundian border. It had been a Tutsi commune surrounded by a swamp with a single bridge as its only exit. On the first night of the genocide, people couldn't get across the bridge, which was watched at both ends. So they fled into the papyrus marshes, where one by one they were tracked down and killed. Those who did manage to hide were either caught later or died of starvation. This fellow had been one of the very few who escaped. When I first met him in the army I wondered if he would ever regain his belief in anything. He moved around like a ghost. Yet with time he changed. At his discharge he had managed to get a small enterprise loan from the government. When we parted, he was going to set up a carpentry workshop in Nyamata. Out of curiosity I asked him if he'd ever hire a Hutu to work for him.

"If he was a good enough carpenter," replied my comrade, "I would hire him."

Then I asked, "What if he was better than a Tutsi, but not a lot better. Would you still hire him?"

After a moment's thought my comrade smiled and said, "I would hire the Tutsi."

When I got to my hill, I found my house was still standing. I was surprised to find that almost nothing was missing inside. Why hadn't it been cleaned out?

Going into the courtyard, I looked at the acacia tree under which my wife and two daughters had been murdered. After sitting in its shade a while, I noticed something on the ground a few feet away. I went over and found a dust-covered plastic comb, my wife's. Then I began to look around for other things. I found pieces of an earthenware jug used for carrying water. It must have been broken during the slaughter. So I picked up those pieces and took them and the comb into the house and put them in the old trunk, where I had last stored the Intore costume, which, again to my surprise, was still there, untouched.

Going back outside, I made sure that the graves had not been disturbed. Then I went to the kraal to confirm what I suspected. All my cattle were gone. Of course they were. But I still wondered about the house, why it hadn't been looted.

The next day I learned from a cousin, who had returned last month, that the woman in the next rugo, the woman whose husband I killed, had persuaded her relatives to guard my house during the worst of the looting. She had saved my house and belongings. But how could I thank her when her husband had helped to kill my family and I had killed him? I thought about that for a week. What had led her to save the house of her husband's killer? Perhaps when we met on the road, I might nod in passing. Perhaps the ninth or tenth time we met, I might say a word or two. Not enough to embarrass us both. "Good morning." "Good evening." Just enough to tell her how grateful I

felt. But her greatness of spirit would remain beyond my under-
standing.

Each morning when I got up, I splashed water in my face five
times just the way my father used to do. My father's father had
entrusted his Hutu garagu with three large herds of cattle. The
garagu could handle the cattle as he pleased, but if he failed to
take care of them properly, my grandfather could ask immediately for their return. It required nothing more than a few words.
"You have neglected your duty. Give me back my cattle." And
it was done. Yet my grandfather was shebuja to that particular
garagu for nearly fifty years without incident. The relationship
between our Tutsi and Hutu families had begun when my grandfather's grandfather and his garagu's grandfather had committed
themselves to the first buhake contract.

One of my great-great-uncles had been an umusizi at court.
His poetry had been favored by one of the greatest of the
mwami. So I came from men of good blood. On my return home,
I often thought of my ancestors. Sometimes at midday I saw
their faces swimming out of the sunlight glare. I was alone in
the rugo, yet these men of the past surrounded me while I
planted a garden patch. I felt ashamed to use a hoe in front of
them, yet I did. My food allotment would run out soon enough,
so I must work like a Hutu farmer.

The truth was I no longer had anything. Of course, I owned
ibikingi, but pasturelands without cattle are merely expanses of
worthless grass. Sometimes I dreamed of cattle and my wife
standing at the edge of a pasture. But she never came close or
spoke to me.

Every day I like to open the trunk and take out the Intore
costume. There for me to look at and admire are the leopard

skin and two strands of beaded chest cloth and my plumed necklace and feathered headband and the set of ankle bells. Picking
up the short dancing spear, I heft it in my hand.

Sayings have been coming back to me. "Rwanda is Imana's
country." "If Imana walks elsewhere during the day, at night he
comes home to Rwanda." The silence of my rugo fills me with
sadness. It's like pouring sand into a gunnysack. At other times
I pace up and down the courtyard in a mindless rage. I feel the
need to kill as I felt it during my first days as an infantryman. I
think of going to one of the abarosi, one of those witches who
brew poisons to rid a client of enemies. If you bring them a
fingernail paring or a couple of hairs from your enemy's head,
they can cast a death spell.

But I ask myself, who is my enemy? They are Hutu and live
all around me on the hill. I pass them every day on the path or
stand next to them in the market.

In the old days there was the biru, a council of wise courtiers
who guarded tradition. They were entrusted with memorizing
court rituals and selecting the mwami's successor. They assured
us of things returning. History was seen as repeating itself endlessly. I would like that. I would like time to come around again
to what it was.

When I had planted the garden and lacked an excuse for
sitting around the rugo, I decided to find my cattle, if any were
still left in the hills. I went from kraal to kraal, both Tutsi and
Hutu, and looked for my cattle. I knew every one of them as if
they were kinfolk, but if necessary I could also identify them by
my brand.

At a Hutu farm, I saw three immediately and went to the
farmer there. "Three cows of mine are in your herd," I told him.

He nodded solemnly. "I was keeping them for you."

"You were keeping them for me. Good," I said, not believing a word of it. I supposed he was afraid of me. "Then I'll take them now." I began to walk toward the herd.

"I am sorry," he said at my back.

I turned and looked at him.

"About your family," he said.

"I wish you good fortune," I told him. "I hope that your herd increases."

"Thank you."

I got my cattle and left. At another farm I found two more from my herd, but this Hutu wasn't happy about giving them up. We examined the brands together and he scratched his head doubtfully. "How do I know this is your brand?"

"Because I tell you it is."

"That isn't enough."

"Yes, it is," I said, looking down at him. "If you want to live, it is."

"Are you threatening me?"

"Of course I'm threatening you."

"I will go to the police."

"Go."

He hesitated a long time, his lips trembling. Then he said, "Take the cows and leave me alone."

"I will do both."

I now have five head of cattle in my kraal. The sight of them gives me hope. I find my lips curving into a smile when I look at them and when I take them out to pasture.

Then an older man, a Tutsi, came up to me at the market yesterday when I was buying some carrots. I knew where he lived and I also knew that he had returned very early to the hill and somehow had regained nearly all of his livestock. Moreover, he had lost only one member of a family of thirteen. He was a very lucky man.

"Your father was my friend," he said, coming up to me. "Can you forgive me my good fortune?"

"I must forgive you," I said, but my body trembled from my confused feelings.

"Just as your father was my friend, I hope you will be my friend too."

"Yes," I said, unable to say more.

"Come to me for help," he persisted.

"Yes."

After he hesitated a moment longer, perhaps hoping for something more to happen between us, he turned and went into the crowd. I told myself to forgive him for having good fortune. Could I let jealousy make a fool of me? How can people live without friends? We need one another. Yet I knew I couldn't forgive him, but somehow, eventually, I would. And I would go to him for help. I must. And I would take up where my father left off and be the man's friend.

I went to see a great-aunt who lived on a nearby hill. Somehow the killers had gone past her little rugo. Maybe they had forgotten that she was still alive. People took care of her, but every day she still managed to sweep the courtyard of her rugo and prepare her own porridge. I sat with her under a shade tree. We said little and her eyes narrowed so that I wondered if she had fallen asleep. Suddenly, she leaned forward and stared at me. "What happened here was ugly. But you mustn't dwell on ugly things. Live with your neighbors and learn what it once was and could be once more." Then her eyes narrowed again, and this time she began to snore, so I got up and left.

Yesterday while weeding in my bean patch, I noticed a man watching me from the road. When my eyes met his, he seemed to take it as an invitation to walk over. I waited for him. When he got closer I recognized him as a Hutu who used to operate a bar that sold potent banana beer.

We greeted one another. He welcomed me back to the hills. I waited for more. He seemed very nervous while explaining what I didn't need to know—that his wife and three kids worked in the fields, that he had a storehouse of beans and sorghum flour, that he no longer feared the RPF units that were billeted in the next commune. I waited.

Then he said in a voice almost too low to hear, "I know what people say. People say I'm a génocidaire."

I waited while he just stood there staring at the ground. I realized he was getting up the courage to say more. "I did kill some people." He looked up and pointed to an opposite hill. "Over there."

"Tutsi?"

"A man and his son." Again he paused. "With a hoe."

"Were they running away?"

"Yes. I hit the son first, then the father."

There was a long silence. Finally I asked, "Why do you tell me?"

"Because," he began and stopped. We stood there in wind gusts. They made a rattling sound like rain when going through a nearby banana grove. "Because," he said again, "I want you to forgive me."

I might have said that I couldn't forgive him for killing people on another hill. I couldn't act on their behalf. I had no authority for such a thing. I had no right to forgive him for killing people of my own tribe. But then I thought of my great-aunt snoring under the shade tree, and I said without hesitation, "I forgive you."

Squinting up at me, the man nodded and walked away.

That night I dreamed of my wife standing at the edge of a pasture. This time, unlike the other times, she began to walk toward me. Her hands were held together beneath her breasts like I remember. For the first time in one of those dreams she was smiling at me. But after a while she turned around and walked beyond the pasture into a mist. That was the last I dreamed of her, maybe because she seemed happy with what I was doing.

Not long after that I heard of some young génocidaires returning. They were militiamen who had avoided arrest at the transit centers. They were walking around the hills as if nothing had happened. I would not seek them out, but when I heard of them strutting free, I kept the war knife strapped to my belt at all times. If the occasion arose, I'd not hesitate to use it.

Surely guilt and fear lay heavy in the hills like fog. Those who participated in the killings, whether charged or not with crimes, must think of their surviving neighbors as the enemy waiting for the right time to kill them.

But after spending a month at home, I decided to put the war knife aside. I forgot the génocidaires. I thought only of tending my garden and my five head of cattle. Men of the past no longer surrounded me when I lifted the hoe. I heard the wind coming through the silence and I liked the sound of it, the long, steady sound of it. I decided to expand my garden. So to get more seeds

I went to the largest market in our commune. It was located on another hill.

When I got there, I asked for directions to the seed stalls. As I was looking for them, I noticed a heavyset woman wearing a yellow cloth turban. She was picking over some onions.

It was Pauline, the chicken diviner, whom I used to meet now and then on the road. I had last seen her on the day I ran from the hills. I had just killed one man and was ready to kill more. That day I had threatened to kill her husband if I saw him.

Now, at the market, when I nodded in polite recognition, the woman gasped at the sight of me and seemed ready to faint. Did she think I was still bloodthirsty? I went to her side and was surprised to see tears in her eyes. "You live," she said. "You live, you live. His father, you live."

I helped her find a seat on a bench near one of the stalls. To give her air, I waved my hand in front of her face like a fan. She was staring at me in wonder.

"You live," she kept saying.

I was puzzled. "Did you think I was dead?"

"We all did. He did."

"Your husband?"

"No, no. Pacifique."

"Pacifique?" I had not spoken his name out loud in a year. "My son?"

"Did you think he was dead?"

"My son Pacifique?"

"He thinks you are dead."

I sat down beside her. We both stared ahead for a while in stunned silence. "Do you know where my son is?"

"Yes. He lives with me."

Our eyes met.

While she explained what had happened since the massacre, I reached out without thinking and gripped her hand hard. When she winced, I let go.

"So you brought him back to the hills," I said. "All the way from Goma?"

"I brought ten back."

"Where is my son now?"

"Playing with other children at home." Shading her eyes, she looked beyond the market. "Way over there." Turning to me, she asked, "Do you want me to go get him?"

"You mean, now?"

"Yes, now. I can do that."

I shook my head. "Please bring him to my house." It seemed important to meet him there. "Will you do that?"

"Yes. Go home now. I'll bring him to you."

I wasn't ready to go just yet and she knew it, so she waited for me to say the last thing. "I will thank you," I said, "until the day I die."

PACIFIQUE

SHE TAKES ME across the hill to another hill. I think I have
seen this hill before, and I grip her hand and stop. "No," I tell
her, because I don't want to go this way again. I came from this
hill when my hands were full of blood and I couldn't put their
heads back on.

I tell her no and pull back, but she keeps me moving forward
and her voice is soft and sweet as it says, "Go on, now, Pacifique,
go on. Don't be afraid. There's nothing to be afraid of. Just
go on."

So I go on because she tells me to in a voice I like and ahead
there's a rugo with the gate open. I think I know this gate. I say
"No," again because I'm scared, but she gives me a little push
in my back and says, "Go on," so I go on past the gate and
there's a courtyard I know I know and the big tree where the
heads were. I turn to run and say, "No."

But she holds my shoulders with both hands and turns me
around again to make me look at the tree. Under the tree stands
a tall man. He wears the feathers and headdress of a crane dancer and carries a short spear. He seems almost as tall as the tree.

My heart is pounding. I go forward slowly when she gives me
a little push.

The tall man comes forward too. He is smiling as he throws down the spear and falls to his knees.

I go forward faster when I see he's not so tall anymore. I'm running with my arms out and I know him, I know him for my father, for my father and dancer, for my father.

I am running and running and his feathers and beads get closer until I reach them and with my arms around him and his arms around me I know I am home, I am back home now forever, and I feel him laughing against me and the feathers tickling and I am laughing too and we are laughing together, one against the other.